The Water Bailiff's Daughter

Yvonne Hendrie

Stairwell Books

Published by Stairwell Books
161 Lowther Street
York, YO31 7LZ

www.stairwellbooks.co.uk
@stairwellbooks

ISBN: 978-1-913432-01-0

Layout design: Alan Gillott
Edited by Rose Drew
Rev 1

Dedicated to Brian and Chloe, with thanks for their love and support, and to Kenji, my constant canine companion as I write; and in memory of Mum and Dad, who was a water bailiff's son.

I would like to thank my sister-in-law, Fiona Hendrie, and my friend, Paula Hamilton, for reading the first draft and for their insights and encouragement. Thanks also to members of Ayr Writers' Club who evaluated the first one thousand words and thought the idea was viable; and last but not least, many thanks to Rose, Alan and Grace at Stairwell Books for their enthusiasm, advice and guidance.

PROLOGUE

May Day, 1928

A young woman ran through the coarse grass. Her long dress, stained with perspiration, clung to her meagre body. She trailed a cloak in one hand, a staff in the other aiding her ascent of the steep slope. When she reached the top of the hill overlooking the village, she stopped, panting, and pulled the cloak around herself. Smoothing her wild hair, she yanked up the hood and tucked stray tendrils of damp spiral curls into it. A balding man down by the stalls at the harbour glanced up at her. His eyes lingered, his gaze keen. She experienced a puzzling jolt of recognition and pulled her hood further forward. She had never seen him before, only heard of him, yet she knew him instantly. Her heart pounded.

She watched as a fishing boat berthed and its crew shouted to the bystanders at the May Day Fete to come and see what they had landed. When a young man stepped forward to inspect the bundle held by one of the fishermen, she let out a small cry; he had looked very different when she had last seen him, barely two months ago. He took the bundle carefully in his arms. Her shoulders slouched then with relief. It wasn't what she had intended, but it was the best outcome in the circumstances. Stumbling with weariness, she made her way down the hill. Now she had to make amends to the only true friend she had left in the world.

PART ONE

March 1928 – August 1933

Chapter 1

A full moon balanced on the horizon. It appeared huge in the sea mist through which it shimmered, and a humped shape stood in silhouette against it. It was the rounded Faerie Isle of Ailsa Craig, and the waves ran shoreward from it to another humped object on the shingle. At first glance, this looked like any old upturned boat, but on closer inspection, a thin crooked chimney pipe could be seen protruding from the side. A wisp of wafting smoke curled upwards on the still night air, and the raven which flew through it scattered it into shreds as it swooped and landed on the ledge of a small round window.

From within, a dull red glow pulsed and flickered, and the raven preened by its light. It raised its head to watch a cloaked figure approaching from the shoreline, striding out and tapping the shingle with a staff. This individual laid down the sack slung over its back and fumbled within the folds of the cloak, producing a large key. Moonlight fell on a fair-skinned hand with long, tapering fingers, inserting the key into the lock of an arched doorway next to the window. As the door hinges creaked open, the hood of the cloak fell away, releasing a tumbling mass of silver-blonde corkscrew curls. The glow from within illuminated the features of a striking woman: not beautiful, but something more than pretty. She could have been any age between fifteen and fifty in that enchanted light. Leaning her staff against the house-boat, and stooping to untie the sack, she threw a small fish to the raven, its dead eye glinting as the bird caught it. Then the woman walked into the upturned hull she called home.

Inside, the red glow proved to emanate from a wood-burning stove, where a young man sat on a three-legged stool, hands outstretched to the meagre fire within. He turned wary eyes as the woman entered, tossing the sack to him with a curl of her lip.

"Here," she said. "I'll be away to my bed, if ye don't mind, and leave ye to it. Yer manners disgust me."

"Ye should have thought o' that," he replied, reaching to open the sack.

'I could put up wi' it, though," she said. "Ye know I would. If ye would join me." She inclined her head towards the bed at the other end of the house-boat.

"That I will never do," he said calmly but firmly, as if this conversation had taken place many times, and he was weary of it. He pulled a fish from the sack and sank his teeth into it. He turned his body so he could stare at her as he ate, blood trickling down his chin, and the chain on his ankle rasped against the rough planking of the floor.

The woman threw off her shabby black velvet cloak. She wore a long dress of grey beneath it, as antique in style as the cloak. Her chest heaved and her face contorted, bringing an ugliness to her otherwise fair features. "Such insolence! I'll feed and clathe ye nae mare!"

"I never asked it o' ye," the man replied through a mouthful of fish, scales clinging to the stubble on his jaw. He spat out some bones. "I didna want tae be brought here tae dae your bidding!"

The woman faltered, her youth suddenly apparent in the quiver of her lip, the pleading of her eyes. "Ye know the Sea Witch o' Ballaness must choose a mate and bear a daughter tae follow her, Sam. I've chosen you."

The man wiped his chin and regarded her. "And you know, Megan, as well as I do, that if I do as ye ask, I'll be a man ever more. I want tae return tae my own kind. I have a mate, and she's in the family way."

Megan the Sea Witch glared at him, and jealousy made her heart harden. "Then go, and feed and clathe yersel as best ye can," she said icily; and as she did so, she pointed her staff of skeletal white driftwood at him. "Go!" she cried. "Get oot! Ye shall have nae mare o' my hospitality!"

The chain on the man's ankle released itself and fell with a clatter. He grinned and massaged the raw skin where it had rubbed, then stood, stretching. "I'll be glad to go. But aren't ye forgetting something?"

"I really dinna think sae."

"Turn me back, Megan!"

"Never!"

6

He held her frozen stare. "This is not you, Megan. Nane o' this is like the friend I valued, for her wit and her funny ways. You are not the same lassie."

"I am what you have made me!"

"No. I don't understand the ways o' women born, but you knew how it was wi' me. Now, turn me back!"

"Never!" cried the sea witch, and her voice carried like the shrieking of gulls on the wind. She raised her staff and held it horizontally above her head. She spread her feet and swayed. "If I cannot have ye, she never shall! Be gone! Go!"

The fire flared and pulsed rhythmically with her words. The young man recoiled at the force her curse unleashed within the room. The sea witch's rage was a wave crashing into him, pushing him through the pointed arch of the door and into the cold spring night beyond. She was suddenly older, the power of something ancient behind her, and it was terrifying. He discovered then that his speed had survived her initial spell as well as his creature appetite for fish, and he ran. He didn't think about where he was running, and he didn't stop to look back.

The raven watched him go. He keeked in the window and saw his mistress kneeling on the floor. Her small frame heaved and shuddered with sobs. He spread his wings and flew low over the shore, in the opposite direction from that taken by the man. When he reached the place where the River Dunn entered the sea, he turned and followed it upstream. He had to go some way before he discovered what he was seeking. The woman for whom he had been looking sat on the river bank, the rising moon silvering her naked skin. One hand rested on her pregnant belly, and she sighed. Then she slipped into the water, turning to float on her back; but the moon shone now upon a creamy underside of fur where fair flesh had been, and reflected in the doleful brown pools of an otter's eyes.

At dawn the next day, Sam lay exhausted in a field. He woke from a dreamless sleep to see the raven strutting in the dew in front of him, cocking its head and regarding him as if impatient for him to stir. It took a few moments for the events of the previous night to flood back into his addled brain. Sam stirred, stretching stiff and soaking limbs. The body of a man didn't cope well with lying long in damp places, unlike that of an otter, which was Sam's natural state. He belonged to an ancient race of otter-folk who could take human form at will. He fixed the raven with a stare.

"Hello, Rab. Has she sent ye after me? Does she intend tae bring me back?"

The raven couldn't answer, as Sam knew. Even as an otter, he hadn't been able to converse with the bird; but, imprisoned in Megan's houseboat, he had felt that the feathered creature had been sympathetic to his plight. Sam stood up and stared as far as he could in every direction. There was no sign of the sea; he had run far and fast, retaining the speed of an otter on land. There was no sign of any cloaked figure in all the vast landscape of fields which surrounded him, either. He had no idea where he was.

"So, until I find my way back an' reason with her, I'm cursed tae make my way in the world as a man," he sighed. "A man who needs a hell of a lot o' fish."

The raven rose into the air at these words, and circled once around his head before flying low in a northerly direction. Sam began to follow. Maybe the bird knew something he didn't. He hoped so, anyway; and before long, he saw what it was. The morning sun glinted on water, and Sam, despite his sore limbs, broke into a run at the prospect of breakfast. He remembered, just at the last minute before diving in, to take off his clothes; he splashed into the river, immersing himself in water for the first time since Megan the sea witch had lured him to her lair. The raven swooped back and forth above his head, croaking in rapture. Sam thanked the bird with sincerity. Rab, he knew, only had so much freedom in the day, and whether it was love or loyalty or fear that took him back – for his mistress was as mercurial as sea mist – he would return to her. The bird made one final swoop, then soared into the clear spring air and became a dot.

Sam, his mouth full of fish, decided he had best take them out to eat once dried and clothed again, so he threw them one by one upon the bank and clambered out. The cold air hit him in a way it never had when he was able to change his form, and he rolled on the grass in an attempt to dry his red, goose-pimpled flesh. Then he dressed in the old shirt and trousers Megan had given him. As he ate, he wondered where he was and which waterway this river was, and whether it linked to other water sources he knew which would lead him home.

8

Sam continued to gnaw at the fish while all this went through his head. He trembled with cold, the thick thatch of his coarse brown hair not drying easily in the chill morning air. His clothing was useless out in the open. He had slept the sleep of the exhausted, having fallen down and slipped into semi-consciousness when his run had become a stumbling walk, and he wasn't refreshed at all. He would need help to get back to Ballaness to confront Megan, but where was he to find it in this strange, empty landscape?

As Sam pondered this, something caught his attention upstream. He thought it was clothing caught in tree roots at first, the lilac colour standing out against the browns and greens of the river bank; but then it moved. He glimpsed a hand, briefly, reaching out to grasp an overhanging branch, and without a second thought he was on his feet and running along the bank. He saw the frail form in the river, the silvery blonde hair floating tangled with weeds, and he plunged, fully clothed, into the deep, dark water.

He grabbed hold of the female and turned her over. The woman, who was not Megan as he had first thought, was gasping for breath. He seized her in both arms to pull her to the bank, but in her panic she struggled against him and they both tumbled into the deeper waters, grappling with each other and battling the current. That was where they were when a gamekeeper, out early on the Craigendon estate, heard the commotion and came running.

William Tully cracked the whip from the seat of his ramshackle cart and goaded his elderly mare into a brisk trot. He was torn between where to go first – the doctor's house, where his daughter Rose was being treated after nearly drowning in the River Duie, or the police station, where his colleague MacAllistair had taken the young man who had been found with her. The gamekeeper had said that he wasn't just going to let him get away. He resented the knowing look which had accompanied MacAllistair's telling of his story. It confirmed what he had been dreading, that word about Rose's condition was out. The police station being closer, he decided to go there first and take a look at this young man. Whether he had been rescuing Rose, or they had fallen in fighting as MacAllistair thought, he might well be the one. It was the only lead he had, because his daughter would tell him nothing about the father of her unborn child.

Constable Harkness greeted him with a handshake and words meant to reassure. "If he's guilty, I'll get him banged to rights. Breach of promise, assault, whatever it takes."

The sympathy in his meaningful look, the complicity, made Tully wince. Just how many people knew about his daughter's fall from grace? "I would appreciate a private chat with him," he said.

"Be my guest," Harkness replied. "Any father would be the same in your shoes." He winked.

Tully winced. "Have ye questioned him?"

"Of course. Suspicious character. Won't answer much at all, and clothes a century oot o' date. Not that he's wearin' them, they're still dryin'. The wife found some old things o' mine for him. I've filled oot a bit over the years wi' her fine cookin'." He patted his paunch and lifted a ring of keys from a hook on the wall. "This way, Mr. Tully."

They went through a door into a small corridor with two cells at one side. The constable unlocked the first and preceded Tully into the room.

"Stand!" he yelled, like a sergeant-major, making Tully jump. There was a crash as the suspect leapt to his feet and sent an empty slop bucket clattering into the corner. As he bent to pick it up, he tripped over his borrowed trousers, which were too long for him. "Sakes, man!" bellowed Harkness, "Roll them up! Why have ye not got the braces on?"

Tully peered round the policeman to see a pathetic sight. The man found struggling with his daughter in the River Duie was small of stature and slight in build, maybe in his mid-twenties. He was holding Harkness's old trousers up with one hand.

"Is that these things, Sir?" he asked, indicating the braces lying on the low bench which took up most of the cell. "I didnae know what tae dae wi' them. I had a thing called a belt wi' my last pair o' troosers."

Constable Harkness turned puce and puffed out his chest, straining the buttons on his jacket. "Insolence!" he cried, and he struck a blow with the back of his hand which sent the young man sprawling on to the bench. He stared up in uncomprehending shock, huge brown eyes filled with fear.

As Harkness launched into a tirade about not giving the likes of him a belt (except a belt round the ear), Tully interrupted. "Will ye not introduce us, Constable, and allow us tae talk as we agreed?"

The policeman breathed deeply and turned to face him. "He says his name is Hailstanes, Sam Hailstanes, frae Ballaness. Not Hailstones, 'stanes'. Never heard that as a name before. Well, Hailstanes," he said, pulling Sam up by the collar of his shirt, "this is Mr. Tully, father of your young lady, and we'll see what he has to say!" With a nod at Tully, he marched from the cell.

Tully rubbed his stubbled chin with his large calloused hand, thinking. Sam Hailstanes was not what he had expected, not at all. "Did ye know my Rose before today?" he asked.

"I telt that man, an' the one wi' the gun, him that found us in the water, that I've never set eyes on her in my life!"

Tully could hardly shift his gaze from Sam's prominent brown eyes. "Hailstanes?" he said. "Is that yer real name?"

"I'm Sam," the young man replied. "They wanted another name, a surname, they said. They kept on and on. It came intae my head. They were batterin' off the roof the night before last…" He tailed off and looked at the floor.

Tully watched him, considering. "I believe ye," he said finally. "Ballaness, ye say? It seems tae me ye need help. Work, a place tae live…since ye saved my daughter, I'll help ye. I'll employ ye, son, and give ye a roof over yer head." Tully smiled wryly. It was a long time since he had had dealings with Sam's kind, or the world around Ballaness, but the two worlds he knew had merged in timely fashion.

Sam was staring at him in disbelief. "Really, Sir? What kind o' work? Where?" He glanced down at his strong hands. He had no doubt he could work like a man, but he had no intention of remaining as one. "I really need tae get back tae Ballaness, though, thanking ye, Sir," he added.

The older man regarded him with pity. "I'm the only one who can get ye oot o' here, lad. Ye can't explain yerself, or what ye were doin' wi' my Rose. They think ye were fightin'. I can help ye. I'm the water bailiff up on Loch Duie. I could take on an assistant. I'm thinkin' maybe ye know a bit aboot fish, Hailstanes?"

"I should say I do, Sir," Sam answered cautiously, "but…"

"Aye, well, that could come in handy," Tully interrupted. "But there are aspects of that ye'll have tae keep tae yourself. Yer work will help wi' that. There are things ye must never mention, lad. Now, let me do the talking while I get ye oot o' here." As he spoke, he helped Sam on with the braces, then went to the door and called Constable Harkness. "Ye need have no more bother wi' this one," he said. "He was savin' Rose. She fell into the water, an accident. I've been in his position, and I know how the victim can panic an' put up a fight."

The policeman blustered, caught off guard. "But his suspicious name, an' the Victorian clothes…An' Rose was a long way frae hame, beggin' yer pardon, sae early in the morn…"

"My Rose's business is none o' yours!" barked Tully. Then, controlling himself, he said, "He's not from these parts. He's from far up north. They've got some strange ways up there. Only lately come tae Ballaness." He put a hand on Harkness's shoulder. "Arrived a few months ago," he said in a confidential tone, forcing himself to wink, hating the whole affair; but Sam's timely arrival could be the saving of Rose in more ways than one. "Ye've done well, Constable, and I thank ye. Matters can be put right now."

The surly policeman looked from Tully to Sam and back. "Whatever ye say, Tully," he said. "Good fortune tae you and yer family."

Outside the police station, Sam, now wrapped in a blanket – which was all that could be found for him to keep out the spring chill – climbed into Tully's cart. The village to which he had been taken, briskly marched by the big man called MacAllistair, who had gripped his arm with one hand and his gun with the other, was called Crosson. Sam had never been here. "Am I far from Ballaness, Sir?" he asked.

"Far enough," answered Tully. "I'm takin' ye further away, up into the hills, near tae Craigendon House. Ye'll like it there. There's the whole o' Loch Duie tae swim in, and all the fish ye can eat."

Sam stared wide-eyed at his companion. "Sir, am I right in thinkin' that…"

"Aye, lad. I knew ye for what ye were the minute I saw ye. I didna always live oot in the wilds o' Craigendon. I lived at Ballaness when I was younger. I was the assistant water bailiff on the River Dunn there for a couple o' years, an' I…experienced some things. Oot at all hours I was, an' I saw your kind – the otter-folk. Other kinds, too. I dinna talk aboot it, for I would be ridiculed. Had ye dealings wi' a woman on the shore at Ballaness, by any chance?"

"Aye!" cried Sam. "Do ye know her?"

"I haven't seen her for many years," Tully replied. "An' I hope never tae see her again! If ye've crossed her, son, and ye must have tae be left in this state, she'll not forget an' she'll not forgive. Ye have tae make the best o' it now, an' I'm offerin' ye a chance ye won't get anywhere else."

Sam stared at his companion, his heart sinking. "She's my friend," he said. "We had a falling out, but I'm sure if I could just talk tae her…"

Tully laughed. "Waste o' time. I knew her well, an' she won't have changed. Anyway, ye owe me now. I've got ye oot o' danger."

They had left the village by this time and were approaching a large house surrounded by a low wall and a garden. Tully drove past before stopping at a row of trees on the road which blocked the house from view.

"That's the doctor's place," he told Sam. "Stay here while I check on Rose." He jumped down from the cart and turned back, saying kindly but firmly, "Don't be daft an' run off an' end up in trouble again."

Sam sat looking around him. He could see the hills ahead – presumably, his new home would be in those hills. Every clip-clop of the horse was taking him further from Ballaness and the life he had known there, where he had been a shore otter. He had lived by the tides, foraging the rock pools at low tide no matter the time of day. At night, though, he would range further, following the course of the Dunn upstream to his mate Jeanette's territory. She wasn't his only mate, but she was his favourite, and she was expecting their first litter.

The thought brought tears to his eyes. As an otter father, he would have taken little to do with the rearing of his cubs, but if he went along with this man Tully he wouldn't see them at all, or Jeanette, ever again. He pictured her, her sleek strength as otter and woman, her fierce independence and the freedom of his bond with her. The only human he had ever befriended was Megan the sea witch. Disoriented and queasy, Sam clutched his blanket closer. He saw by the sun that a long time had passed since breakfast at dawn, and he was hungry for another feed of fish.

Tully reappeared after ten minutes or so. He took up the reins in silence and remained drawn into himself for the next few miles. Finally, he spoke. "Rose will be spending the night at the doctor's house, to recover fully," he said.

"I'm glad she'll be well," said Sam.

"I haven't thanked ye properly for savin' her," said Tully.

"I thought she was the woman ye knew, Sir," said Sam, "the sea witch. Similar hair…"

Tully barked a wry laugh which made Sam jump. "Oh aye, she'll still have that, and here's me near bald! I had a head o' hair not dissimilar once, ye know – took it from ma mother, an' passed it on tae Rose. Of course, I kept mine short, but it grew like a bush when I was younger, though ye would never believe it now." He stopped speaking, lost in thought, before hissing, "The sea witch and her wiles! Ways tae go against nature, lad, ye know?"

Sam didn't know what he was talking about, but he kept quiet. Finally, he picked up courage to ask, "Do you know so much, Sir, because you're… maybe like one o' the creatures around Ballaness?"

Tully frowned. "No. I'm a man through and through. Nothing hidden about me, son. Except that I'm a man wi' a problem, Sam Hailstanes, one ye can help me with. In truth, ye have little choice."

Sam glanced at his companion and wondered what was coming next. He shivered, the blanket round his shoulders providing little warmth against the breezy March day. Tully noticed.

"At least it's not rainin'," he said.

"I was warm in the water this mornin'," mused Sam. "It was just like usual, until I got oot."

"Well, it's all change now," said Tully. He cleared his throat. "Let's discuss the deal."

Sam's heart began to hammer. "I…I don't know much about the dealings o' men, Sir…" he stammered.

"That's why ye need me, Sam. More than I need you, as it happens. But I do need ye. As does Rose. My daughter has need of a husband."

Sam sat very still. His mind went numb while his body tensed in every muscle. Megan had wanted a man and had trapped him in her houseboat, waiting for his surrender. Now it seemed he was wanted for mating with this man's daughter.

"Megan the sea witch wanted me for that," he said.

Tully reined the mare in so suddenly that the cart jolted. "No, that's not what she would want! Not marriage, in the sight o' God. Her kind dinna bide by the same laws, so ye canna go by what ye've learned from her. Marriage is vows and commitment to one person for your whole life. It's for bringin' children into the world, and raisin' them properly with a mother and a father."

14

Sam shrugged. That sounded like what Megan had been after – him to be hers, and hers alone, and to give her the daughter she said she must have, as the Sea Witch o' Ballaness. There was something in Tully's countenance which stopped him saying so, though.

"Look, lad," said Tully. "Marriage is the place for children tae be born tae the likes o' us. An' Rose is tae have a child. She's stuck wi' that, an' you're stuck wi' your problem, for I've told ye, ye've crossed the sea witch an' she'll not forgive. I'm offerin' a solution to both problems, yours and mine."

Sam was silent. He was being asked to take on another human woman; not one such as Megan, but she would no doubt impose the same bounds, she and her father in their house among the hills. He had a choice, but he knew it would mean stepping down from this cart right now, in this strange countryside, and being back where he had been this morning, before he set eyes on Rose in the river. He was hungry again, and cold, lost and afraid.

"I'll do it," he said. It came out as barely a whisper.

Tully held out his hand. "Shake, lad."

Sam hesitated, then held out his left hand uncertainly and touched Tully's fingertips. Tully smiled.

"I'm guessin' I have a lot tae teach ye. An' I will, for although we bide oot in the wilds an' I could keep ye there – an' ye would be happy enough – I want a normal life for Rose. I do not want for her to suspect you are anything but a man, understand? Any creature habits ye have, ye'll take care tae hide them. Yer work will help wi' that. There are no otters up at Loch Duie, of your kind or any other, so ye'll not be troubled that way. In return, I won't interfere. You an' Rose must work things oot between ye as man an' wife. But ye must never lift a hand tae her. Ye'll regret it if ye ever dae."

Sam could see from the set of his jaw that he meant it. "That's a worry ye need never have, Sir," he said, raising his chin, his dignity asserting itself. "The code by which otters live is better than that o' some men."

Tully nodded. He took up the reins again, and they set off at a trot.

Chapter 2

Two weeks later, on a crisp and clear Sunday morning, Sam woke in the hayloft which was his temporary abode until he and Rose were married. Whenever he wakened now, his fate was upon him in an instant. He didn't even have the few seconds of blissful ignorance he had known at first, when he believed himself to be safe in his holt, with waves crunching the shingle nearby, and the promise of freedom to frolic and fish on the shore. When his memory had tricked him in these moments, he had clearly seen the Dunn where it flowed into the sea, and the great hump of Ailsa Craig out there in the brine. He used to converse with seals who swam ashore from their colony there, selkies who could take human form as he did. He could almost feel the wind and taste the salt on it. It had all receded now, though, replaced by the practicalities of life as a man; a man who had to feed the appetite of an otter.

Sam yawned and stretched, and pulled on the clothes with which Tully had provided him. They were second-hand, but they fitted him, and were warm and comfortable. Before, in his times as a human, he had been content to be naked like all his kind. They didn't feel the cold. Now, cursed to remain as a man, he was only oblivious to the cold, strangely enough, when he was in the water. He picked up his towel, clambered down the hayloft ladder and pushed open the barn door. The beauty of the April day flooded in. Sam walked outside, drenching himself in sunlight. The loch lay before him, so different from the Irish Sea at Ballaness. Wooded hillsides surrounded the flat expanse of water, which mirrored a sky of intense blue dotted with white puffs of clouds floating on a slight breeze. It didn't even ruffle the surface of the loch. Sam walked around the shore to a clump of bushes which hid him from view of the water bailiff's cottage. He pulled off his clothes then ran into the water with a rush of joy, and swam at speed up the loch. He would fish well away from prying eyes.

Rose Tully shut the cottage door behind her and leaned back against it, eyes closed. She had seen her intended setting out for his habitual morning swim. At least he had been dressed. She recalled with a shudder the day she had been leaning against the wall outside, weak with morning sickness, and he had emerged naked from the barn and rushed straight into the water. She had lived near lochs and rivers all her life, but had never known anyone so keen on swimming. He was from the far north of Scotland, her father had told her, where they had strange ways. He was an uneducated man, an orphan, and as well as telling her that she was to marry him, her father had instructed her to teach him to read and write.

Rose felt the child stir within her. It caused her to recoil in guilt and horror, that she had sought to kill both it and herself in the waters of the River Duie. She patted her stomach and set about preparing breakfast, although it turned her heart. At least there was plenty of porridge left in the drawer. Rose had been taught when young, by the housekeeper who had worked for them for a while after her mother died, to make large pots of porridge which were then poured into a drawer to solidify. Pieces could be cut and heated with water at breakfast time, and thus fresh stuff didn't have to be made every day. She still had to fry bacon and eggs, though.

A tear escaped her eye, and she brushed if off her cheek. She and Da used to be close. It had broken her heart as well as his to bring shame on him, and to refuse to say who was responsible. There was no point. The father of her child had gone, and knowing herself abandoned, Rose had sought to drown herself. She had left home early that fateful March morning and plunged into the loch where it overflowed into the countryside as the River Duie, and allowed the current to take her. She could swim, though, and she couldn't help the sudden urge to live that came upon her; that's when Sam had found her, struggling for life. When Da arrived to collect her from the doctor's house next day, and told her of the arrangement he had made with her rescuer, she had felt sick with fear. Her beloved father was prepared to marry her off to the first comer

17

in order to cover their shame, and she had no choice. It was a relief that Sam, despite his odd ways, had turned out to be a quiet and decent sort.

She heard footsteps clattering down the wooden treads of the stairs, but she didn't turn to greet her father with a smile as she would once have done. "Morning, Da," she murmured, stirring the pot. "I'll have your fry ready soon. I was...you know."

"Yer mother was the same wi' you," said Tully.

Rose turned and looked at him then, startled by her father's words. He spoke them in a tone he hadn't previously used when speaking of her condition, a conversational tone as if things were normal. He seemed aware of her surprise. He cleared his throat.

"Look, Rose, this bairn is a fact o' life. It's my first grandchild, an' I might wish the circumstances tae be different, but things are as they are. I'm sorry ye won't tell me who the father is. I'm even sorrier ye saw fit tae dae what ye did. I lost yer mother, and I dinna want tae lose you."

As Rose broke down over the range, tears streaming, Tully went to her and took her in his arms. "Oh Da, I'm so sorry," she sobbed.

"I've fixed it, lass," he said, "I've fixed it as best I can. Sam will look after ye. I'll see to it, for he'll do as I say."

Rose looked up at him, and he took a handkerchief from his pocket and began to dry her tears. "But why, Da? Why does he do your biddin'? Do ye know of some trouble he's been in...do ye have some hold over him?"

Tully released her and sat down at the table. "There's no trouble," he said. "Put that out of yer head. Look, he's a Highland laddie of no family who canna even read. He's wandered down here, odd-jobbin' here and there, nowhere tae lay his head at times. He's no prospects. I've given him work an' a home for life if he learns well. An' he's a lucky man tae be marryin' you intae the bargain."

Rose sat down opposite her father. "I wish I could thank ye, Da, but it's askin' a lot for me to marry a man I hardly know."

Tully was silent a moment. "And how well did ye know the father o' yer bairn before ye lay down wi' him, Rose?" As she began to cry again, he said, "Come now, lass, get the breakfast. I'm goin' tae teach Sam how tae fish wi' a line later, and ye'll have tae fry fish for breakfast from now on."

"Whatever for?" asked Rose, wiping her eyes.

"Because your future husband has a taste for it," said Tully. "He craves it, an' it's your duty tae please him."

At that moment, Sam walked in the door. Rose saw something silver glinting on the stubble of his chin, but before she could remark on it, he had swiped his hand across it.

A few hours later, Sam sat with his fiancée and her father in the stark stone building they called "the kirk", for which purpose Tully had provided him with clothes only to be worn on Sundays and special occasions – such as his forthcoming wedding, for which the banns were being read today for the second time. The minister stood in the pulpit, looking down at them over the rims of his spectacles. He announced that Rose Annette Tully, spinster of this parish, was to be married to Samuel Hailstanes from the parish of Buckraddie. It was a backwater in the mysterious northern regions from which he was supposed to have come, Tully had told him, and nobody would bother to check.

The minister was looming over them, menacing in his black clerical robes. His piercing brown eyes, golden-flecked beneath his neat fringe of tawny hair, burnt into Sam. Instinct told him that Rev. Neville O'Neill neither liked nor approved of him. He ran a finger round the stiff collar of his shirt. He was perspiring with anxiety, and his hands shook slightly as he fumbled to hold the book of psalms he couldn't yet read, and which Rose had surreptitiously opened at the right place and left on the shelf of the pew. He remembered Tully's advice just to open and close his mouth. Plenty of folk mumbled their way through, he had said. Sam was aware of the glances of other worshippers, heads turned in curiosity, some matronly mouths pursed in judgment. He glanced up at the vaulted wooden ceiling, which reminded him of Megan's upturned boat-house. He had a dizzying sensation of looking down on himself as if he was somebody else, and for a moment he longed to run as he had run from Megan at Ballaness.

Afterwards, Rose asked him if he would care to walk home with her instead of riding in the cart with her father. Sam shrugged and consented. He gave in to most things they wanted. They were kind to him, and cowed with grief for his old life, overwhelmed by his new responsibilities, he went along with their wishes. They walked in silence for a while. Rose's head was down, her brow pinched. Sam glanced sidelong at her. She was painfully thin, and the pregnancy showed as a rounding of her belly totally out of character with her gaunt face and legs like those of a bird. They were to be married the day after the calling of the last banns, one week and one day away.

Suddenly, she cleared her throat.

"Why are ye doin' this, Sam?"

He wasn't surprised by the question. It had been a while in coming. "For the reasons yer father gave ye," he replied.

"But ye could work for somebody else! Ye've nae need tae marry for work!"

Tully had prepared him for this. "I stand tae take over from yer da. Since he has no sons, if I prove myself able, I'll be the next water bailiff at Loch Duie."

Rose nodded. "So it's true – ye would marry a stranger for a chance like that." She stopped walking and regarded him for a moment as if he was an oddity. "An' I get to bide in the cottage where I've been since I was seven years old, except for in the Great War when Da was away," she added, in an undertone.

"Aye. Ye'll never have tae leave yer home,"said Sam, with feeling.

Rose made a sound somewhere between a laugh and a cry, causing Sam to jump. "Ha! I'll be here on Loch Duie, tied tae him and now tae you, for the rest o' my days!"

It was Sam's turn to stare at her. "Why would ye want to leave? I can understand ye not bein' keen on marryin' me, but why would anybody want to leave their home and their family?"

"For a chance tae be somebody, and achieve somethin', and just tae see life!" cried Rose. Suddenly, her expression changed. "Oh, I'm sorry, Sam. I forgot ye were raised in an orphanage. Have ye never had a settled home since? Not some kindly farmin' family tae take ye in and treat ye well?"

Sam sifted his weary and confused brain for the personal history Tully had concocted for him. "No. I had tae keep movin', no matter how hard I worked," he said, parrot fashion.

Rose, her eyes narrowed, was peering into his wide eyes as if she would read his soul. He shifted uncomfortably, and looked away. She spoke at last.

"Well, for what it's worth, Sam Hailstanes, I see ye're a decent man, if a bit deep an' quiet. But I suppose I would be, tae, if I was takin' on a woman I didna ken, and bringin' up anither man's bairn." She gulped.

Sam opened his mouth and closed it again. Hearing such words from her lips brought the enormity of their situation home. He was expected to do more than marry her – he was to be a father to her unborn child. The fact that it was another man's meant nothing to him, for he wasn't even a man in truth, and had no interest in Rose that way; indeed, Jeanette had given birth to pups that weren't his. It didn't matter, for he had nothing to do with their rearing; it didn't matter in any sense, for this was not an issue in their world, so the paternity of Rose's baby hadn't interested him at all. But hearing it said out loud that he was expected to bring the child up in the manner of human fathers made his throat constrict.

"Why have ye never asked me, Sam?" Rose asked, softly.

"Asked what?" said Sam, lost in his own uncomfortable thoughts.

"Who the father o' ma bairn is! What else?" Her face was incredulous.

Sam thought quickly. Had Tully instructed him on this? Yes. "I'm not likely to know him," he replied, as he had been schooled. "Comin' frae up north, as I dae. So long as…" he struggled to recall Tully's words; "So long as ye never see him again!" The words, spoken quickly before he lost the thread of them, came out with convincing vehemence.

"I won't, Sam. He was somebody passin' through, workin' up at the big hoose. Ye deserve tae know that much. He'll never bother us again. He charmed me, an' I thought I loved him. I'm not wanton, Sam. He was the first, and it was only once."

Sam knew this was more than she had told her father. The thought made him feel warm towards Rose. "Thank you," he mumbled.

"Dae ye think ye can like me at all, Sam?" she said, in barely a whisper. "I'll be a good wife tae ye," she added. "I may not have shown it, but I am grateful ye'll give the bairn a name, even if it is for job prospects an' a home more than anythin'."

Sam felt more out of his depth than ever. These human females were complicated creatures! "Of course I like ye, Rose," he said. He was surprised to find how much he meant it. She wasn't strong and wise like Jeanette, she wasn't fascinating like Megan, but she was gentle and smart and caring.

She hooked her arm through his, and they began to walk on. Rose seemed happier, comfortable with the silence between them now. Sam felt her boney elbow digging into his ribs, and he closed his big hand over her frail little one. He didn't notice the raven on the fence, head cocked, studying them both.

Down by the coast at Ballaness, the wind was getting up as morning gave way to afternoon. Megan the sea witch had clambered on to the curved roof of her house-boat, where she sat with a leg either side of the hull. Her fair hair was uncharacteristically greasy, and tendrils of it lifted and floated around her face like seaweed. There were dark circles under her eyes. She regarded herself in an ornate mirror she held in her hand, the kind you would expect to see on the dressing table of a grand lady. "This is what lovin' a man brings ye tae!" she said. "Ma warned me, but I never took heed."

Lowering the mirror, she raised her head and scanned the skies. "Rab! Rab! Where the hell does that bird get to?" She placed the mirror carefully between her legs, put her fingers to her lips and whistled. A sudden gust almost unseated her, and the mirror tumbled towards the pebbled beach below. At that moment, before it hit the ground, Rab appeared. He swooped down and scooped the handle into his bill, returning the precious mirror to his mistress. She took it from him gently and stroked his head. Reaching into her pocket, she found a nut for him. "Ye've redeemed yersel' for bein' gone so long. I hope ye have news for me." Rab flapped as if he would take flight again, but she caught him in one arm and pulled him under her armpit, holding him firmly. "Oh no, Rab. Let's see what ye've been up tae. Let's hope ye've found him. Or her. Her most of all."

She held the mirror up so that it reflected the bird. He turned his head this way and that, cocking it, making circles with his beak. Megan squeezed him until he was still, though quivering slightly. His reflection in the mirror trembled more than he did: it began to undulate like waves, then dissolved until another image altogether appeared there. It was a building of the kind Megan most despised – a church. "Tsst!' she hissed. People began to file out of the arched double doors at the front. She stared with interest. Just as a young woman with blonde hair not unlike

22

her own appeared, Rab made a choking noise and spat out the nut she had fed him. It hit the mirror and the scene evaporated.

In her shock and frustration, Megan let the bird go. She gave a cry of rage. "That was the best yet! It might have led tae somethin'!" On reflection, though, she had to admit it was unlikely. What would Sam or his mate have to do with a kirk? Rab was eyeing her from the end of the hull. "I dinna think ye're doin' my bidding, bird," she said. "I dinna send ye oot for a wee day in the country. I want to know where Sam is. But more than that, I want to know where his mate is. And you will lead me to them. Sooner or later." Her staff, never far from her, was sticking out of the man's belt she wore with her faded Victorian day dress, forming a rod to her back. She reached above her head, whipping it out, and before Rab could spread his wings, he found himself tethered by the leg to a nail jutting out of the hull.

Megan returned her staff to its holding place and concentrated afresh on the mirror. Gripping it in both hands, she turned it this way and that, not looking at her reflection, but casting about the beach. The tide was low, and rock pools glinted black amongst jagged boulders. She sighed, for she saw nothing. No glimpse of a naked woman searching for shellfish and crabs in the rock pools; a naked woman who, she knew, would simply be a shore otter if she turned around, for she would be unaware that an enchanted looking glass revealed her secret form. "I will have you yet," hissed Megan.

Chapter 3

On the morning of the wedding, Tully met Sam as he emerged from the loch, mouth full of fish. Sam froze and stared at him wide-eyed, caught out. Tully had taught him how to fish like a man. He took his catch home for Rose to cook. Tully had hoped this would wean Sam away from his creature habits. To his relief, his future father-in-law just smiled.

"Come ashore and eat yer fill, lad," he said. "Breakfast's not up tae much the day, for I'll have tae get it. Ye canna see the bride. Bad luck."

Sam removed the fish. "I'm sorry for this. I'm nervous. I just wanted tae fish in my old way, one last time. I promise I'll content myself wi' cooked fish from now on."

Sam had been banished from the house since tea time yesterday. He was surprised to find he would miss Rose's breakfast. Human food took a bit of getting used to, but he was. He hadn't cared for Megan's offerings during his week's imprisonment – only the porridge was palatable – but Rose's efforts tasted fine, especially now fish was on the menu. He longed for the greater variety offered by the sea and the rock pools at Ballaness, though. It was, after all, why he had chosen to be a shore otter. He sat beside his boss and soon-to-be father-in-law, and ate as daintily as he could manage.

When he had finished, they returned to the cottage. William Tully cut chunks of porridge from the drawer and heated them.

"How did ye manage when Rose was a bairn?" Sam asked him. "I mean, when your wife died, an' Rose sae young?"

A darkness passed over Tully's face. The smile he had worn dropped suddenly, and his cheeks seemed to deflate. He looked gaunt.

"I'm sorry…" stammered Sam.

"Dinna fash yersel', lad," said Tully. Turning away, he continued. "I had a woman come in tae keep hoose for a couple o' years, until Rose could manage. She taught her what tae dae. She could manage fine by the time she was seven. Ye're gettin' a good wife, Hailstanes."

They could hear Rose stirring in her bedroom upstairs. Tully prepared a tray and carried it up to her. When he came back, he said that Sam should dress and set out on foot. His colleague, the gamekeeper MacAllistair who had found Sam and Rose in the river, would act as a witness along with his wife. Tully would drive Rose down in the cart – the bride and her father would arrive last, as was fitting.

"But before ye don yer weddin' finery," said Tully. "We've a job tae dae while Rose feeds the chickens. We'll move my things into Rose's room, and her belongings – and yours, such as they are – into mine. Ye have need o' a double bed, an' I don't."

Sam gulped his tea, the tight feeling seizing his throat again. He nodded.

There were light showers that late April morning. The loch wore its grey face, reflecting the uncertain sky. The smell of vegetation was sweet, though, as the morning admitted the warmth of the coming summer. Daffodils were still in full bloom high up among the hills, and Sam squatted down and buried his head in a clump of them outside the church, their sharp tang a balm to the rising nausea of his nerves. He imagined he was an otter again, nosing through a cluster of blooms on the banks of the Dunn deep in Jeanette's territory, on his way to her warm welcome. It would be night, of course, for that was her preferred time to forage and hunt. He could almost feel the night air alive with promise, and see the moonlight shining on her magnificent pelt.

"Are ye ready, Mr. Hailstanes?"

The voice startled him, and he fell backwards. He sat on the stony graveyard path and looked up into the features of the minister. Sam was beginning to be able to distinguish differences among humans now. This man, he knew, was much younger than William Tully. Sam compared the face before him to his own, which he had taken to studying in mirrors and reflections in the loch. He judged he was around the same age as himself. Tully had told him to tell folk he was twenty-five. The minister had a fierce look about him.

"Aye," said Sam. "Ready." He supposed he should look happier as a bridegroom. He forced a smile and hoped it didn't look too much like an animal baring of teeth. Something about the minister made him wary.

"And the banns have been cried in the parish of your birth, as the law demands?"

"Aye." Sam raised his chin and stared him out, although he knew otherwise.

"And you have the licence?"

Footsteps crunched on the path. "I have that," said another voice. Sam turned to see the head gamekeeper on Craigendon estate, the same who had found him with Rose that fateful morning last month.

"This whole matter is a tad...irregular," said the minister, peering over his hooked nose. "It is my duty to ensure all is done according to the law of the land."

"It has been. It is," said Jock MacAllistair. He stood legs apart, a solid pillar of a man, and even without the gun he habitually carried in the course of his work, he looked powerful and fearsome.

"The laws of God have already been defied, in the conceiving of a child out of wedlock," said the minister.

"Then it's your job to set things right in His sight, Reverend," MacAllistair said, pleasantly enough. Nobody else would have dared speak to a kirk minister like that.

Sam was still sitting on the path. He almost felt like an otter again. He didn't belong among men who hid murky meanings under their words. MacAllistair issued a soft kick to his back, and he remembered he had a role to play. He had a role to play for the rest of his life. He stood up quickly, swaying from the sudden rush of blood to his head.

MacAllistair thumped him on the back and held up a pewter hip flask. "Here, son. Ye'll be needin' a bit o' courage."

Sam detected the tang of barley in the stuff men called whisky. Tully had bid him drink it before. As on that occasion, he waved the flask away with thanks. There were other things in there that didn't seem so wholesome. The minister flushed crimson at the sight of the flask and stalked away.

"It's a fine thing ye dae this mornin', lad," said MacAllistair, taking a swig. "Rose is a good lass, and worthy of standin' by. Come on, now, and dinna mind that parsimonious ba…buzzard." He winked at Sam.

They walked into the church together. Mrs. MacAllistair, a kindly matron in her best tweed suit, said she was waiting at the door for Rose to arrive. The pews were deserted. The only sign a wedding was to take place was the large display of flowers on a stand. These had been gifted by Lady Craigendon, from the hot houses up at the manor where the employer of Tully and MacAllistair lived in grandeur. Sam was not officially an employee of the estate. His arrangement was purely with Tully, for bed and board and the money he would spare him when necessary. Sam winced at the strong scent from the flowers. He had no idea what they were; nothing like that grew in the wild. He and MacAllistair stood at the front of the plain little church. It was freezing cold. Despite the dampness of the day, outside was warmer.

There was a cough from the back, and Sam turned to see the minister leading Rose and her father down the aisle, Mrs. MacAllistair bringing up the rear. Rose wore a light blue dress and jacket he hadn't seen before. She carried a bouquet of the same exotic flowers as were in the vase, and she had given one to Mrs. MacAllistair, for the woman wore it pinned into her brooch. They walked in silence. There was no-one playing the organ, for there were to be no hymns. Tully delivered Rose to Sam's side. The minister took his place facing them. MacAllistair had been right, Sam reflected; there was something hawkish about him. He was staring at Rose with a glint of the hunter in his eye.

"Who gives this woman to be married?" he intoned.

"I do," said Tully. He let go of Rose's arm, not meeting her beseeching eyes, and stepped back.

Sam saw the bouquet tremble in Rose's hands. "She's a wee moose," he thought. He didn't mean it as an insult. She was mouse-like in her way. He supposed she was attractive, though. He couldn't judge such things, but he had looked around at church and not seen hair as bonny as hers on any of the other women. It was particularly beautiful today, freshly washed and brushed and arranged over her shoulders in those tumbling corkscrew curls that reminded him of Megan. His thoughts wandered, heart-wrenchingly, to Jeanette and her river of rich brunette locks.

Rev. O'Neill was preaching at them. The words went over Sam's head. Finally, they came to the vows, in which he had been well schooled. "I do," he said, when called upon, and Rose did likewise; both playing their parts, puppets in a play, their strings being pulled by others. Sam was aware of the heavy wooden vault of the church roof above him. He felt claustrophobic, as if it was bearing down on him. In his mind's eye, it was becoming Megan's boat-house, and he was shackled again. He closed his eyes against the sensation, snapping them open when he heard that he and Rose were now pronounced man and wife. It was done, apart from signing the papers. He had laboriously practised his signature all that week, and he signed himself away. He was Samuel Hailstanes now, husband and father-to-be, and unpaid water bailiff's assistant.

Mrs. MacAllistair laid on a spread for them back at the gamekeeper's cottage. It was simple fare, and the newly-weds cut a sponge cake decorated with their initials in a heart, for there had been no time to make the traditional fruit cake which would have needed soaking with brandy at regular intervals for two months at least. There was, however, a large Cloutie Dumpling. Sam thought he had never tasted anything so delicious in his life, and said so. Mrs. MacAllistair promised the recipe to Rose. Tully cleared his throat and made a speech. He spoke of Rose's grace and loveliness; he said how she reminded him of her mother, and that he was proud of the way she had taken on the household. He said Sam was a fine young man. There were tears in everybody's eyes except Sam's, helped on no doubt by the whisky liberally dished out by MacAllistair, of which even Rose partook in good measure. Sam didn't judge. No doubt she needed courage as much as he did.

Once they had eaten and drunk their fill, Tully took the young couple aside and told them he would be spending the night with the MacAllistairs, to give them time alone together. The water bailiff's cottage was all theirs today and tonight, as indeed it would be in time to come. "For," he said, placing a fatherly hand on Sam's shoulder, yet pinching it hard to convey his meaning, "I know ye'll always do right by my daughter, and by me."

Sam and Rose rode back to the cottage in the cart in strained silence. It was mid-afternoon, and the rest of the day stretched endlessly ahead. Rose took the reins because Sam hadn't learned how to drive the cart yet. He was just learning about the horse and other animals the Tullies kept. At least the fact there were still jobs to be done would fill in the day. In the end, it was just the same as any other afternoon and evening, apart from the expectation of the night looming over them. They both seemed keen to push any thoughts of it away, however, in a zealous flurry of work. They stayed apart as much as possible. When it came time for tea, Rose left Sam a loaf and a fresh pot of jam, and some cheese and butter, saying she wasn't hungry after the wedding meal, and had gone for a walk. It was twilight when she returned. The issue couldn't be avoided much longer.

Sam was gazing at the loch, exhausted with unnecessary work he had done, and with feeling numb and yet overwhelmed by emotions all at the same time. Rose sidled up to him and took his hand. It was the first time their fingers had intertwined. She said nothing, and wouldn't meet his gaze, but she led him to the cottage and up the stairs to her father's former bedroom. He noticed that the bed had been changed. A much finer bedspread covered it now.

"My mother made it for her bridal bed," said Rose. She rolled off her stockings, fumbled with her buttons and let her dress slip to the floor. She climbed beneath the sheets in her underwear and lay waiting, resignation on her face.

Sam remembered she had said her bairn's conception had been her only time. He had made love with Jeanette in human form. He knew what was expected of him. Taking her lead, he stripped down to his underwear and climbed in beside her. She lay stiffly, her fingers clawing the sheet which covered the mattress. Her chest rose and fell as she gulped air in great breaths, and he knew her heart thudded. His did, too. He leaned over and inhaled her scent. She smelt of flowers. Why did women do that, he wondered? Why did they mask nature's smells?

Puzzled, she turned to look at him. "It's only rose water. The gardener at the big hoose spares me some of the fallen petals frae ma favourites, and I make it."

Sam didn't answer. He sought another scent, and he didn't find it. There was no smell to indicate that this young woman desired him, no scent that marked her as ready to be his mate. As with the farce at the kirk this morning, they were playing their parts, strings pulled by others who called the rules of human conventions. Well, he had learned enough to know that he was master in this marriage now. What went on between them was their business, and nobody else's.

In truth, he did desire her, now he lay close to her semi-naked body. It was weeks since he had lain with a female, and this was the time of year he was at his most active that way, when the sap was rising all around. It disgusted him, though, to think that he could take her because of a few words in a church and a couple of signatures. It made him sick to know that these things gave him permission to do with her as he would. He owned her now, as her father had owned her and could marry her off to a total stranger to save face. He wondered at the ways of men. He would never have paid attention to Jeanette, or any female, in that way, unless her scent had marked her as being receptive. Even then, if she didn't want him, making it plain, he would back off. Yet this frail creature lay next to him, not wanting him yet presenting herself for his taking. He jumped from the bed and began to pull his clothes back on.

"Sam, what...?" cried Rose.

"We'll try again after the bairn's born," he said. "Until then, I'll leave ye in peace."

Her pretty face was a mask of confusion. He bent down and kissed her tenderly on the lips.

"All in good time," he said.

Sam was content to move back into the barn. He had an old horsehair mattress in the hayloft on which to rest his human bones, and blankets to make up for lack of the pelt he would never feel upon him again. He liked it out there, waking to find spiders spinning above his head as he had been used to in his holt. Tully returned to the cottage, but made no remark upon the arrangement. It was clear no grudge was held on either side, for the young couple continued as before, but with an added warmth and amiability between them which led Sam to believe that he could live happily enough here as Rose's husband. He continued with his training as a water bailiff, and with his literacy lessons from Rose. The instruction he feared to ask, however, was how to be a parent to a human child, for he still had no idea what that was about.

Then, a week after the wedding, he had no need to worry any more. Passing the outdoor privy after his morning swim, he heard sobbing. On knocking at the door and asking if she was alright, Rose's distraught face appeared as she opened the door a crack and informed him that she had lost the baby. If Sam seemed indifferent, it was put down to the fact that the child wasn't his. Only Tully discerned the relief behind the young man's mask.

"I hope ye realise this makes nae difference," he said to Sam. "Ye've sworn vows tae Rose, before God and witnesses. Give her some time tae recover, then join her in your room. Father bairns o' yer own."

"Of course," Sam replied. "I had no thought tae dae otherwise."

The older man patted him on the shoulder. "It's May Day the morn, lad. Rose'll no' be up tae it, but we should go tae the fete doon at Ballaness."

When Sam looked at him in surprise, he continued swiftly, "Dinna get ideas. A certain wild woman never shows her face at such things, an' you will not go lookin', Sam. We made a gentleman's agreement by the shaking of hands, and ye're tied tae Rose in the sight o' God and the law," said Tully. "Put it all behind ye. Ye have a new life. We should let it be seen that we're family. And an added bonus would be tae stock up on salt water fish, freshly caught, maybe even some crabs. How about it – eh, son?"

Chapter 4

It was the early hours of May Day and still dark when Megan pushed the door of her house-boat shut and locked it. She looked in the round window and curled her lip at Rab the raven, feathers drooping, head under his wing, pathetically tethered by two chains. "We got there in the end," she said to him. "Ye've led me tae one o' them, at least. Ye surely weren't sae stupid as tae think I would let ye give warnin'?"

She headed south along the shore. The shingle was slippery with spray, and the air tingled with early morning dew laced with salt. It was calm, though, and the darkness enveloped her as she strode out with her staff, sure-footed on ground she knew well. She heard the Dunn before she saw it, rushing over pebbles to pour itself into the sea. Standing on the bank, she set her sights upriver, and determinedly began to plod her way, keeping close to the edge, head turned towards the gurgling water. She had assumed Sam's mate was a shore otter like him, but she had been mistaken, and had wasted enough time. The darkness began to thin out as dawn approached, and she hurried her pace, for sunrise brought other deeds that day.

Megan smiled as she came upon what she was looking for sooner than she had expected, and in a way which allowed no mistake. Where the ruined castle of the Earls of Ballaness perched on its mound above the Dunn sat a young woman. She was naked, her flesh as milky as the hawthorn which surrounded her. Her hair tumbled around her shoulders in rich brown tresses. It covered her breasts and the two infants who suckled there. She smiled at them, but when she looked up, her gaze was seawards, and there was despair and longing in her eyes. Megan approached silently until she stood looking down on them.

"Ye'll be seeking Sam?"

Jeanette turned a startled face towards the sea witch. One of the babes, a boy, lost its hold on her breast and let out a cry. Megan took in the appearance of her rival; the strong cheekbones and jaw, the prominent brown eyes, the small but lithe and muscular body, the dark river of hair. She herself was dainty of feature, and fair, and proud of it.

"Are they Sam's?" she asked. It had mystified her at first that Sam refused to lie with her, saying he had a mate. Jeanette wasn't his only mate, and no doubt Sam wasn't hers. It seemed she was his true love, however, and he knew that Megan wanted that position for herself. He had feared that lying with her would trap him in human form forever, he had said; well, that was, after all, what she had intended, and she had seen to it anyway, precisely because he would not sleep with her. Yet he could still meet with his otter woman any night she chose to change her form.

Jeanette recovered from her shock, and hope dawned in her eyes. "Have ye seen him lately? Aye, these are his pups. Bairns," she corrected herself.

"I've seen him, though not lately," said Megan. "I've known him a while, as man and beast. I know fine what ye are. Ye wouldn't find human mothers feedin' their brats naked oot in the wilds, no' even on May Day."

Jeanette paled at the harsh words, her gaze taking in the strange woman and her staff. "You're Megan, the sea witch."

Megan blinked, eyes wide. "He told you of me?"

"We had no secrets," said Jeanette. "He said you were his friend."

Megan reddened as if she had been slapped.

"Dae ye know where he is?" Jeanette asked, placing the girl infant in her lap while burping the boy over her shoulder.

"No," Megan replied, aware that the otter woman feared nothing from her. She smiled, drawing herself up so that she reared above the sitting mother, helpless with her babes. "And you never will, either. Or if ye do find oot, there'll not be a thing ye can dae aboot it!"

As she raised her staff, Jeanette realised the danger, but too late. Blue light flashed from the tip as Megan mumbled, twisting the staff, and Jeanette regressed to otter form. Megan paced the curse with deliberate languor, so she could enjoy seeing fur grow on the rounded breasts, belly and limbs of her rival, and whiskers sprout on that handsome face. The spell took in the children, too, but in her shock, Jeanette let the one on her lap, the girl, slip into the river before the curse hit. Soon, Jeanette and her other child were in the water also, as otters. The female infant remained human. Megan pointed her staff at the baby where she floundered in the current, but she found that the spell didn't work. Somehow, the mother and the boy were consigned to otter form forever, but the girl remained human.

Megan shrank back, dismayed; then she threw off her cloak and launched herself into the river, swimming expertly in her water element despite her clinging skirts. She seized the child and carried her to the river bank, laying her down awkwardly in the long grass. The babe let out a pitiful wail. Casting a glance at the mother and her pup swimming wild-eyed in mid-stream, she shrugged. "I'm sorry. I didn't mean for this tae happen." She gathered herself together and headed along the bank towards the sea. She held her hands over her ears to shut out the cries of the infant she had left, but to no avail. Looking back, she saw that Jeanette had hauled herself out and was pawing around her child. The otter-woman made pitiful creature noises of her own to add to her daughter's cacophony, and she had managed to scratch the baby's fine flesh with her claw; blood dribbled on to the grass.

Megan turned round and began to run back towards the pair on the bank. Jeanette saw her coming and raced at her. She seized her skirt in her teeth and pulled. "Let go!" yelled Megan. "I've turned back tae help her!" Jeanette ignored her, nosing under her petticoats and sinking her teeth into Megan's ankle. As she withdrew and reared on to her hind legs, ready to launch herself at Megan, the sea witch pointed her staff and froze the creature where she stood, teeth bared. She was small, but she was a fearsome sight. Megan took off her cloak and wrapped the helpless baby in it.

"I'm sorry, Jeanette!" Megan cried. "I'll do what I can tae help." She pointed her staff again, and the otter fell gracefully on to her front paws and regarded Megan expectantly, her deep breaths alone revealing her turmoil. "I can't reverse the spell," said Megan. "I would if I could, but my magic isn't powerful enough. My mother died before…before we were both ready. I can't change some things I've done, I don't know how!" Jeanette's head drooped. "Look, help me, if ye can," said Megan, "gather grasses, an' some heather an' moss."

34

The two of them set to work. Jeanette's paws were dexterous, and she plucked and pulled as eagerly as the sea witch, employing her mouth, too. Before long, a heap of natural materials lay on the bank of the Dunn. Megan pointed her staff and closed her eyes, directing the picture in her mind down her arm and out into the bleached ash wood staff. A mist gathered, and when it cleared, a basket of woven grass lined with moss, with a blanket of softest moss and heather, stood waiting for its cargo. Jeanette gave a cry as Megan removed the infant, who had fallen asleep, from her cloak, wrapped her in the blanket she had conjured, and placed her in the basket.

"It's fully protected," said Megan to the distraught mother. "Watertight as any boat, an' I'll watch tae see she's safe. I give you my word, Jeanette."

She carried the basket down the bank and waded into the river, swimming out to the middle, pushing the infant ahead of her and launching the basket into the current. Jeanette scrambled in after her, and swam beside her child as Megan pulled herself from the water and set off on foot to follow the basket's course to the sea.

"Ye live in different worlds now, Jeanette," she called to the otter. "Go back and tend tae yer son!"

The mother's huge eyes were molten beacons of pain as she watched a few seconds more, then she turned tail and swam for her holt.

The sky was just a shade lighter than Megan's grey dress, but she didn't turn her feet in the direction of the ancient spring beside the so-called saint's cave that May Day. The cave was the haunt of ancient sea witches, her ancestors, and she knew she had broken faith with them in her treatment of Sam and his family. She usually visited it well before the sun was above the horizon, just as darkness was dispersing, because she revelled in grey times of transition. The blackness of night was for those witches darker than she, and the daylight was for mortals who knew only superstition and not magic.

The locals arrived every year at sunrise to wash their faces in St. Bride's Spring, for the blessings of St. Bride upon their health and fertility. They were unaware that the strange, striking woman never seen without her hooded cloak, who dwelt in the old up-turned boat on the shore and had been held in suspicion and fear for generations, had already squatted on the holy stone from which the spring emerged. She had cupped her hands and bathed her naked body from top to toe in the sacred spring, renewing her beauty and vitality. Not on this May Day of 1928, however. Megan the Sea Witch o' Ballaness stood still as a rock on the shore, staring at a speck in the water only her witch's eye could perceive by now, carrying it on the tide of her will towards the Faerie Isle of Ailsa Craig. Tears coursed down her cheeks as she wept for her mother, and the motherless bairn borne upon the brine.

Tully and Sam set off for Ballaness that May Day afternoon, Sam at the reins of the cart since Tully said he had to learn. Tully also wanted to take Sam's mind off his return to home territory. It had to be faced some time, for Rose was fond of Ballaness, and Tully was determined that his daughter and son-in-law would live the life of any normal married couple. He also had to make sure he could trust Sam not to seek the sea witch. Rose waved them away from the bedroom window. She was going for a nap, recovering as she was from her miscarriage. Tully glanced at Sam on the seat beside him. This was a test of how well he would pass himself off, not just with handling the cart, but as a man out socializing. When Rose lost the baby, Tully had cursed himself for an interfering fool for marrying her off to Sam, but then he had reconsidered. Her condition had been known, so it was as well the marriage had taken place; and Sam was a biddable son-in-law who would remain so, because he needed Tully. All things considered, the water bailiff quietly congratulated himself.

The fete wasn't far from its conclusion when the pair arrived at Ballaness. Tully took the reins for the last few miles, concerned that Sam would drive them into a ditch. His hands were sweating at the sight of Ailsa Craig rearing from the sea, like a mountaintop from a kingdom hidden beneath the waves. They stopped and changed places, Tully telling the young man to compose himself. Their main reason for going was to purchase fish, he said. Other than that, they were just showing face, as he normally would with Rose. Her recent loss was an excuse for their tardy arrival.

Rev. Neville O'Neill had been invited to judge the home baking competition that year, and he patrolled the tables in the large marquee with his colleague from Ballaness parish acting as host. Tully peered in and smiled wryly at O'Neill's discomfort. It was well known that the May Day Fete, beginning with the superstitious dawn pilgrimage to the ancient spring on the shore, did not meet with the minister's approval. Something moved at the edge of Tully's vision, and he gazed up the hill to where a figure shrouded in long clothing stood starkly against the sky. He couldn't believe what he was seeing, and shot a startled glance at Sam. To his relief, the younger man's attention was out at sea, where it had been most of the time since they arrived; he wasn't doing well at being sociable with the acquaintances Tully introduced to him. Now, Tully could see that he was focusing on an approaching fishing boat, no doubt glad that they could buy fish soon and depart.

As the boat berthed, however, there came a cry from one of the fishermen: "We've landed more than fish the day!" He clambered ashore and turned to take a bundle from his ship mate, who was stripped to the waist. The bundle was given and received with great care, although it seemed to be no more than the half-naked fisherman's sweater; but then a tiny hand and arm poked out, clawing at its coverings, and a plaintive mewling rent the air. The big man rocked the bundle and cooed.

Prize judging forgotten, everybody rushed to see the strange catch. Answering many questions at once, the crew climbed out on to the quayside to display a basket woven of grasses and moss. They said they had found the infant, a girl, floating in it out near Ailsa Craig. She had slept like somebody drugged until they berthed. They pulled back the folds of the sweater to reveal a blanket of what appeared to be moss and heather somehow knitted seamlessly together. Nobody there had ever seen anything like it.

Tully stared as some in the crowd shrank away from the child, and others crossed themselves. An old woman, watery eyes filled with fear, said the babe was surely a changeling, found floating out there by the Faerie Isle. Rev. O'Neill tutted – had there not been enough superstitious nonsense that day, he asked. He tried to take charge, saying the police should be called, and that the mother should be found and held responsible for abandoning what was no doubt the consequence of fornication. Tully flushed and looked at the ground, suddenly remembering Sam and wondering what he was making of it. Sam was no longer at his side. He had gone right up to the fisherman and was staring at the baby with a rapt expression. Tully watched as he bent over the child until his nose was almost buried in the bundle of clothing. Abruptly, he straightened up and spoke.

"We'll take the bairn. My wife and I will look after her."

Tully's mouth fell open. He noticed the MacAllistairs in the crowd for the first time. Mrs. MacAllistair stepped forward and asked Sam, with meaning in her concerned expression, if Rose was well enough. Sam was adamant. There were murmurs, and a young woman spoke up and invited Sam to bring the infant to her cottage. She said she could lend him baby clothes and blankets, for the infant had soiled her coverings, and they could spoon-feed her some evaporated milk, for her cries indicated growing hunger. She would do fine on evaporated milk, she said. Tully pushed through the people standing in front of him.

"Sam!" he said. "Ye can't do this. Ye canna just take a strange bairn home an' expect Rose tae take it on!"

In response, Sam merely looked back at him and held his gaze, eyes blazing with spirit Tully hadn't yet encountered in the young man. Tully looked away first. He glanced up the hill, but the cloaked figure on the skyline had gone.

Megan dragged herself along the shingle to her house-boat, her body as heavy now as her spirits. She let herself in and pointed her staff at the chains which bound Rab. It took an effort, and when he was free, she dropped the staff and fell upon her bed. The raven cocked his head and hopped on to her pillow, pecking at a curl of hair, lifting it to peer at his mistress's face. Tears ran unchecked down her cheeks, soundless in her exhaustion.

"I've done wicked things," she whispered to her bird. She pictured the basket bearing the baby on the waves of the Irish Sea and the waves of her will. Her target had been the cave in the great granite rock which directly faced Ballaness. If she had managed to guide the basket there, the child would have found a safe haven, for Ailsa Craig was a gateway to the hidden world from which her otter-folk ancestors had come centuries ago. Other creatures came and went from there also, and would have known her for what she was. Megan hadn't been strong enough, however. The basket's course had been slow and erratic, and she had watched helplessly as the fishing boat scooped it up in its nets and bore the mysterious cargo back to Ballaness. She had run along the beach then, and up on to the high ground overlooking the village, well away from the throng at the fete. She was bewildered by Sam's presence there, with that man, the one who she knew used to be a water bailiff in these parts. No matter; the child was with her father, and it was the best thing to have happened in the circumstances.

"I need time tae recover," Megan told Rab. "I'm drained. Then ye'll have tae look for them for me. I need tae find oot if they're well, and can cope. I canna change what I've done, but I can maybe help. No more meddlin', I swear that on the memory o' my mother."

Her body slumped as she fell into a faint. Rab pulled at her cloak to gather it snugly around her.

Tully drove the cart back into the hills as Sam nursed the thrashing infant in her borrowed wrappings, struggling to hold her. "That's no newborn bairn," he said, glancing sidelong. "So, ye recognised yer own, then?"

"She has my scent and her mother's," said Sam. "And nothin' ye can say or do will stop me carin' for my daughter."

"This'll be the sea witch's doing. She was on the hill."

Sam looked surprised. "I guessed she was behind it. But I thought ye said she never came near the fete?"

"She doesn't. She was obviously watchin' tae see what happened. I suppose yer mate will be lookin' for the child – and you."

Sam's voice came out on a sob. "If Jeanette was alright, or even cursed tae remain a human like me an' the bairn, she would be with her. The bairn wouldn't be floatin' at sea in a basket only the sea witch could conjure." He had flung the woven vessel over a hedge once they were clear of Ballaness; let it rot.

"Ye'll not be lookin' tae join her, then?"

Sam's head drooped. "I doubt she's alive. But I can't believe that my old friend would be capable of murder!"

Tully hesitated. "I can't, either. Many's a thing, meddlin' and mischief, but not that."

Sam looked at him gratefully. "I'll not condemn her, then, when I don't know what happened. Maybe she just took the bairn, then couldn't cope. She wanted a daughter."

"Oh aye, she always does," said Tully.

39

Sam frowned. "It canna be the same woman, Tully. Not the one you knew. She looks younger than Rose."

Tully laughed wryly. "I told ye she could go against nature. It's St. Bride's Spring, lad, the one near the cave. It renews her in every way. I've seen her there with my own two eyes, naked like the heathen she is, sittin' on the stone and cuppin' the water in her hands tae bathe hersel'."

"So, how old is she?"

"God alone knows. Or the Devil. She's his spawn. Dae ye not know the legend? The Sea Witch o' Ballaness has been there as long as folk remember. She seeks a mate tae make a daughter every few years, but she sends him packin' and the child is never seen. She sends her back as tribute tae the Faerie Isle, so the story goes, tae the faeries who gave her her powers. The holy spring runs fresh frae an underground stream fed by a lake deep inside the Faerie Isle, and that renews her every year on May Day." He paused. "Ye intend tae keep this spawn o' yours, then, an' foist her on Rose?"

"Aye," said Sam, "as I would have kept and cared for Rose's bairn. I know this wee one's lost tae our race, like me," he said. "I won't seek her mother." He was puzzling over Tully's words, though, for he knew Megan loved him and had wanted him to stay with her. She wouldn't have let him go once a child had been conceived, he was certain. The explanation that she had taken the infant to replace the daughter he wouldn't give her made sense, but he had never heard this strange tale about the Faerie Isle.

Tully's face was grim. "Rose must never know the truth. Make out ye're replacin' what she lost, tryin' tae help in a clumsy way."

"Why are ye so keen she shouldn't know there's more tae this world than most folks understand?" Sam asked. "She would believe us, not ridicule ye as ye fear others would if ye told them things ye saw long ago. It's time she was told the truth."

"No!" barked Tully. "She's delicate. It would be too much for her."

"She's stronger than you think," said Sam. "But I'll go along with what ye say. For now."

The baby had fallen asleep by the time they arrived back at the water bailiff's cottage. They found Rose in the kitchen baking scones. Sam carried his precious bundle in, looking to Tully for help, but his father-in-law made a gesture that clearly said explanations were all down to him.

"What's that ye've got there?" asked Rose.

"It's a bairn, a wee lassie, that's been abandoned. She was found oot at sea, floatin' like Moses in a basket, an…"

Tully interrupted him in an undertone. "Nothin' holy aboot that bairn, if ye ask me."

Rose looked from one man to the other. "Ye've brought an abandoned bairn back here? Why?"

"I thought," said Sam, taking a deep breath, and with a glance at Tully, "that since ye've lost one, ye might like this wee one tae console ye."

Rose stared at him, shocked. "I hadn't even got used tae the idea o' havin' my own," she said.

"Well, the bairn needs a home," said Sam awkwardly, "and I thought we may as well take her."

"Have the police been informed?" asked Rose, still not moving from her stance at the kitchen table. "Are they not lookin' for the mother?"

Tully spoke. "Rev. O'Neill was there, and he said he would inform them. But I doubt anything will come of their enquiries."

"So," said Sam, "we'll raise her as ours. The woman who lent us these clothes thinks she's maybe eight or nine weeks old."

Still Rose didn't move. Sam carried the baby over to her, and she peered at it hesitantly. "I have no idea how tae look after this bairn," she said. "I expected it would come naturally wi' my own…"

Tully rounded on Sam. "I told ye this was a bad idea. I think we should hand her over tae the police. They'll take her tae the orphanage in Ayr…"

"We'll do no such thing," said Sam. His eyes blazed with meaning. Tully made a gesture of submission and was silent.

"I want tae keep this lass, Rose. I want tae raise her as I would have raised the one you lost. I was expected tae dae that, an' I'm not askin' any more o' you."

"But why?" asked Rose.

Sam thought quickly. "Am I not an orphan myself? Can I not take pity on one abandoned like me, an' spare her what I went through?" He shot a triumphant glance at Tully. "We'll call her Jeanette."

Rose dusted her floury hands on her apron, and lifted the edge of the blanket to look closely at the infant. "I don't like that name," she said. "If I'm tae take her on, I think the choice should be mine."

Sam shrugged, relieved to see her coming round to the idea. "Fair enough, as ye wish, Rose."

"Helena," she said. "Helena Hailstanes. It has a ring to it. But I still want the police tae look for the mother, mind."

Sam smiled. "Pour some of yer whisky, Tully. I might even try a sip. We'll drink tae Helena Hailstanes, the new water bailiff's daughter!"

Rose took the baby from him. Helena woke and stared at Rose with large brown eyes. Tully picked up his whisky bottle and stalked out of the kitchen.

A few days later, at Ballaness, Megan sifted through the chest of clothes she kept, most handed down from those who had gone before her, or items found while beach combing. She pulled out garments she thought suitable and set to altering them. Hours later, she changed into a dress she had cut down, so it wasn't as long as her usual attire. She thought it would pass. There was a coat there, too, which would do. She packed two more dresses into an ancient leather bag, with stockings and undergarments. Hesitating, she finally decided to add one of the long grey gowns she habitually wore, and her cloak. Among the clothes, she tucked her precious mirror and a number of small glass bottles and phials. The mixtures contained in these were the only means she had ever known to make money, not that she had ever needed much, following her mother in making remedies to sell to those brave or desperate enough to seek out the sea witch. She believed she knew where she could pursue this livelihood, now that she judged herself unworthy of her heritage. This done, she sighed and turned her attention to her staff.

Hands shaking, she caressed it before sitting with it over her knees. Then she took a knife and, tears streaming down her face, cut a length off the tip and began to whittle away at it. Megan felt as if she had severed an arm and she had a sensation of growing weaker with every stroke of the knife. She gritted her teeth and reminded herself the weakening of her power had already begun because of what she had done, and could only increase, though slowly.

That night, hair tamed and pinned at the back of her head, and passing for any young woman of modest means in that era, she pulled the door of her house-boat shut behind her, whistled to Rab to follow, and set off into the darkness.

※

Chapter 5

Sam could hear his daughter crying from where he lay curled up in the hayloft, wondering about the fate of Jeanette and any other pups there may have been. He hoped they were still alive and well. He was certain Megan would not have killed to obtain Helena, but his disappearance and her abduction would be hard on Jeanette. Unable to bear the crying any longer, he made a decision. He climbed down the ladder and headed for the cottage. Tully was sitting in the kitchen, whisky glass in hand.

"See what ye've done?" he said as Sam entered. "There'll be sleep for none of us from now on!"

Sam shrugged. "It would have been the same wi' Rose's own bairn."

"That's different! She would have wanted it, and it would have taken comfort from its mother. She's not this one's mother, an' she doesn't want it, Hailstanes!"

"Let me tell her the truth, Tully."

The older man's eyes narrowed. "No. Never. Or you and your brat can get oot."

Sam clenched his fists and bit his tongue. He had no more idea how to look after Helena than he would have any other baby, but he had come to help, and he would waste no more time on his father-in-law. He walked over to the stairs which led up from the kitchen, and went up to the bedroom he hadn't seen since their wedding night.

Rose was pacing the bedroom floor, Helena over her shoulder. The baby's face was puce with crying, her mop of soft dark hair soaked with sweat. Rose stopped and stared at Sam as he came in. "Sam, this really isn't the night to…"

He held up a hand to silence her. "I've come tae help, Rose, no other reason. What dae ye take me for?"

She shouted at him over the baby's cries. "A man, Sam, a man! Only a man would have tried to replace a lost bairn with one found, like…like bringin' home a stray cat tae cheer up a child that had lost its pet!"

"Here, give her tae me!" yelled Sam.

Rose handed Helena over and collapsed on to the bed. Sam began to pace the floor with her. She stopped struggling and relaxed against him. Her cries lessened and died away. Rose looked both relieved and offended.

"I'm glad one of us has the touch," she said.

"Has she had more milk?" he asked.

"It takes so long tae get it intae her, Sam. We need a bottle. I can't go on wi' just a spoon."

"I'll try when she cries again," he said.

"Ye will?" Rose looked astonished.

"Of course," said Sam. "She's my responsibility. I mean, I brought her here."

Rose laughed. "Ye're a strange one, and no mistake, Sam Hailstanes. Even a bairn's real father doesn't do much tae help!"

Sam looked at the child in his arms, avoiding Rose's eyes. His daughter gazed back at him. He knew in that moment that he would do anything to protect her, always.

Two days later, Sam and Tully were about their duties on the estate when a knock came at the back door, and Rev. O'Neill peered round it. Rose sat in one of the chairs by the fire, feeding Helena evaporated milk with the baby's bottle Mrs. MacAllistair had borrowed when she had gone asking young mothers on the estate if they had any baby clothes and bedding they could spare. She put the bottle down and began to struggle to her feet, the baby protesting.

"Good afternoon, Minister," she said.

"Good afternoon, Mrs. Hailstanes," the reverend replied. "I would tell you not to get up, seeing how you are occupied, but I must inform you that Her Ladyship is at the front door, in her motor car."

Rose stared at him in shock. "Lady Craigendon? Whatever for?"

"She has brought gifts for the child," he replied, removing his hat. His tawny hair gleamed with flecks of gold in the sunlight streaming in the doorway, and his eyes were piercing. His shadow loomed over Rose, and she shrank back a little. He had had that effect on her ever since his arrival in the parish a year ago.

She tried to master her tired brain. Lady Craigendon wasn't known for playing the lady bountiful – she sent gifts as a duty, she didn't bring them. "I'll open up the good room, if ye could give me a few minutes. Go back tae Her Ladyship and I'll let you both in the front door," she said, laying Helena in the old borrowed crib at her feet, where she began to cry lustily.

As the minister let himself out, Rose pulled off her apron and closed the door on Helena's screams. She ran down the passageway from the kitchen to the seldom used parlour. There were dust sheets over the furniture which had been bought by her mother and father for their nuptials twenty-seven years ago, and she tugged them off and pushed them into a cupboard. Then she tidied her hair as she went to open the front door.

To her surprise, Lady Craigendon was at the wheel of the car, her chauffeur in the passenger seat. He went round and opened the door for her. She climbed out and he came after her, bearing a large basket. "Good afternoon, Mrs. Hailstanes," she said. "Jamieson here was giving me a driving lesson today, and I thought I may as well call by with some gifts for the new arrival. Rev. O'Neill was visiting, and told me all about her." As Rose dipped a curtsey, she breezed past her and entered the cottage as if she owned it – which she virtually did, it belonging to her husband's estate.

Rose tried to still her trembling hands and followed Her Ladyship, Rev. O'Neill and the chauffeur following on behind. Lady Craigendon found the parlour (which wasn't hard in a cottage) and took possession, instructing Jamieson to lay the basket down and take the reverend back to his home. Then she sat on the sofa and indicated to Rose to sit in one of the chairs.

It was unheard of for Lady Craigendon to visit the home of an estate employee, and Rose didn't know how to react. While she tried to find the words to offer tea, Rev.O'Neill prodded her in the back to do as Her Ladyship bid, then, taking off his hat, he said that, with Lady

46

Craigendon's permission, he would like to stay and offer his congratulations, too.

Rose sat in the chair indicated, the reverend taking the one on the opposite side of the fire. Jamieson left the room quietly, and Lady Craigendon opened the basket and began laying baby garments on the sofa beside her.

"These are from the nursery at Craigendon House," she said brightly. "No doubt Lord Craigendon's sister wore them, and maybe others before her. I thought you may as well have them. It's not as if I will ever have any use for them."

Lady Craigendon's childlessness was a great sadness to the couple in the manor house. She was in her mid-forties now, so what she said was probably true. The clothes were the finest children's garments Rose had ever seen, classic pieces of knitwear and little dresses of the kind still in fashion for infants. She didn't know what to say.

"Thank you, Your Ladyship. This is most generous. However, I'm not sure we'll be keeping the baby. The police are looking for her mother..."

Rev. O'Neill cleared his throat. "I think there's little likelihood of finding her, Mrs. Hailstanes."

Rose let the words lie between them in strained silence. She couldn't quite accept that Helena would be staying, that this was her life from now on, chained to the demands of a baby who wasn't even hers.

Lady Craigendon peered at her and seemed to be choosing her words carefully, which was unlike her. "Of course, I must also congratulate you on your recent marriage. And commiserate over the loss of your own child."

Rose flushed crimson, lost for words. Rev. O'Neill leaned forward and placed one of his great hands over hers as she twisted them in her lap. She did not find it a comfort, and struggled to keep herself from withdrawing her hands from beneath the talon-like fingers which groped to intertwine with her own. She couldn't meet his eye, or Lady Craigendon's.

He spoke. "I know that Mrs. Hailstanes was overwhelmed by the flowers Your Ladyship so kindly sent for her wedding," he said, squeezing Rose's hand.

"I was, yes, thank you. Very beautiful," she managed to say.

"And are you recovering, my dear?" her ladyship asked.

Rose glanced from one to the other. She had never known such shame, not even when she had to admit to her father that she was pregnant. They were both staring at her, eyes keen like hunters after prey.

"I'm well, thank you," she said in a whisper.

"And your husband hails from up north, I hear? How did you meet?"

"One day when I was out with a friend at Ballaness," mumbled Rose. It was what Tully had told her to say. She caught the look that passed between her visitors. They didn't believe her. Rev. O'Neill wore a hint of a smile which spoke of triumph.

"Well," said Lady Craigendon, "I'm sorry for your loss, but I think it admirable that you have taken in the waif. What a wonderful story, like a fairy tale, a child in a basket floating away out by Ailsa Craig. In recognition of your generosity, His Lordship will be offering proper, paid employment to Mr. Hailstanes, as official Assistant Water Bailiff."

O'Neill, whose fingers had still been massaging Rose's hands, pulled his hand away and sat up straight. "Really, Your Ladyship?"

"Oh yes," she said. "It's the least he can do."

"And does he know about it?" asked the minister, immediately clapping his hand to his lips at the impropriety of his question.

"No, Reverend, but he will," she replied icily. "I'm sure I can look to my husband to favour my idea."

Rose felt sick with nerves. It was well known that Lord Craigendon had recently had an affair with a house guest, a friend of Lady Craigendon, whom she had invited because the son was a talented artist. She had commissioned him to paint her portrait as a gift for her husband. The affair was the talk of the estate. Rose couldn't look either of her guests in the eye.

"I thank Your Ladyship," she managed to say.

"Well, since I hear the infant is wanting you, I'll be on my way," said Lady Craigendon. "Reverend, I shall drive you home."

The minister scratched his hooked nose. "Your Ladyship is too kind, but I'm happy to walk, thank you." He sounded as if he meant it. His eye met Rose's, and despite her nerves, her lips twitched at his obvious unwillingness to submit himself to the back seat of that car again.

He lingered after Rose had seen her important visitor away. "May I see the new arrival, please, Mrs. Hailstanes?"

Rose led the way to the kitchen and picked Helena up. The baby cried even louder than before and clawed at her dress. The minister peered down his nose at the infant, his eyes keen and curious.

Rose struggled with Helena and looked at him, puzzled. "Minister…" she said, "do ye have any idea who the mother might be? Is she maybe…dead, and relatives could have abandoned the bairn?"

He directed his gaze from Helena to her. "Do I have any idea who the mother might be? Oh no, Mrs. Hailstanes, not the mother. Well, I'll be on my way and let ye get on. You have your hands full. Perhaps more than ye realise."

Chapter 6

September 1929

Sam arrived home to find Helena tethered by a rope round her waist to the leg of the kitchen table. Ignoring her excited calls for his attention, and hiding his dismay, for the rope reminded him of being chained in the sea witch's abode, he walked to the stove and wrapped his arms around his wife, nuzzling into her neck.

"Unless ye want burned, get off me, Sam!" said Rose, but she was laughing. She turned her head briefly from staring at the saucepan she was stirring, and kissed him on the lips.

Seeing that she was in a good mood, Sam ventured to speak his mind. "Is it really necessary tae tie Helena like that?" he asked, squatting down to the child, who held plump arms out to her daddy and began to tell him the game she had been playing with her rag doll. Reckoning her birth date as March the previous year, she was by now eighteen months old, and her speech was advanced for that. If only the same could have been said for her potty training abilities.

"We've been through this, Sam," said Rose. "You're out most o' the day. She's a handful, an' if I turn ma back she's away an' there's pee and skitter in corners all over the hoose, just like a dirty pup! This way, I've a chance tae set her on the pot before she does it."

As if prompted, Helena abruptly tugged down her pants and squatted. Sam dismissed the thought that she might have done it on purpose. He picked her up gently and placed her on the potty which sat ready beside her. "This is where we pee, wee lass," he said. She looked into his eyes and giggled, and there was complicity there. He couldn't deny it. She knew full well what she was doing.

"I wish ye would let me take her swimmin', Rose," said Sam. "Oh I know, we've been through that, too!"

Rose sighed. "Ye would have had her in that loch from her youngest day! It's not natural, Sam. I grew up around water, an' I learned when I was four or five. Time enough."

"It would help burn off some energy, though, Rose. She would get intae less mischief."

Helena was, as Rose had said, a handful. She was tireless, exploring the cottage and croft and looking for things to be up to all day. She had walked at nine months, could talk in sentences by the time she was a year, and she ran Rose ragged. At least she had begun sleeping through the night at an early stage, something for which her parents were grateful...and it had enhanced their marriage in unforeseen ways. Sam hadn't been sure if they would ever have a proper marriage, but they did, and if it wasn't like falling in love with the partners they had known before, it was still, amazingly, love.

Rose was struggling with a heavy dish of fish pie she was taking out of the oven. Sam's mouth watered. He only ate cooked fish these days. He had managed to wean himself off hunting like an otter in the loch. She set it down and looked at him as he helped Helena tidy herself and picked up the potty to take outside.

"I'm sure swimmin' would only make her pee more," she said, lips pursed.

Sam glanced away to hide the familiar sadness he felt when Rose was sarcastic about Helena. At that moment, Tully came in. He wrinkled his nose in distaste at the potty Sam carried past him.

"I swear that infant stinks like an animal," he said.

Sam clenched his free fist and walked outside. He emptied the pot and rinsed it under the outdoor tap, went back in, untied Helena and set her on his knee. He picked up her comb and began to untangle her dark hair, which was long and thick for her age. Tully was sitting in his favourite chair, reading the newspaper. Rose continued to busy herself about the kitchen. Helena watched her.

"I like Mammy's fish pie!" she said. "I'm hungry!" She was beaming at Rose, showing dimples and sharp little teeth.

51

Rose didn't respond in any way. Tully didn't look up from his paper. Helena began to struggle on Sam's lap. She freed herself from his grasp and toddled across the kitchen.

"Mammy! Mammy!"

Rose slammed the lid on a pan of turnip and turned to glare down at her. "Ye'll get yer tea soon enough!" she said, hands on hips. "If ye hadn't kept me back, it would have been ready fifteen minutes ago!"

Sam sighed and rubbed his hand over his face. In the time it took him to do that, there was a screech from Rose, and his eyes snapped open to see Helena on the floor by her left ankle. She was chewing something, and there was blood on her chin and also trickling from Rose's leg.

"She bit me!" Rose yelled, tears of pain and rage blinding her eyes.

Things happened quickly then. Sam launched himself across the kitchen and slapped Helena on the back to dislodge the piece of Rose's flesh, swept her up and carried her outside. Rose, hanging over the kitchen sink nauseated and faint, watched him stride to the edge of the loch, cast off his boots while still gripping the infant under one arm, and wade in, clothes and all. Tully, his paper flung aside, ran to her aid and put his arm around her to comfort and support her as they watched him fling Helena into the depths.

"Oh, dear God!" cried Rose.

"I sometimes wonder if he even exists," said Tully, weeping. He had only wept in front of Rose once, and he wasn't crying as he had then, when Rose's mother had died, but in a high-pitched gibbering. Rose stared at him in shock.

"Da! He's goin' tae drown her! Stop him, Da!"

"She'll no' drown. More's the pity," he answered.

Rose turned her attention back to the loch, where two heads bobbed on the surface. Sam had hold of Helena again, but he kept letting her go and throwing her off him when she returned to cling. After a few endless minutes of watching, Rose saw Helena swim away suddenly as if she had been born to it. She dived under the water and came up heart-stopping seconds later. She did it again and again, swimming and ducking under the cold water, then breaking the surface, triumphant. Sam applauded, and Helena laughed, her infant gurgles carrying up to the cottage to send a chill into Rose's soul.

"What is she?" she whispered, heart pounding. "What are they?"

Tully didn't answer. When they came back, dripping wet and triumphant, Helena had a trout in her podgy little hands and she was gnawing on it happily. Rose sat down, legs shaking, and gripped the table.

"Pack yer bags, Hailstanes," said Tully. "I'll give ye money. I'll give ye whatever ye want. But take yer spawn and go!"

"No," said Rose. "Nobody is going anywhere until ye tell me what's been going on here!"

Rose emerged from upstairs, tear-stained but calm, an hour or so after the two men in her life had explained the manner in which she had been deceived into marriage, then into adopting a child. She had grown up with tales of selkies, witches and fairies, and even water horses and all the other fanciful creatures of her Celtic heritage, and she was struggling to come to terms with what they had told her. Most tales, Sam had said, had some foundation in truth. They both turned wary faces to her as she entered the room. Tully set down his glass, cheeks flushed. How did her solemn, religious father cope with this knowledge of creatures from a hidden world? Maybe that was why he drank more than he should at times.

She came straight to the point. "It seems tae me we're all trapped," she said.

"No, Rose," said Tully, rising to go to her and putting his hands on her shoulders. "I did wrong tae start all this. I was tryin' tae save us from shame. But if he goes now, and takes the brat, it'll be a seven days' wonder, an' everybody will be on your side. We've known for a long time that Rev. O'Neill has had his suspicions aboot Sam. He never believed he was the father o' yer lost bairn, but he suspected he was Helena's. I don't think he was the only one. We'll just put the story out that Hailstanes had another woman, an' he's found her and gone back tae her."

Rose shrugged her father's hands away and stared at him as if she didn't know him. "An' don't ye think that would shame me, Da? Tae be abandoned for somebody else? Anyway," she added, "I've been left once before when I was in the family way. I'm not going to let it happen this time."

It took a few seconds for the news to sink in. Tully went pale and strode out the back door, while Sam smiled hesitantly, tears in his eyes.

Six months later, Rose went into labour. It had been a difficult time, the three adults adjusting to the truth of their situation. Helena was still a demanding child, but less so now that Sam took her swimming every day. Catching fish was a highlight for her, however, and one which meant they had to be careful to keep her away from prying eyes, and try to teach her not to mention it in her constant chatter to other people. It wasn't difficult, because there had been fewer visitors to the water bailiff's cottage ever since her arrival. Superstitions died out slowly in country places, and although people's lives weren't ruled by them in the late 1920s, they came to mind readily enough when something happened to spark a folk memory – and a baby found floating in a strange basket out near the Faerie Isle was more than enough to do that. Rose had even seen people cross themselves when she walked out with the pram. Once she knew that she was indeed raising a changeling, she became less inclined to mix in general.

In the days of her deepening relationship with Sam, before she discovered the truth about him and Helena, she hadn't felt lonely, though. They were a young family, happy in their own company. Rose supposed it had been a sort of falling in love, different to what she had known before, but absorbing in a gentler way. Learning the truth had changed things. She had been deceived by her father and husband and was part of their conspiracy. Sam's awkwardness and lack of education made sense now, as did Helena's behaviour, and both had to be dealt with. It became easier just to avoid company, and of course, Rose didn't know what to expect from the birth of this child she was carrying. The time had arrived when she would find out.

"Ye have tae let me fetch help!" Tully pleaded. "If not the doctor, Mrs. MacAllistair. Just Mrs. MacAllistair."

Rose cried out as another contraction gripped her. She had been labouring for fourteen hours now. It was four in the morning. "No! What happens if it's got fur or claws? Neither of ye thought, did ye? Senseless men, ye thought o' nothin' but what you stood tae gain!"

Sam sponged her forehead. "Rose, Rose…look at me an' Helena…we're perfectly human tae look at. Nobody knows!"

"Not unless they see ye swimmin' – a bairn divin' an' catchin' fish wi' her teeth!"

"I'll train her, Rose! She'll stop. I manage as long as I eat plenty o' cooked fish."

Tully dropped the cup of water he was fetching as Rose screamed. It smashed, but he left it and ran to her side. "It's near," he said. "Her mother screamed like that near the finish of it."

"The pain!" screamed Rose. "It's tearin' me apart!" She was writhing, her body convulsing on the bed.

Tully took her shoulders and pressed down to keep her still. "Push, lass! I think that's whit happens now!"

"I already am!"

Sam lifted the sheet laid across her for modesty in front of her father. "I see the head!"

"Is it human?" yelled Rose. "Tell me it's human!"

"It is... *he* is!" cried Sam, as Rose pushed with a great scream and their son slithered out into his hands. Tears of relief and joy coursed down his cheeks. "He's perfect, Rose, perfect."

"Let me see!"

Sam held the baby out to Rose. He wailed, and despite his red, squashed face, she loved him the minute she looked at him. She held out her arms to receive him and knew her fears that she might reject her baby had been unfounded.

"Angus William," she said, with significant looks at both men.

Sam, who had insisted on Helena being christened Helena Jeanette, was in no position to disagree. The new grandfather, William Tully, didn't look as pleased as he might have done.

Sam watched Helena carefully for any signs of jealousy, especially with Rose so obviously preferring her own flesh and blood. Rose believed she was jealous, but Sam viewed the matter differently. Helena wanted the baby's attention, not Rose's. She was, in fact, doting towards him. She wanted to spend time with him, to hold him and fuss over him, and Rose was grudging in allowing her that.

"It doesn't do tae breed divisions," Sam said to her. He also insisted that he should teach Angus to swim, but Rose was having none of it. He was a more docile child than Helena had ever been, she said, and she believed "her half of him" was stronger in his personality. So Sam and Helena continued to take to the loch alone, as he tried to wean her off catching fish while she was still young enough to forget she ever had.

Then, one day when Angus was six months old, Sam woke to an eerie feeling that his son wasn't asleep in the cradle in their bedroom. He jumped out of bed and went to look. The cradle was empty. The bedroom door was lying ajar, and he bolted out of it to Helena's room. She wasn't in her bed. He looked out of the window and saw her, sure-footed on the shingle, striding towards the loch in her nightgown with her brother grasped in both arms. He ran for the stairs, meeting Rose coming out of their room.

"Where's Angus?" she asked. "I thought you must have him!"

He didn't answer, but raced downstairs in his bare feet and out the open back door, Rose on his heels. Helena was already in the water, Angus protesting.

"She's going tae drown him!" cried Rose, rushing after Sam.

"She's not!" Sam answered. "Ye thought that aboot me wi' Helena. This is the same thing." Nevertheless, he caught up with his children and waded into the loch with them, allowing Helena to keep hold of Angus as she kicked to keep them both afloat. She ducked him under a few times as he continued to thrash and cry, and then instinct kicked in and he got the idea, as she had before him, and began to swim.

Rose stood on the shore with her hands over her mouth and tears of fear and fury running down her cheeks, shivering and waiting for her family to return to her. Sam didn't allow them to linger long, coming out with Angus under one arm and dragging Helena by the hand. His wife seized their son and marched into the cottage. His explanation that Helena was following the instincts of an otter mother did not go down well.

Chapter 7

August 1933

Three years later, Helena Jeanette Hailstanes, daughter of the younger water bailiff on Loch Duie, Craigendon estate, stood before the mirror in her parents' bedroom and admired her reflection. She was ready for her first day at school. She had two brothers by this time, for James Samuel had been born a few months ago. As fiercely devoted to Jamie as she still was to Angus, she was torn between wanting to stay with them and the desire to do something new.

Helena rarely left the water bailiff's cottage and its surroundings. Neither did her father or her brothers. Her mother and grandfather took the cart to Crosson for weekly supplies, and sometimes went to places further afield with fancy-sounding names which made Helena wonder about them – Ballaness, Ayr, and once they were gone for two days to Glasgow, which Rose told her was a great city, not just a village or a town.

Helena had no idea what the difference could be. She had been to Crosson only twice that she could remember, and it had been strange enough with its long main street of houses, its shops and post office, police station and public house. There had been lots of people walking about, and some had stared at her. Last time, two had done something with their hands, touching their foreheads, chest and shoulders, and Rose had jerked her by the hand and pulled her away. She passed her days in the cottage or playing outside. Rose gave her chores to do, which she did half-heartedly and haphazardly, making her mother angry, so she

57

was always glad to escape. She swam whenever she felt like it now, with or without Sam and Angus. She looked forward to teaching Jamie, too.

Helena turned this way and that, admiring her new school uniform and how well she looked in it. She hadn't thought much about clothes until now, or about her appearance, but seeing herself in the mirror, she knew that the pinafore, blouse and tie made her look different somehow. She liked that and felt a thrill at the thought of the day ahead. Rose's voice trilled up the staircase:

"Helena! I hope you're stayin' neat and tidy, and don't dare loosen a single hair on one o' yer plaits!"

"I am, Mammy," Helena called back, "and I haven't!" She hastily tried to tuck some stray hairs back into place where she had been scratching her head because of the tightness of her two long plaits. Rose had said she was making them especially tight so that they would last the day at school, and woe betide her if she undid them, as was her usual trick. Then her father called up the stairs that he had to go, and wished her a good first day.

"And remember what I said!" he added. "Stay away from the water!"

"Yes, Daddy!" Helena yelled. Overcome by the need to see him before he left, she made to head down the stairs. At the top of them, she heard him speak in a low voice to Rose.

"I'm still not sure we're doin' the right thing."

"Sam, it's the law! She has to get her education. And you and the children need to mix more. I've been sayin' it for years now. We can't all stay cooped up in this cottage forever!"

"You know what folk think o' Helena. And they all wonder aboot me."

"Well, we should show them!" said Rose. "She's quite civilised now, and you're like any other man."

Their voices trailed away as they both stepped out the back door. Helena stood puzzling for a moment, then shrugged her shoulders and ran back to the bedroom, throwing the window open and calling and waving to Sam as he set off towards Craigendon House. Then Rose said it was time to go, and Helena prepared for the biggest adventure of her life.

🐾

By the end of the week, Helena was less enthusiastic. She was finding it hard to make friends. It was a small school, with all thirty children in the same classroom and taught by the same master, no matter what their age. Only two other girls were new besides herself, and they were friends already and made it clear they didn't want her around. Anyway, she was used to her brothers and would have preferred boys as friends, but they all gave her funny looks and scorned her company. She had never had any friends, since her family didn't mix with others on the estate.

Helena stood alone in the yard at break. She was comforted by the sound of the stream nearby, trickling over the stepping stones she crossed on her way to school. Finding the school was near water had instantly made her feel better, but Sam had told her firmly she must concentrate on her lessons and never think of it, never go near it. Yet it would be so good just to see it flowing... She wandered out of the schoolyard and stood staring into the clear water, relaxing and feeling better. Being near water always made her feel this way. Totally absorbed, she didn't hear anybody coming up behind her.

Suddenly, somebody grasped her plaits and she was jerked back. She found herself looking up into the face of one of the older boys.

"I've caught the selkie!" he yelled, as his friends came running to join him. "Come on, show us what ye really are!"

Helena shrieked at the pain as he pulled her hair harder. "Let me go!"

The boys surrounded her, jeering and prodding. "There's one sure way tae make her show her true form," said the tallest boy. "Fling her in!" Several pairs of hands grabbed her then, and she was lifted off the ground. They held her menacingly over the water, teasing her with their intentions, before dropping her in it.

The stream was shallow there by the stepping stones, and Helena made only a slight splash, turning quickly on to her front and grazing her knees on the stony bed. It didn't distress her to be in the water, but the manner of her entering it did. She felt its coolness flow into her, filling her with ice-cold fury and something more...a surge of willpower, wild yet controlled. She would deal with these boys. She rose slowly, her prominent brown eyes blazing. The boys' expressions changed.

"Dae ye think she really...?"

Helena launched herself from the river like a wildcat. She was five years old, a bedraggled wee lassie, and of course they shouldn't have been scared of her, but they were. Her anger was bigger than she was, it was a wall crashing down on them, and they ran from the force of it. She chased them as they raced for the safety of school, and she was too fast for them, although they were twice her age. She caught one easily, and brought him down. She dug her nails into his scalp as her mouth closed over his throat. Just at that moment, much larger hands gripped her firmly by her clothing and hauled her away…

When she looked back on the incident later, the one clear image in Helena's mind was of a raven staring at her intently from the top of the schoolyard wall, as she was borne away in the schoolmaster's firm grip.

Rose arrived with dry clothes for her as she sat wrapped in a blanket in the master's house, where he had carried her, kicking and struggling. Helena had given her version of events, but the boys refused to speak of anything. As she pulled on the clothing, Helena looked into her mother's face. "What's a selkie, Mammy?" she asked. Rose rarely looked her in the eye unless she was giving her into trouble, but her startled gaze met Helena's puzzled one now.

"Come on," was all she said. "I have permission tae take ye hame."

That evening, they sat round the fire as Da told the legend of the selkies, seals who could transform into people. Her mother was in the rocking chair, Jamie clamped to her breast, and her grandfather stared into the hearth. Angus was in bed.

"Why would they think I was a selkie?" Helena asked.

"We are unusual in swimmin' so much…" her father replied, his voice trailing off.

"Tell her, Sam," said Rose quietly. "Tell her the bit we can't hide any longer." She had winced then, saying that Jamie's teeth would be the death of her and it was the bottle for him soon. Tully rose and left the room in silence, as was often his way when he felt uncomfortable. Sam Hailstanes swallowed, took a breath, and told Helena of a baby in a basket, floating on the Irish Sea out near Ailsa Craig, which some people called the Faerie Isle. Her real mother would have had her reasons, he said, and they loved her as much as if she was their own child. Stupid people just made up tales when nobody knew the true story. She was definitely not a selkie, he reassured her.

Sam didn't think they should go to church that Sunday. Tully was angry. "You an' the lassie can dae as ye please, but my daughter and grandsons still have a chance tae be normal. I'm takin' Rose an' the boys, an' that's that!"

Rose thought they should all go. "Please, Sam," she pleaded, "dinna cut us off any more than we are already. Dinna make us any more different."

"But ye both know what's said aboot Helena," he replied. "Oh aye, we've told her the truth as far as we're able, but think what folk must be sayin' after what happened the other day! She thinks it's normal, the way she behaved, but everybody knows it wasn't!"

"The boys are so ashamed o' bein' scared o' a wee lassie, that they're not talkin', Sam," Rose reasoned.

"Not what I've heard," said Tully. They turned to him. "John McDowall's father heard rumours and beat him until he had the story," he continued. "Then, he beat him some more for lettin' a tiny lassie get the better o' him. There'll be talk, alright – a five-year-old runnin' at that speed, an' bringin' a big laddie down! What I don't understand is why they ran? How could Helena scare them that much?"

That had been puzzling Sam, too. "I've no idea," he admitted. "It's all the more reason tae keep away from folk!"

"You and her, if ye so choose," said Tully, "but not Rose an' the boys. They're half our blood, and young enough that we can curb any other instincts. We've done it wi' the fishin' already, wi' Angus. We'll just take more care. As for her, Helena, it's too late. She's wild, that one."

As Sam's face reddened with rage, Rose intervened. "Look," she said, "Helena has tae go back tae school on Monday. There's no way round that. Goin' tae church will give her – and us – a chance tae face everybody. Please, Sam, see reason."

He had to concede defeat.

Much to Sam's surprise, Sunday morning was not the trial he had feared. Despite his dislike of Rev. O'Neill and the disdain with which the cleric treated him, the minister had developed a soft spot for Helena. He hinted whenever he could that he was as suspicious of Sam as ever, but he didn't take it out on the child and for that Sam respected him. He had obviously heard what had happened at school, for his sermon was about believing in God and not the foolish superstitions some continued to hold. He spoke of Ailsa Craig, which was an extinct volcano and not a Faerie Isle. He mentioned the cave and the spring at Ballaness and said he had been able to find no trace of an ancient saint who had lived there – that the people were, in fact, continuing a pagan rite in visiting it every May Day sunrise. It was a sin which should be stamped out.

Quite a few were fidgeting and looking at the floor as the minister's keen eyes raked the congregation. Sam gazed up at the vaulted wooden ceiling, thinking of the knowledge he and his family hid, smiling at how wrong the pompous cleric was, yet at how much his words helped to protect them. As always, the ceiling made him think of Megan and her curious upturned house-boat. Tully had brought back word from Ballaness long ago that she was gone, and her home falling to ruin. Sam wondered where she was, and why she had left, but he chose to keep himself and Helena well away from Ballaness nevertheless. He fully intended to do likewise with his sons, no matter what Rose and Tully might say.

He wasn't paying attention to the rapt look on Helena's face at the mention of these superstitions and far-away places. Nor did he see the kindly wink Rev. O'Neill gave her when he said that people should stop letting their imaginations run away with them, but he looked down in time to see the radiant smile she bestowed on the man. Not for the first time, Sam marvelled at what a bonny lass she was, the sun shining on her long thick chestnut tresses, her eyes like great dark pools ablaze with inner light. She was her real mother's daughter, and more.

PART TWO

May Day – Midsummer's Eve 1942

Chapter 8

May Day 1942

Since she was out earlier than any of the others, Helena Hailstanes stripped off the knitted swimsuit her mother insisted she wore, and launched herself gracefully into the loch. She had read that young maidens should bathe their faces in the morning dew at sunrise on May Day, to ensure beauty, but she had bathed every morning in Loch Duie for as long as she could remember, and hoped that was even better. The loch was certainly a special place – she experienced a joy and calmness in its waters that she didn't know anywhere else – but for some time now, she had yearned to explore further afield. The locals down at Ballaness washed their faces in a holy spring at St. Bride's Cave on this day. The minister, the one who had baptised her and under whose hawk-like gaze she had fidgeted every week for fourteen years, said every year that it was superstitious nonsense and time it was ended in this new age, especially now there was a war on. It was time, he said, for humanity to grow up and stop believing in such things. His words fell on deaf ears, as usual. Old ways died hard in the countryside.

Helena flipped on to her back. The sun was up. There was a steely grey cover of cloud, but the air was warm and she hoped it might disperse. The others would be out soon. She turned and swam at speed up the loch to a favourite spot. Arriving, she saw what she was seeking and swam towards the bank, creeping up on the creature with practised skill. She seized the toad, banged it on the nearest rock to kill it, and settled down to enjoy her secret pleasure. She couldn't see what the problem was with eating toads' legs. The French, she had learned, ate frogs' legs and were considered sophisticated. First, she had to strip the legs of their poisonous skin. No-one had ever told her this, and she had no idea how she knew. She did it with her sharp little teeth, then ate with relish. She choked as her father suddenly appeared, for he could swim just as fast and with as much stealth as she could.

"Helena! What have I told ye? How many times?"

"There's nobody here tae see me but you!" she laughed. "And what does it matter if it's not what a young lady should do? I'm not likely ever tae be one, or tae go anywhere, ever!"

Helena sighed. She went to church and school, but both had been built for those who lived on Craigendon, and she had no wider acquaintance. She couldn't recall the last time she had been away from the estate.

"It's safer here," was all Sam said. It was all he ever said on the matter.

Helena eyed him sulkily. "I would have liked tae work at the big hoose. It would have been a change, at least."

"That subject is closed," her father said. "Get back along the shore an' get yer costume on. The boys have seen it, an' know what ye're up tae. Ye should be settin' an example." He launched himself back into the water.

Helena rolled her eyes. Da was becoming as bad as Ma these days. At least Ma would have let her work as a maid at Craigendon House. A raven was watching her from a nearby rock, the same one which had shown up from time to time for years now. At first, she hadn't been sure it really was the same bird, but over time she had seen it age gradually. Now, it had a few white feathers, while its black ones had become iridescent with age. In the steely early morning light, they glowed deep purple, green and blue against the grey of loch and sky. Helena regarded the creature with interest for a moment, then hissed, "Catch yer ain breakfast!" She finished her toads' legs at leisure, ran her finger up her chin to catch the juices, and sucked it thoughtfully.

By the time she arrived home, her brothers were flailing at each other with their wet towels as they capered back to the farmhouse, which was further away from the loch shore than the water bailiff's cottage had been. They had moved there five years ago after her grandfather had suffered the first of a series of strokes. At that time, he was no longer able to fulfil his duties as water bailiff, but he could still tend some livestock with help from his family, so Lord Craigendon had settled them further up the loch near his own sprawling mansion, on a croft which required new tenants. Sam had become the sole water bailiff. Now he was also the farmer, as Tully had suffered further ill health. This meant he had not had to go to war, as he was providing an essential service. Helena was relieved about that, because the thought of losing her father either temporarily or permanently terrified her – what would her life be like if she was left with just her mother?

Helena scuttled into the farmhouse, hugging her damp towel around her, but Rose Hailstanes wasn't fooled. She glanced at her eldest child, her mouth a firm line, before deftly grabbing at the towel to reveal the dry swimsuit underneath.

"How dare ye defy me again?" she cried.

"It itches," said Rose. "It itches when it's dry, and when it's wet, it sags and weighs a ton!"

"There's a war on, and not much money in this hoose, madam!" screeched Rose. "Ye'll be thankful for what ye have, especially when I have tae knit a new one every few months!"

Helena wrapped her arms around herself against the chill of the kitchen. "It's been a whole year," she replied. "I've stopped growing. Up the way, at least. It stretches for these." She cupped her breasts and brushed past Rose, heading into the hallway. She didn't need to turn back to see the look on Rose's face; she could feel it burning into the fair flesh of her back, where her dark hair tumbled, damp and tangled, to her waist.

After breakfast, Rose cleared away the mess her two daughters had made in attempting to tidy the kitchen. How they could both manage such chaos when trying to achieve the opposite, and when they were so very different in temperament, Rose would never know. Helena's post-swim mood had altered, though, for she had been lost in thought in that intense way she had – the way that Rose recognised as a presentiment of trouble ahead. She tried to imagine what she might be scheming now. Over the years, she had learned the need to stay one step ahead of this stranger her husband had brought to their home, at a time when he was little more than a stranger himself.

The girls reappeared. Six-year-old Sadie was smiling, her sober little face lent sudden vivacity by some scheme or other. It was a game Helena had promised to play with her, she said. They would pretend to be explorers in the woods. Might they make jam sandwiches – "pieces", as they called them – and stay out all day?

"Wonders will never cease," murmured Rose. She said it loud enough to be heard – just – with a sideways glance at Helena. "Okay – make your pieces. But I've just got this place in order, so try no' tae make too much mess."

The girls set to work, slopping Rose's bramble jam on grey slices of wartime National Loaf.

"Go easy on that jam!" their mother cried. "Ye know sugar's rationed – it has tae last a while!"

Sam came through the back door, carrying fuel for the stove, and learned of the plans from Sadie, so excited she was jumping on the spot. "That's lovely, Sadie, and how thoughtful of you, Helena, tae play wi' yer sister on yer holiday."

Helena launched herself at him and wrapped her arms around his neck. He returned her embrace, then disentangled himself and scooped Sadie up in his arms. Rose flicked at crumbs with a tea towel that cracked the table like a whip. Sam put his youngest child down and told them to have a great day. "And mind ye do as your big sister says!" he called to Sadie, as they scampered out the door.

"She's up to no good," said Rose, scrubbing at the table top with vigour.

"She's being nice to Sadie!" Sam exclaimed. "That's an improvement. Ye should praise her for what she does right. Ach, we've been through this before!" He pulled on his waders and stormed out of the house.

In the sudden quiet of the kitchen, Rose heard a tap-tapping from above. Sighing, she ran up the stairs. The door to her father's room was open. His walking stick had fallen to the floor after he had summoned her with his tapping, and she picked it up and laid it on the bed.

"I'll get ye washed now, Da," she said, stroking his forehead. "Did ye enjoy yer breakfast?" She picked up the napkin on his tray and wiped jam and saliva from around his mouth. "It's a bit grey for the first o' May."

68

The old man's eyes filled with tears, and he choked on a sob. He had lost the power of speech with his last stroke. He took his good hand – the left one – and clutched her wrist, his eyes glistening and beseeching. Rose kissed his damp cheek.

"Oh, Da, Da," she cooed. "Ye canna blame yersel'. I've never blamed ye, not once."

A succession of memories flitted through her mind; a handsome face, unsmiling, leaving her; Sam, as a young man, overwhelmed; the changeling, brought to her home on May Day fourteen years ago. For that was what she called Helena in the silence of her heart – the changeling.

Helena led Sadie away from the house, but not towards the woods as promised. She was turning over in her mind if there was any way to be rid of her little sister, for she would rather have done this alone; but Sadie was her cover. If she hadn't shown willing to look after her on this May Day holiday from school, no doubt Rose would have found more chores for her to do. She thought about playing hide and seek, and taking herself off, leaving Sadie to seek until she panicked and cried. Sadie would reach that stage far too soon, however, and run home full of the tale. They might be able to stop Helena before she could put her plan into action.

"The woods are over there, Helena," said Sadie.

"We're goin' on a bigger adventure than I told you," Helena confided in the little girl. She knelt down so she was Sadie's height, and took her hands. Sadie coloured with pleasure at the unexpected intimacy. It was pathetic, Helena thought, how easily pleased she was, how easily she could be led. She imagined Rose was the same once. "We're goin' to Ballaness – to the May Day Fete!" It didn't have the effect Helena had expected. She retained a frozen smile in the face of her sister's evident bewilderment.

"Why?"

"Because it'll be exciting! Because…because…don't you get fed up here, goin' frae hame tae school tae the kirk, week in, week oot?"

"I've never thought aboot it." Sadie's bottom lip began to tremble.

"It's where Da found me," Helena reasoned. "Ye know the story, Sadie – how I was floatin' like Moses oot by the Faerie Isle, rescued by fishermen? We've never even seen the Faerie Isle. Ye like fairy stories, Sadie… come on. It's a quest…ye're comin' wi' me to find where I came frae. I've chosen you as my companion. Not the boys, oh no. I might discover I'm the Faerie Queen, and you will be my princess sister."

Sadie skewed her mouth to one side, thinking. "Alright."

"Good girl!" said Helena. "Now, we must await our carriage. But we'll walk down the road while we do." She drew Sadie into the shelter of the hedgerow on the verge, the better to hide them from view of any prying eyes. Her brothers were out with Da, and she had no idea which part of the estate they were in.

As they walked, Helena listened for the sound she wanted to hear and kept looking hopefully over her shoulder. Finally, the hum of an engine cut through the May morning birdsong. It was just what she had wished for – the vehicle she considered her best bet. An ambulance, really a converted furniture store van, thrummed its way from the big house, which was being used as a convalescent hospital for the military.

"Here's our carriage!" she giggled.

"That?" said Sadie. "I thought ye meant one like a pumpkin, wi' horses."

"Tchht!" Helena pinched her arm. "I'm fed up bumpin' behind a horse! I want a motor!"

"Owww!" Sadie began to whine.

Helena stepped out into the road, dragging her sister with her. She waved at the ambulance. The driver honked the horn and didn't slow down. Sadie panicked and tried to break free, but Helena held on to her and stood her ground. The ambulance grated to a halt.

The driver opened the window and leaned out. "What the devil do you think you're doing?"

To Helena's dismay, it was Lady Craigendon. She had forgotten that her ladyship had involved herself in war work, like all the women were doing now – even Ma. She thought quickly. Lady Craigendon wouldn't know what she was and wasn't allowed to do. She took scant interest in the estate workers.

Helena took a deep breath. "Father is working even although it's May Day," she said. "He's training my brothers to look after His Lordship's estate. Mother has to stay with Grandpa, who served Craigendon for so many years. But they said we might go to the fete if someone would take us." She smiled sweetly.

Lady Craigendon flushed scarlet. "I'm on war business, girl! I do not take estate workers' children on holiday jaunts in this or any other vehicle! Your parents shall hear of this." She let down the handbrake and accelerated, engaging the gear with a crunch.

Helena had to pull Sadie out of the way as she darted to the verge. The younger child was rooted to the road in awe and terror. The ambulance screeched past in a cloud of dust. Helena stared after it, and her rage was greater than anything she had ever known; and that was saying something. Helena's temper was legendary.

"Ye told a lie, Helena!" Sadie sobbed. "An' she'll tell Ma and Da!"

Helena barely heard her. Enraged, she stared after the vehicle and her lips worked, although no sound came out. A feeling that she had come to recognise flowed over her, and she felt as if she was underwater, as if nothing else existed, and time had been suspended. She was in her element and it welled up through her, empowering her with elemental energy. The curse fell from her lips and surged through the air after the speeding ambulance.

Helena saw Sadie's tear-stained face and registered her terror. "I am the Faerie Queen from the Isle of Faerie," she said; "And you are my Princess. She shall not betray us. I will not allow it!"

Sadie stopped snuffling and stared at Helena. Helena put a hand to her forehead and shut her eyes for a few seconds. She shuddered, suddenly cold as when she stepped out of the loch after swimming, although it felt like a warm bath when she was in it.

"Come on, Sadie. We've started on this quest, and we'll finish."

Twenty minutes later, they were still walking. Neither had said another word. The sun had broken through, and it was growing hot. Bees droned and blossom drifted on the slight breeze. When Helena heard the second vehicle, she knew, in the way she sometimes did, that this was the one for them. She had been mistaken in her first choice. She didn't know what kind of vehicle it was, or who was driving, but she knew she need do nothing. Afterwards, she couldn't explain moments like this, but they happened now and again. The car drew alongside them and stopped, engine labouring.

"And where might the bonny Hailstanes lasses be going today?"

It was the well-known voice of Rev. O'Neill. Sadie broke into a smile, pushing damp blonde ringlets, so like her mother's, off her forehead to shade her eyes and look at him. Helena felt an inner surge of triumph.

"To the fete, Rev. O'Neill."

"I don't think I've ever known you to go there," the minister replied.

"I'm allowed to take Sadie, now I'm so near to leavin' school, Reverend," said Helena. "Ma and Da dinna hold wi' May Day, but they said we might go if we met somebody who would…(she searched for the word)…chaperone us."

Rev. O'Neill hesitated. Another voice boomed from the passenger seat. "Oh, make your mind up, Neville. Take them or don't, but hurry up!" Mrs. O'Neill, whom he had married four years ago, was not known for patience or tolerance. The minister looked at Helena. Her hair had dried in waves which glistened. It flowed over her bare white shoulders like a dark river. He swallowed.

"Jump in," he said.

Chapter 9

The girls knew the story of Dick Whittington, who ran away to London. Ballaness was a fishing village, but it couldn't have been any more exciting to them, especially decked out in its fete finery, bunting flapping in the salt-air breeze, and marquees, stalls and barrows everywhere. The drive there was adventure enough in itself, their first ride in a car, the steep road winding down the hillside, the busier roads as they approached the village, their first glimpse of the sea. At sight of the heaving blue mass of the Irish Sea, something stirred in Helena; she felt a yearning, heard the crash of waves as they drew nearer, felt her heart hammer in rhythm. When she saw Ailsa Craig, she wept.

Mrs. O'Neill had talked most of the way, mostly about herself and the deprivations of war, but she tailed off as she caught sight of the tears streaming down Helena's cheeks. "Whatever is it, child?"

"I came frae oot there," the girl mumbled, the vastness of the scene overwhelming her.

The car swept down to the harbour where Helena had been brought ashore.

Helena held her sister's hand, and for once she admitted to herself that it was more than holding Sadie to her will, pulling her along with her schemes. They were giving mutual courage and comfort, standing there on the quayside surrounded by strangers and unfamiliar sights, sounds and smells. Then she heard a sound she recognised. It sliced through all the other noise, familiar and welcome; the single "Kr…rr…k!" of a raven. Helena looked and saw the creature nearby, cocking its head and appraising her with its glassy eyes. It was the same one which had watched her earlier that morning, she knew it without a moment's doubt, although her reason told her there must be many old ravens.

"You're a long way from home," she said.

"Why are ye talkin' to a bird?" asked Sadie.

Helena ignored her, her intuition compelling her to watch the raven, and when it moved, hopping and flying low, flitting from stall to stall, she followed. She and Sadie took in the delights along the way. They had no money to buy anything, but it was enough to feast their eyes. After a while, they came to a marquee smaller and shabbier than the others, and the raven alighted on the pinnacle of it with a resounding "Krr...rr...k! Krr...rr..k!" which caused them to jump. Somebody pushed the flap aside, and a woman wearing a headscarf tied in the gypsy manner emerged. She had a sunburned, careworn countenance. Two tendrils of curling blonde hair had escaped from her scarf, and she pushed them back in with long, work-roughened fingers. She glanced first at Sadie, who was studying her with a puzzled expression, then she stared at Helena and held her gaze rather longer than was comfortable.

"Come away in," she said, and Helena, curious and wondering, gave Sadie's hand a tug and followed.

Inside, a round table draped with a purple cloth held a crystal ball. The woman herself wore long flowing clothes, a grey dress with flimsy purple scarves tied at neck and waist.

Helena gasped. "Are ye a fortune teller?" She had read stories, and the mystery of it filled her with excitement. "We have no silver tae cross yer palm," she added, her face falling.

"I think I can make an exception for two bonny lasses on their first trip oot intae the big world," the woman smiled.

Helena paled at the same time as her heart thrilled. "How did ye know that?"

"Is it not my business tae know such things?" she replied. "You first, wee one," she said to Sadie.

"I'm the oldest!" cried Helena.

"Then you should learn patience," replied the woman.

Helena blushed, and stepped back into the shadows of the shrouded marquee, while her sister sat and offered a trembling hand to the fortune teller.

"I see a long and happy life for you," she said. "Ye'll do well at school, and one day meet a handsome…"

"You're a fraud!" said Helena.

The woman glanced up, startled.

"She's too young for the lines on her palm tae show much. And anyway, ye're just tellin' her a fairy story, the kind o' thing she wants tae hear. And ye've got fair hair. Whoever heard o' a blonde gypsy?"

The fortune teller gaped open-mouthed at her insolence. "Then sit you down, Madame, an' I'll deal with you!" she said. She gave Sadie's hand a squeeze as she stood up and vacated the stool for her sister. "There's nothin' tae fear for you, dear. Things will be simple for ye, smooth."

Helena bumped down and stuck out her hand. The woman stretched out her own hesitantly, and slid it under the back of Helena's hand slowly and with contact barely being made. Even so, they both felt the tingling sensation which crawled up their arms like a rash and made even their scalps feel alive with electricity.

"How dae ye dae that?" Helena demanded.

"Maybe because I'm not a fraud after all," the fortune teller said, and her fingers folded round Helena's hand. "I see trouble for you if ye keep runnin' awa' frae hame, missy. There's nae fairy story for you – a twisted tale is your fate, if ye dinna heed this warnin'."

Helena winced at her grip. "Let me go! Ye're not even lookin' at my hand!"

"I dinna need tae." The woman's eyes were wild, staring into Helena's.

Helena tried to pull her hand away. A kind of electricity still crackled up her arm, into her head and even her heart, which thudded out of rhythm, and she couldn't let go. The fortune teller seemed as afraid as she was, now. She couldn't seem to prise her fingers away. Finally, they separated with an effort which threw Helena off the stool. She landed on the trampled earth on which the marquee stood, and the fortune teller slumped across her table. The crystal ball toppled and smashed. Sadie let out a cry, and Helena picked herself up and fled, her sister on her heels. A few yards from the door, somebody grabbed her upper arm. It was Rev. O'Neill.

"Don't tell me you were in there?" he asked.

Helena stifled a sob in response.

"Such things are not Christian! Such people are not to be trusted. They'll say anything for money, and all they do is feed dreams or nightmares according to their mood!"

Helena considered this. "But she didna take money. We have none."

Sadie was watching, trembling with fright. The minister turned to her. "Is that yer lunch in that bag ye have there? I think I can do better than that." He held open the brown paper bag he carried, and the girls glimpsed two pies with cakes sitting on top of them. Such things were a rare treat in wartime. "Sadie, you go over there and eat your share, while I talk to Helena."

Helena felt as if she couldn't eat a thing, but she saw Sadie's face brighten in the sudden way young children do when their mind is distracted from a situation, especially when hungry. The girl took the bag eagerly and did as she was told.

"Come with me, Helena," said Rev. O'Neill, "just behind here." With a furtive glance around him, he led her behind the large marquee where the home baking, such as it was in these days of rationing, was set out waiting for judging by his wife. It was more a contest of ingenuity than anything, the good lady had said on the drive down. He stood close, bending over her, his hawk-like face inches from hers. "I gather yer father doesn't wish ye to work at Craigendon House?"

"No, Sir," Helena replied, backing away a little from his breath.

O'Neill smiled. "I hear," he continued, "that you make a very fine pupil-teacher."

Helena folded her hands and cocked her head. "Thank you, Sir." She had enjoyed the last few months, as her own school career drew to a close, helping with the younger children. Some evacuees had arrived after the Clydebank Blitz in March, and her efforts with them had been noted.

"Ye have the brains to become a teacher," the cleric said. "Just think what that would mean, Helena. Going to college in Edinburgh, meeting new people, learning new things…the wide world would be yours."

Helena felt warmth surge through every part of her. "I would love that, Sir!"

"It's just a shame that your parents' circumstances will not allow it."

Her smile faltered and the light in her eyes faded. The man allowed a beat to fall.

"However, I think I might be able to help."

"How so, Sir?" Helena leaned towards him, eager for any crumb of hope.

"Firstly, I could arrange for ye tae remain at school, as an unpaid assistant, while ye gain more experience and mature a bit. And I would personally tutor ye in some aspects tae help yer application."

Helena beamed. "Thank you, Rev. O'Neill! That is so kind!"

"Well, Mrs. O'Neill and I…we have no children of our own. I've come tae think o' ye as bein' like a niece, Helena." He swooped forward suddenly and kissed her cheek.

Taken by surprise, Helena's mouth fell open, and before she could close it, his lips were on hers. She tried to push him away, but he bore down harder. Disgusted, she felt the tip of his tongue touch hers, and their teeth clashed. She reached up and clawed at his cheek. He grabbed her then, one hand in her hair and the other exploring her back, settling on her bottom, fingers kneading. She dug her nails into his face until he pulled away in shock and rage at the pain. Then she ran. Like her father fourteen years before her, she took to her heels with the swiftness of an otter on land, her one thought to get away from Ballaness. She ran from the fete, forgetting everything but her own safety.

Sadie was left at the fete, sitting munching in the sunshine. Meanwhile, among the hills on Craigendon estate, an ambulance lay on its side in a ditch. The tree into which Her Ladyship had crashed was bent and broken, as was Lady Craigendon herself.

Chapter 10

Unaware of Lady Craigendon's fate, Helena was deep in the countryside, lost. She had run at a speed of which no normal girl was capable, then walked, stumbling with exertion, until she came to a river. She thought this river was the River Duie which flowed from Loch Duie, in fact she had been sure of it, with that intuition she couldn't explain; and so, she had begun to follow it in a northerly direction, up into the hills.

It was hot, and she was ravenous, so she stripped off her clothing and immersed herself in the cold, clear water, eyes peeled for toads as she swam. Finding none, but aware of the fish darting around her, and the hunger gnawing in her stomach, a strange sensation came over Helena and she went under and bit at a passing trout with her teeth. She caught it and ate it as it was, no need for flensing as with toads' legs. Helena whooped with joy then, and went wild catching fish of all sizes, filling her belly, revelling in the taste and the blood and juices trickling down her face, the scales silvering her chin. Vague memories began to stir. It seemed to her she had done this before, and her brothers, too, when they were all much younger. She wondered if all children did this as infants, but grew out of it. Even as she thought it, though, the differences between her family and others, of which she had long been aware, began to surface and nag at her mind; and anyway, it occurred to her that she had never known Sadie catch fish like this. Her memories of her as a baby were clear.

Having eaten her fill, she dragged herself out of the river and lay behind some hawthorn bushes to dry off. She felt relaxed, warm, and drowsy in the heady scent wafting from the blossom, and she drifted into a delicious sleep. When she woke, the afternoon had worn on and a chill breeze was beginning to creep from the west. Helena pulled on her clothing, inadequate though it now was. She had expected to be home by this time. She would, of course, have had to confess how she and Sadie spent the day, but at least she would have been to Ballaness. Any punishment then would have been worth it. She frowned as a brief concern for Sadie flitted across her mind, then she shrugged and decided it would do her good not to be cosseted for once in her life. Somebody would help her to get home. It was she, Helena, who was lost.

She began walking again, sometimes running, to keep the chill at bay, but it was becoming colder as she headed up into the hills. Their shapes as she walked began to look familiar, which meant she must be approaching home territory, but she still had no idea how far away she was. She stopped to stoop and drink some water, cupping her hands; she shivered violently afterwards, and wished for a warm cardigan. Gathering herself together and plodding on, she couldn't believe her eyes when, half an hour later, she saw a red cardigan hanging from the branch of a tree a few yards away. She pulled it down. It was a little large, but all the better; she bundled herself up in it and walked on, worrying as dusk began to fall if she was going to be out all night, and wondering if she might find a coat.

Three quarters of an hour later, she came across a sack lying at the base of a huge oak tree which arched over the river. She prodded the sack with her foot and found it was clean and dry and worth investigating. She could rip it open and use it to keep herself warm. Helena untied it and found it wasn't filled with the grasses or hay she had been expecting, but a cloak. It was a black velvet cloak of the type worn long ago. It had seen better days, but like the cardigan, it was clean. As far as Helena was concerned, it was better than any coat. She wrapped herself in it as she sat under the tree and thought soberly about her situation. Looking around, she could see no sign of any habitation. It was getting dark. Sighing, tired again and her courage dwindling, she leaned back – and cried aloud as the ground beneath her gave way and she toppled into a hollow among the roots of the tree. She was surprised to find it was snug and warm, and she felt safe there. Helena drew the cloak around her and went to sleep, with an owl hooting in the branches above her, and bats beginning to flutter from their haunts.

She woke many hours later to see sunlight filtering through the branches of the tree, dappling her in shifting grey shadows as the fresh young leaves stirred in the stiff morning breeze. A spider quivered in its web just above her head. How Sadie would have screamed at that! The thought of her little sister brought everything flooding back, and Helena, who had thought herself dreaming at first, remembered where she was – not that she really knew. Yet pushing herself out of the convenient hollow which had cradled her all night, she felt her sense of adventure renewed. She had coped, she had survived, and the river lay before her with all its joys, including breakfast! Casting off the cloak and all her clothing, she launched in and relished the most pleasant morning swim she could remember, delighting in pitching her strength against the current, diving under and catching fish with ease.

Helena never felt the cold when she was in the water, but afterwards she did, and that spring morning, it gnawed into her. Realising she had no towel, no warm house into which to retreat, and no cooked breakfast waiting on a table at which her family would be gathering, her mood changed abruptly. She dried herself with the cloak, and pulled on all her other clothing, but her bare legs were purple with cold. Helena succumbed to something she rarely did then, and began to cry. Between sobs and sniffs, she rubbed at her raw legs and wished for socks. No – long stockings! She longed for the woolen stockings Rose knitted her for winter days.

After crying piteously for some time, she decided the only way to keep warm was to move on and continue her quest to get home. As she stood and dusted herself down, there was a "Swoosh!" among the branches of the tree. Looking up, she saw a large raven perched above her, with something trailing from its beak. It couldn't be! Helena's mouth fell open when she saw the grey woolen stockings. The bird dropped them on her head and fluttered down to stand in front of her. The creature eyed her, and she recognised intelligence and knowledge in those black eyes.

"It's been you all along, hasn't it?" she said, picking the stockings up and examining them one at a time. "Are they *my* stockings?" She let out a peel of hysterical laughter. "If ye answer me, bird, I'll know I've gone mad! It's a coincidence. All a coincidence. I just happened tae find things I needed tae keep me warm, and you've just happened tae steal stockings off a washin' line." Nevertheless, as she looked at the raven, daring it to respond, she knew it was the bird who had hung around her for years, and who had been at the fete. When it persisted in returning her gaze, she flapped her hands at it. "Shoo!" Then she pulled on the stockings, looked around, and began to walk. She wore the cardigan, but left the wet cloak where it lay. Surely, she thought, she would reach home today. They must be looking for her, and if she didn't find her way, maybe they would find her first.

As she walked, the gurgling of the river lulled her into a reverie. What would she do now, once she got back? She had seen Ballaness and the Ailsa Craig, for all the good it had done her. She felt more overwhelmed at the lack of knowledge about her origins than ever, and now she had made enemies of Lady Craigendon and Rev. O'Neill, two important people in her small world, people who could have helped her. Her future had been the subject of discussion for the last few months, since her school days were almost over. Rose could have secured her a job at Craigendon House, where she was volunteering with the wounded servicemen in the hospital. Lady Craigendon had said there were places below stairs for new staff, and Rose had mentioned Helena to her, but Sam had said there was no way she was going into service. Anyway, after her encounter yesterday with Her Ladyship, Helena was certain that door was firmly closed now. Yet what else could she do, stuck out in the wilds of Craigendon? Rev. O'Neill seemed to be offering her a lifeline, but even as she had greeted his words with hope, before the cleric had frightened her, she knew her father would never agree. He seemed to want to keep her at home. Why? It's not as if he was even her real father, although they loved each other as surely as if he was. Where did she come from, and where was she going – and why, why had she always felt different?

Helena was hungry again. She had been alternately running and walking at pace, desperate to be home, and she had shed the cardigan and even the longed-for stockings as the sun began to grow in strength. They lay where she had discarded them, for she refused to believe that she would need them again. She would not be spending another night out in the wilds. Lacking her previous enthusiasm, she removed her remaining clothes and lowered herself into the river to fish. After she had eaten a few, she spotted a toad, and it distracted her from her troubles for a while as she flensed the legs of their skin and savoured the change from fish that they offered.

On emerging from the water and drying in the sunlight, closing her eyes to doze, she was awakened by a sharp "Krr...rr...k!" right in her ear. The sound ripped through the dream she was having, and caused her to sit bolt upright. There beside her was the raven. He – she had always been sure of that – was peering at her with head cocked to one side.

Helena felt conscious of her nakedness before this intelligent bird. "Excuse me while I dress," she said, reaching for her clothes. Her flesh tingled when the creature actually turned its back to her; the bird gave her the creeps.

"Ye're not the most grateful child, are ye?" said a voice.

Helena had begun to pull on her dress, and it was covering her face. She stiffened, then yanked it down and whisked her head round. A woman stood silhouetted against the light, the river shimmering behind her. She wore the uniform of the Women's Land Army. The raven flapped on to her head, and only then did Helena recognise the fortune teller from the fete. She carried the cardigan, cloak and stockings which Helena had cast aside, and she was smiling at her discomfort.

"His name's Rab," the woman said, "and I'm Megan."

Helena stood up. "Have ye been followin' me all the time?"

"In a manner of speaking," smiled Megan. "I get Rab tae dae my bidding as much as possible."

Helena eyed her warily. "It was you who left the clothes for me to find, then! How did ye know I wanted them? I know ye aren't a real fortune teller," she added, although why she was so sure of her words, she didn't know.

Megan gave a little laugh. "Oh, Rab has been watchin' you, Helena Hailstanes, for a long time."

Helena's dark eyes were huge with fear-tinged curiosity. "Why? Who are you? What do you want with me? And how can a bird spy on me for you? Does he speak?"

Megan reached into a large sackcloth bag she had swung across her body. She pulled an ornate hand mirror out of the bag, then she called to Rab, who fluttered from her head and tucked himself under her arm.

"Sit, Helena," she said. "I dinna bite. Unlike you, at times," she added.

Helena flushed red as Megan's words sunk in. She did as she was told.

Megan sat beside her and held the mirror up so that it reflected Rab. Then the glass became hazy and wavering lines appeared, clearing into images of herself running, walking, swimming, fishing, sitting, thinking.

Helena could hardly speak for the hammering of her heart. "How did you do that?" she asked.

"I see what Rab has seen," Megan replied, "and in my mind, I hear what he has heard. Even if what he heard was only spoken silently inside your head. So, I arranged for ye tae have the clothes ye needed. Are ye not goin' tae thank me, child?"

Although her legs were shaking, Helena raised herself to her feet and backed away from Megan. "I don't know who ye are, but ye should leave me alone now," she said. "I'm goin' home."

"Not so fast," said Megan, jumping up and grabbing her arm. "We need to talk."

"Why? I don't know you. I don't know what ye want with me!"

Megan sighed. " Ye're a lot like me, Helena. I can help ye. That's what I want. That's all, I swear. I know ye want answers tae some questions, and I can give ye them. Now, if I let ye go, ye'll not run?"

Helena slumped on to the riverbank, trembling. "Can you tell me why I'm different?" she whispered. "Do you know where I came from?"

Megan released her grip and put the mirror away in her bag, rummaging for something else. She pulled out a stick of white wood, tapered to a point at one end. She pointed it at Helena's head, where her long hair was tangled and frizzed for lack of a comb. Helena felt a warm sensation begin at her crown and spread down the length of each dark tress, as if someone was running fingers through her hair, like when Da used to play with it as he brushed it when she was younger. When Rose did it, she pulled and yanked and lost her temper with the tangles. Megan waved the wand with graceful flicks of her wrist all around Helena's head, before bringing it to rest in her lap.

Helena closed her eyes, and when she opened them, she said, "I am a changeling, aren't I? A fairy child. Is that what you are, too?"

Megan's raucous laughter wiped the serene smile from her face. "Nothin' so grand, sadly! And neither am I."

"But that's a…"

"A wand. Yes, it's a wand. It's all that's left of my staff. I made my staff myself, from driftwood on the shore at Ballaness. This is more convenient to my new way of life." Megan indicated her Women's Land

Army uniform. "I'm doin' my bit for the war effort, but…I'm a witch, lass. A witch."

Helena stared. "There's nae such thing as witches."

"Oh yes, there is, lassie. I'm one. And so, Helena Hailstanes, are you. Why dae ye look sae surprised? A minute ago, ye thought ye were a fairy!"

Helena blushed to the roots of her newly-combed hair and waited for Megan to tell her more.

As Megan departed, having pointed out the way home to Helena, she congratulated herself on having taken a step to right the wrongs she had done. For many years she had watched and wondered how she could help, aware of Sam's difficulties with his new family and Helena's ignorance of her origins. When Rab had alerted her to the fact that Helena was bound for Ballaness that May Day, she had rejoined the travelling people who had welcomed her among them when she turned her back on her life as a sea witch, seeing an opportunity to speak to Helena. Things had not gone well in the tent, and she had been in despair when O'Neill caused the girl to flee, but she was confident that she had sorted it all out now.

She hadn't told the whole truth, in deference to Sam and his family, but she had told some of it, embellished here and there. Helena might not be the biological daughter of a witch as Megan had led her to believe, but somehow, because of the events of May Day fourteen years ago – the curse which missed her, the basket and the spell to protect her – she was exactly what Megan had said she was. Some of her powers had transferred to the girl, there was no doubt. Megan smiled at the remembrance of Helena's face when she had related various incidents she had witnessed, warning the girl that she needed to learn to control her gifts. It was only a beginning, of course. Megan had a bond with Helena, and she had every intention of playing a part in her life from now on.

After Megan left, Helena sat for a while, thinking. So, she was different. It hadn't all been in her imagination. She was a witch. At least one of her parents must have been a witch, too, Megan had said. They might never know why she had been set adrift, but she wouldn't have survived out on the Irish Sea in a basket if she hadn't been protected by enchantments. Megan had seen her brought into the harbour at Ballaness, and had recognised that magic had been at play straight away. At first, the news had filled Helena with elation. Then she had felt frustration at still not knowing the whole truth about her origins. Now, mixed emotions coursed through her as Megan's words about her powers and the way she needed to learn to control them – or risk causing real harm – sank in. Her will, especially if reinforced by strong emotions, could have consequences. Helena thought of events – some trifling, some more serious – when things had happened around her. She remembered how scared those big boys had been when she was only five.

Megan knew why she had fled from the fete. Rab the raven had been watching from the top of her marquee, but by the time Megan had deployed the mirror, Helena was long gone. Megan had searched for Sadie instead, to ensure her safety.

Helena asked if she had bewitched Rev. O' Neill. *"Yes,"* Megan had replied, *"but not in the way ye're thinkin'. Not wi' magic. Bonny lasses bewitch men by natural means. In fact,"* she had added with a sigh, *"it's the only true way. Tryin' to bewitch a man otherwise never has the outcome ye would want."* She had fallen into a reverie then, and was far away when Helena asked, *"So…it wasn't my magic that made Rev. O'Neill dae what he did, but it was still my fault?"* Megan had snapped out of her private thoughts at that. *"No, lass! It was not. Ye've done nothin' wrong. It's him. He's a dirty old man tae even think o' a young lassie that way, let alone touch ye. I'm glad ye hurt him, he deserved it."*

Helena lay back and pondered all the things she had learned from Megan. The witch had told her she wasn't far from home and had pointed her in the right direction. However, Helena felt the need to be alone with her new knowledge. A smile began to play around her lips. She picked up the cloak Megan had left her and put it on with a frisson of excitement at the turn her life had taken. Retracing her steps, moving at speed with renewed energy, she returned to the old oak which arched over the river. She decided she would camp here for a night or two, sleeping in the shelter of the tree's roots while she thought about her new-found knowledge and made plans.

85

The first decision she made was that she wanted a staff. Megan said she had cut hers down to make a wand. It had been impressive in what it could do, but a staff sounded like a much more powerful tool. In vain, she tried to take a branch from the oak, but either her strength was too little, or the oak would not yield to her wishes. She laughed at herself for having such a fancy. Rose had seen to it that she was raised a good Presbyterian girl, and personalities were not ascribed to inanimate objects; and yet, thought Helena as she frowned up at the tree, *You're a living thing, too.* Defeated by the tree's obstinacy, her thoughts turned to Sam, whose wartime duties now included some forestry work. She remembered him talking about the quality of different woods and how they could be used.

Suddenly, she knew that the only wood which would suffice for her staff was the wood of the ash tree. She didn't have to look long before she found one. By chance – or was it something more, she asked herself – there was a perfect branch already almost severed, and all she had to do was break it off. She did this with unaccustomed gentleness, as if the tree could feel it; and indeed, Sam had said that freshly sawn ash wood was uncannily like human flesh. He had also told his family that it made the best tool handles, and the boys had been interested to hear it produced the finest arrows. *It will be my tool to do my will,* thought Helena. *It will send my will flying like an arrow, straight to the target.* She thanked the tree for its gift. Helena was pleased with herself. Now she looked like a witch, with her cloak and staff. She returned to the ancient oak and sat beneath it, staff in hand and eyes far away.

Chapter 11

On the day of Lady Craigendon's funeral, Sam Hailstanes grudgingly dressed himself in the best clothes his father-in-law had given him fourteen years ago. As an estate employee, he had to pay his respects, but her ladyship's death was secondary to the fact that his eldest child was missing. Helena had been gone four days now. They had been alerted late in the afternoon on May Day by the gamekeeper's wife, Mrs. MacAllistair, turning up at their door with a distraught Sadie. A hue and cry had arisen at the fete when the fortune teller discovered the young child alone and in great distress, saying that her sister hadn't come back for her. She had taken her to the organiser's tent, where the chairman of the village committee made an announcement by loudspeaker. Mrs. MacAllistair was there with friends for the day and could hardly believe her ears. What was Sadie doing at the fete? She had gone to comfort the child, while others searched for Helena. After an hour, during which volunteers had hurried out to St. Bride's Cave and other places in the vicinity, there seemed no hope of finding Helena, so Mrs. MacAllistair had brought Sadie home.

When questioned at the fete, Sadie said that Helena hadn't come back after going to have a word with the minister. Rev. O'Neill was sought out; they found him in a nearby cottage, bathing his cheek where a toddler in a tantrum, whom he had been seeking to distract and amuse, had scratched him. He hadn't seen Helena after their conversation ended, he said. They had been discussing her education and prospects, and she had parted with him in fine fettle, for he had offered to help her future career. He confirmed that he and his wife had taken the girls to the fete, being assured they were allowed to go. He was most concerned.

A handful of people reported seeing a girl running from the fete. She ran like the wind, they said, and was a fine lassie, small and lithe with long dark hair streaming behind her.

"That place is cursed!" Sam spat at the mirror, as he fastened his tie. "Cursed, as I was in it, and my otter family, too!" Sadie had described in detail what had happened in the fortune teller's tent, and from that and the description she gave, he had suspicions straight away. When she mentioned a raven on the top of the marquee, he was sure he was right. Yet Sadie said the fortune teller had been nothing but kind to her, although she and Helena had had a sort of row and Helena had fallen over. "Did the fortune teller push her?" he asked. No, the child replied, she fell over because they were trying to let go of each other's hands, and couldn't, and it had been scary. Sam had puzzled over that, but could make no sense of it. Helena had not disappeared straight after, however; she had been composed enough to speak with the minister, and part from him happy and well. There, though, was the dead end. Nobody knew what had made her flee. Sam didn't know what to think – except that he acknowledged, with dreadful certainty, that the Sea Witch o' Ballaness was back in his life.

Downstairs, the boys and Sadie ate their breakfast in silence. Rose was putting on a display of normality, badgering them about everyday matters, determined to get them out the door and away to school.

"Can we not stay off and search again?" asked Angus.

"Please?" Jamie mumbled, his mouth full.

At least they were eating. Sadie wasn't. She had hardly touched a morsel since Thursday, when she had been found wailing in distress and clutching a bag containing her sister's share of the lunch Rev. O'Neill had so kindly bought them. Rose thought that if they ever found her, Helena would pay for causing such harm to Sadie, the most timid of her siblings. On the day she was born, Rose's father had fondled Sadie's fair downy head, so different from the mop of dark hair with which the other children had been born, and he had said, "This one's a Tully." Sadie was a miniature version of Rose. She had none of the creature inclinations of her siblings, either – she didn't even like swimming. Helena had shown scant interest in or love for her, all her devotion being for her brothers.

"No, boys," said Rose. "We've searched for days. The police are looking, too. Word is out everywhere. We've done all we can for now. We must carry on with the things that need doing. I'm sure Helena will return in her own time."

She was certain of what she said. Rose had no doubt that Helena would survive in the countryside; wasn't she half-wild already? Fully wild, she reminded herself, the daughter of Sam and Jeanette. She had to swim every day to deal with her animal energy. She didn't even feel the cold when she was in the water. Sam had managed to tame her of catching fish, or so he said. They had to eat so much fish, even her sons, that the house stank of it constantly. In the early days, she remarked to Sam on what visitors must think. He said it was surely no unusual thing in a water bailiff's house, to smell fish; and anyway, after a while, the visitors tailed off. Even the MacAllistairs had to be discouraged as the other children arrived and the need for secrecy grew. The familiar tapping of Tully's stick sounded from above. Rose sighed. Her father had told her years ago that he swore Sam to secrecy about his past, wanting a normal life for her. It was a pity he hadn't thought things through.

When Rose returned from seeing to Tully, she was surprised to find a small boy with a shock of ginger hair standing in the kitchen. Angus introduced him as his new pal, Billy, an evacuee. She wiped the frown from her face and fixed a smile. They didn't encourage the children to invite friends.

"He just turned up, Ma," said Angus, as if reading her thoughts.

"Oh yes," she said, collecting herself. "Ye're with the McDowalls over at Fernglass, aren't ye?" There had been enmity between the Hailstanes and McDowall families ever since Helena had attacked John McDowall in her first week at school, nine years ago now.

"Aye. I mean, yes, Mrs.Hailstanes." The lad scratched his head and studied her with anxious blue eyes so clear they were almost opaque.

"Have ye eaten, Billy?" Rose knew the McDowalls were a mean lot. They would have taken in an evacuee purely for the unpaid work they could get out of him. Well, she reckoned they must be disappointed in this one: late to the choosing, or had him foisted upon them. His wee white legs, sticking out of his shorts, were like twigs. The only touch of colour on his pallid face was given by a rash of freckles.

"Yes, Mrs," he replied, his eyes betraying his hunger by straying to the scrambled egg growing cold on Sadie's plate.

"Well, I'm sure a growing boy could save me from havin' to throw this in the bin," she said, picking up the plate and setting it at a vacant place at the table.

Billy swooped into the seat. When she turned back from fetching cutlery from the drawer, she was startled to see him eating with his fingers, cramming the slippery egg into his mouth as best he could.

"He's frae Glesga," said Jamie, as if being Glaswegian explained everything.

Rose suffered an unbidden memory of Jamie stuffing himself with raw fish as a toddler, and kept quiet. She handed the boy a knife and fork. He picked them up and set about the egg again with limited success. She went back to the drawer and offered a spoon in their place. He accepted gratefully.

Rose was moved by the little lad, so scraggy next to her sons. "Ye'll have tae come and have tea with us one day, Billy," she said. Her children looked at her in surprise. "Once we find Helena, of course. When she comes back."

"I like Helena," the boy said.

"I'll say he does!" laughed Angus.

Billy blushed, and Sadie giggled.

"She's kind to me!" he protested. "I hope she's safe an' comes back, that's all."

"Well, we all hope that, Billy," said Rose.

Sam clattered downstairs in his seldom-worn good shoes. "If you bairns are ready, ye can walk part o' the way wi' yer Ma and me."

Rose slipped her apron off and her jacket on, and prepared to pay her respects to Lady Craigendon.

The little church was so crowded with family and friends of the deceased that most of the estate workers and tenants had to remain outside. They formed sombre lines either side of the pathway, as the coffin was carried from the horse-drawn funeral hearse and into the church. Rev. O'Neill stood in the doorway to lead the procession. Sam was close enough to see the marks on his cheek from the day of the fete. He had certainly been mauled, his face left red-scarred and bruised.

They couldn't hear any of the service out there, but when the congregation inside sang the hymns, they took their cue and joined in. They needed no hymn books for the well-known words of "The Lord's My Shepherd" and "I to the Hills will Lift Mine Eyes". Sam had hardly known her ladyship at all, but Rose had become more familiar with her in the last year or so since she had begun volunteering with the wounded soldiers and airmen at the big house. Formidable and aloof, Lady Craigendon had nevertheless willingly thrown open her doors to the wounded and astounded everyone by proving herself a competent ambulance driver, ferrying injured soldiers from all over the place out to the manor house in one of a fleet of converted delivery vans. No other vehicles seemed to have been involved in the accident – it was assumed she had lost control of it for some reason. Maybe a deer had startled her. Sadie had been strangely affected by her death, but perhaps it was the shock of it coming on top of Helena's disappearance. She was a sensitive wee soul, Sam mused.

When the service was over, and after the great crowd of mourners had gathered around the family vault in the churchyard to see her ladyship interred with her husband's ancestors, Sam lingered in the hopes of catching a private word with the minister. Seeing his chance, he took Rose's arm and drew her along with him for moral support. Rev. O'Neill was politely dismissive, however; he was so sorry about Helena, he hoped she would be found soon, but he had promised to drive some guests to the funeral tea up at Craigendon House, and would have to go...

It was a perfectly reasonable exchange, but it nettled Sam. Something was nagging at him. The MacAllistairs hailed Rose to jump in the car which Jock now merited as head gamekeeper, having arranged that they should drive her to the tea. Sam hadn't intended to go, but he changed his mind. On arriving at the house, he was annoyed to find that Rev. O'Neill was included among the guests invited to refreshments indoors. He and other employees were served in a marquee on the lawn. He caught a glimpse of the cleric as he helped one of his elderly passengers into the house, though, and that was when it struck him about the scar. He and Rose had both been clawed by Helena when a toddler, and Helena had been stronger than your average toddler, but the damage

91

hadn't been as great as that displayed on the reverend's face. Sam was certain a larger hand had made those marks. He drew Rose aside.

"Rose, I have to go to Ballaness."

Her eyes widened in surprise. "Why there, of all places?"

"I think the fortune teller might be Megan, the sea witch."

"What makes ye think that? She left years ago."

"Sadie said her hair, under her scarf, was like yours and hers – ye don't get many fortune tellers wi' fair hair, let alone the head of curls you and Sadie have," he said, reaching out and wrapping his index finger round one of her spiral tresses.

Rose smiled at the intimacy, although she batted his hand away in pretended displeasure. "These fortune tellers are never real. She might not even be one o' the travellers wi' the fair, just a local dressed up."

"There's the raven, though," he said. "Sadie said she had a pet raven."

"She surely wouldn't have the same bird after fourteen years?"

"Tame ravens live longer than they would in the wild," Sam replied. "And anyway, he's not your average raven."

Rose was silent a moment. "Dae ye think she recognised Helena?"

"I'm certain. She is a witch, after all. And somethin' strange happened between them."

Rose gave a shake of her head. "Sadie's an imaginative wee lassie. All that aboot Helena fallin' off her stool, an' the crystal ball smashin' – I'm sure it was just an accident. Sadie's built it up into more than it was."

Sam rubbed his chin. "Maybe ye're right. But I still think she might know somethin'."

"She was interviewed by the police. She found Sadie, an' looked after her, saw her to safety. She knows no more than that, Sam, even if she is Megan."

Sam frowned. "I feel in my gut that she does. Helena could have gone back tae the tent after she spoke tae the minister. She might have frightened her even more."

Rose let a beat fall. "Sam, leave it. I'm askin' ye, for the sake of our children, tae leave it. Don't get mixed up wi' her again."

"But Helena's our child, an' she's lost, Rose – I have to do what I can!"

"Helena is your child, Sam. Not mine. I'm interested in protecting mine."

Sam drew back as if he had been slapped. "Who knows what Megan might have said to her?" he cried. "She could be oot o' her wits because she knows what she is, what I am! She could be lyin' in a ditch wi' a broken leg or somethin', an' you're worryin' aboot the other three who're safe wi' us! Yes, Helena is my responsibility, therefore I have to go!"

Rose's mouth was a tight line. "Ye'll go alone, then!"

"Of course! I expected nothin' else. Just give me money for the bus, please." Sam held out his hand. He never had any money on him, for he had no need of it on the estate, and he hadn't been off it for a long time.

Rose fished in her bag for her purse. Her hands were shaking as she gave Sam a generous amount. "How do I know ye'll be back, Sam?" she asked plaintively. "Has it not occurred tae ye that this could be a trap so she can get ye back?"

He placed a hand on Rose's shoulder. "Get me back?" he asked. "She never had me, Rose, except as a friend and then her prisoner. If that's what she wanted, I think she would have tried long before now."

"But maybe, just meetin' Helena like that, an' recognisin' her – if she did – she saw a chance…"

"Rose." Sam's voice was low and firm. "I have to go."

Sam walked to where the main road passed through Craigendon estate. Within an hour, he was sitting on the bus with crofters' wives on their way to the shops in surrounding villages, some taking produce to sell. The townsfolk were happy to buy it in these times of rationing. They were fortunate out in the country, with far fewer deprivations thanks to their own livestock and crops. One or two women greeted him pleasantly and with surprise, for they had never seen him away from the rolling hills and rivers around Loch Duie. They asked if there was any news of Helena and expressed sympathy when he said no.

He climbed off the bus at Ballaness and wished he hadn't come. His legs shook for a few seconds as he gathered his wits and headed from the long main street with its low whitewashed houses, down to the harbour. There, he turned south and began to walk along the shore until he left the village behind. There was no noise from any human source the further he went. Time seemed to dissolve, and it might have been many years ago. The tide was out, and he recognised the larger rocks

93

and stones, he knew every pool. He recalled being an otter less and less these days, but the sensation of how it felt to be a magnificent creature clambering among the stones came back to him now. He also remembered his human form as he had been then, a fine supple young man naked in the moonlight, or even warmed by the sun when no-one else was around. Megan had been there often, though, by night or by day. In his innocence, he hadn't considered his lack of clothing an issue. He was far from innocent now, and he was feeling his years; years of being a man. His thick brown hair was flecked with grey, lines appearing where his face had been smooth.

Finally, Sam saw the hulk of the old upturned boat. He was able to see from a distance that it was still uninhabited – the sea witch had not returned to her abode. The arched door was hanging off its hinges, and the chimney pipe was rusted, bent and pointing to the ground. He didn't even bother to go nearer. If Megan wasn't here, however, where was she? Did she live in her fortune teller's tent now – did she perhaps travel from place to place with the small funfair which visited the fete?

He stared along the shore to where he could see the River Dunn glistening as it flowed into the sea. Following its course upriver with his eyes, he could just make out Ballaness Castle on its rugged promontory. It had been a favourite place for him and Jeanette, for it was where their territories bordered each other. They had swum in the river there and frolicked in human form among the ruins. He had heard once, several years ago, that the castle was haunted by naked wraiths. Poachers used to see them sometimes and run in fright, but they hadn't been seen for a while, the teller of tales said. Sam knew that Jeanette and any others he had known – even his own children – would no longer roam these territories or anywhere else. It was like a dream now. He had the lifespan of a human, and so did Helena. She had to be found, and helped to survive in a world where she must conform or remain secluded forever.

Sam turned and walked back to the village. He was perspiring in his best clothes. He looked in his pocket and examined the money he had left from his bus fare. Was it enough for a cup of tea? He had no idea. Rose handled all the money. It occurred to him that his children didn't know how to use it, either. He walked down the main street until he found a cafe. The menu outside reassured him that he had more than enough for tea and a biscuit. He sat in the window so that he could survey the street, and placed his order. When the waitress returned with

94

his tea, he took a breath to steady himself and enquired as to a woman who used to live on the shore.

"She's not lived there for a while," the woman said. "My mother used to tell me when I was a bairn that she had been there hundreds of years," she laughed. "Fancy folk believing that, just a few years ago! She was a recluse, of course, but she changed her ways."

"What dae ye mean?" asked Sam.

"Upped and left, all of a sudden. Nobody realised she was gone for a while. Two years later, she turned up at the fete, callin' herself a fortune teller. She had medicines she sold, too, things she had made herself from plants and the like. Well, they did say she was a witch! She travelled wi' the fair, sellin' her wares, as far as I know."

Sam smiled to himself. "Was she here last week?"

"Aye," said the woman. "She's the one that found the wee lassie in a state because her sister had disappeared...not been found yet, last I heard. Terrible business. Such a worry for the family. She's the daughter o' the water bailiff on Loch Duie, they say. Did ye know the witch woman, then?"

"We met a long time ago," said Sam. He drained his cup and fumbled in his pocket to pay the bill. "I'll have tae be gettin' on. Thanks for the tea."

Sam caught the bus back to the road end at Craigendon. His heart was heavy. Anything could have happened to Helena. The police had checked the hospitals in the area, so he knew she hadn't been taken in anywhere, but she might be lying hurt or dead of exposure somewhere. He brushed away the tears which had begun to run down his cheeks. He loved all his children, but he felt especially responsible for Helena. She was also his last link to his past. As for Megan, she could be anywhere now if she had joined the travelling people. He was sure she and Rev. O'Neill could shed a lot more light than they had already.

A figure stepped out into the path in front of him. She had been concealed in the bushes. Startled, Sam stopped mid-stride. He looked at the Land Army uniform, at the scarf around her head, from which one fair spiral curl fell in front of her ear.

"Hello, Sam," said Megan.

Meanwhile, back at the cottage, Rose was clattering buckets, mops and brushes as she cleaned every corner in an effort to burn off her frustration. She had offered to stay after the funeral to help at the hospital as normal, but she had been told her services weren't required up at Craigendon House, not while her girl was missing. Rose loved her voluntary work at the big house. She was assisting the nurses with patients' hygiene needs and performing simple tasks for the men, like reading to them or helping them write letters home to their loved ones, or even just darning their socks. The men talked to her and were grateful for her company. She felt needed in a different way from the way she was needed at home, and it was a change from the monotony of her routine. She had even been out on trips with the more able patients, and they were as much a treat to her as they were to them, for she never had pleasure trips.

A tap-tapping noise came from upstairs, faint at first. Tully was summoning her. It wasn't long since she had looked in on him and seen to his needs. She tried to ignore it, but it became louder. Rose flung her scrubbing brush into the tin pail, clanking the side of it and sending a shower of soap suds into her face. She sat back on her heels and wept.

Megan smiled at Sam. "No need tae look so surprised," she said. "Dae ye never think o' Rab when ye see ravens these days, Sam? Not even after what Helena must have told ye?"

Sam looked at her, dumbfounded.

"Come on," she said. "I expected ye would make enquiries tae find oot exactly where I was. I didna tell Helena that. Sorry I never caught ye before ye went. I could have saved ye a journey, if Rab had seen ye and reported back tae me earlier."

Sam found his voice. "When did ye see Helena? Dae ye mean at the fete?"

"No," said Megan frowning. "I mean two days ago, when I set her on the road home. I told her certain things she must say to you, and you alone. What's wrong?"

96

The noise of Tully's stick on the floorboards above became a hammering. Rose had never heard him make such a racket, hadn't known he had the strength to do so. She blew her nose and ran upstairs to see what he wanted. His bed faced the window. He liked to be able to look out on to the loch. His eyes just now, as he stared out, were wide and wild. He jabbed his stick at the window, and Rose looked out. On the pathway by the loch's edge was a figure. It wore a long black cloak, hood up despite the clement weather, and it tapped the ground with a staff as it marched steadily towards the farmhouse.

"You told her *what?*" Sam demanded. Megan had filled him in on her meeting with Helena.

"It's the truth. I had tae tell her somethin' tae explain things, tae help her take control…"

"That, Megan, is what I'm afraid of!"

Sam tried hard to gather his thoughts. "Let me get this straight…the curse went wrong. Jeanette and the other pup…*my son*…lost the ability to become human, as you intended…but Helena fell in the water and escaped? And was like me, then, stuck as a human?"

"Yes. I've told ye."

"Tell me the next bit again."

They were sitting behind the bushes at the side of the road. Megan had rolled a cigarette and was smoking, taking nervous puffs. Sam stared in disbelief at the modern woman beside him. He could see that she had aged, which went against what Tully said – that the witch never changed, for she had ways to renew her youth. Megan had travelled for a while with the funfair, she had told him, then enlisted for service, and was billeted at Fernglass, the McDowall's farm. She liked to catch up with her traveller friends when they were in the area, though – they had been good to her, and still let her have a tent to tell fortunes when she could join them. She continued with her story of May Day fourteen years ago.

"I rescued her from the river and laid her on the bank. I told Jeanette I was sorry. I never meant for it tae happen like that, but I couldn't undo it, or send her tae join them. It was a complicated spell. I walked away, but then my conscience got the better o' me…" Megan's voice faltered.

Sam balled his hands into fists and thrust them into his pockets. "Just tell me what ye did!"

Megan took a long draw on her roll-up. "I conjured the basket and a blanket from grasses and heather, and I put a protection spell on them. I floated her in the river. I tried to will the basket to enter the cave in the Faerie Isle. The fae folk there would have taken care o' her, would have known what she was."

"So ye didn't take her for your own, an' offer her as tribute?"

"That's superstitious nonsense, Sam. The legend folks have made up is laughable!"

"I'm not laughing, Megan. So you're not hundreds of years old, then?"

She became serious. "No. We're mortals, though magical. The Sea Witches o' Ballaness stay lookin' young by certain means – the spring at St. Bride's Cave, for one. We tricked people, that's all. Our ancestors did too, only bein' seen in long cloaks and hoods. Mother and daughter both looked young and we let folk think we were one person – right up to near the time Ma died, as all those before us have done. It made folks frightened o' us, protected us, kept folk away unless they were desperate for what we could give. The only bit o' the legend that's right is that the Sea Witch o' Ballaness is solitary, but seeks a man to father a daughter. She always has a daughter." Megan looked away.

Sam remembered what Tully had told him about seeing the witch at the sacred spring, but he said nothing. It must have been her mother. He addressed the main point of the story she had told him. "Ye really think yer powers transferred tae Helena?"

Megan sighed. This was why she had sought to warn Helena, and now him. "I'm sure of it. I've watched all these years. I felt a bond wi' Helena from the first. Then I started seein' things that happened, like wi' those boys at school. Because of my magic, she's more mine than Jeanette's. I wanted tae have a daughter wi' ye, Sam, and I do. She's our lassie."

Sam stood up, his mind reeling. "Don't be ridiculous, woman! Jeanette brought her into this world, and Rose has brought her up! I should thank ye for savin' her life. I do. But I've struggled for fourteen years to make her *normal*...I've hidden what she really is from her."

"So have I! I didna tell her anything except about her gifts as a witch. I told her I saw her being brought ashore, and knew her for what she was. I said she must be from fae folk – I gave no clue about her real parents, you and Jeanette. She's a witch first and foremost, Sam, an' she needs tae learn how tae control her gifts, or…"

"That's supposin' we ever get her back!" Sam interrupted. "And as for O'Neill…"

"There's no way you're supposed tae know that, except from Helena's lips. I can take ye tae where I left her. She'll just be takin' some time tae adjust."

"A pity ye didna think tae have Rab spy on her this time!"

"I was bein' respectful, lettin' her return tae her family. Anyway, Rab can't be everywhere, all at once." Megan stubbed her cigarette out and jumped to her feet. "Come on, I'll take ye, Sam."

"A bit late tae show respect, after fourteen years o' spyin' on us! You can get back tae the farm an' carry on yer new life, Megan. Stick tae that. Ye've done enough. Just tell me where ye left her."

At the moment that her father parted from Megan the former sea witch, Helena strode into the farmhouse, and called, "I'm home!"

Rose stood at the top of the stairs. She had seen the cloaked figure enter the house, and like her father, she thought it was the sea witch. She feared Sam had found her and fallen prey to her malice again. When she looked down and saw Helena throw back the hood and stare up at her with a smile, she grasped the bannister in relief. Despite all she had said and the worse things she had thought, she was glad to see the girl alive and well. Legs shaking, she ran down the stairs.

"Lassie! Where have ye been? Why ever did ye flee the fete? Are ye alright?" She hugged the girl in the embarrassed fashion of one who wasn't used to doing it.

"Yes, Ma," said Helena. "I got lost, but I'm fine."

"What happened, though? Why did ye run, and leave Sadie like that? What happened, Helena?"

The girl hesitated. "Where is everybody?" she asked. "Grandpa must be here if nobody else is – I must see Grandpa!"

With that, Helena brushed past Rose and made straight up to her grandfather's bedroom. She still carried the staff and wore the cloak. Rose recovered herself and ran up after her.

"Look, Da, it was Helena we saw – she's back!"

The old man stared at Helena. His good arm, still holding his stick, began to tremble so that the tip of the cane juddered off the floorboards. Rose went and took it from him, holding his hand.

"Hello, Grandpa," said Helena. "Ye look as if you've seen a ghost!"

"See," said Rose, "did I not tell ye she'd be back safe and sound?"

Helena went to the side of the bed, bent down and kissed Tully's white-bristled cheek. He flinched.

"What is it, Grandpa?" she asked.

"I must get word tae yer father, Helena," said Rose. "And where did ye find that old thing ye're wearin' ? And bringin' a tree branch inside? Worse than yer brothers!"

Despite the fact Rose didn't say it unkindly, Helena rolled her eyes as she left the room. She looked down at Tully. "Dae I remind ye o' somebody?" she asked quietly. *"Ask yer grandfather,"* Megan had said. *"He saw me on the hill at Ballaness. I watched ye bein' brought ashore, Helena, and I knew the truth o' the matter. I think yer grandpa guessed ye were fae, and he would know I was the sea witch. Nobody else noticed me."* "But my Grandpa can't speak since his last stroke," Helena had said. Megan had hesitated. *"Then ask yer father. He didn't see me that day, but he knows me. He knows me. And the things I tell ye, ye must only repeat tae him."*

"Now I know why ye've never liked me, Grandpa. Ye knew what I was, didn't ye? Well, now I do, too." As Tully's eyes widened in shock, she continued, "I'm a witch, but it's goin' tae be our little secret, since you can't talk." She saw a puzzled expression come into the old man's eyes, but he often looked a bit quizzical. She laughed, turned tail, and went to the room she shared with Sadie. There, she stashed the cloak and staff (although it *was* just a branch of a tree, until she did some work on it) under her bed.

Sam met Rose as he walked back from the spot Megan had shown him, the place where she had parted with Helena. There had been no sign of her, but Rose running towards him, and her excited cries, could mean only one thing. He ran into the cottage and took the stairs two at a time, finding Helena in her room. She flung herself into his arms.

"Ye're safe, lass, ye're safe," he said, kissing the top of her head. Holding her away from him, he looked into her eyes. "What happened tae frighten ye, Helena, tae make ye run like that?"

"It doesn't matter now," she replied.

"Was it anythin' to do wi' Rev. O'Neill?" he asked, hoping she would tell him. It was all he could do, since Megan had sworn him to secrecy.

Helena looked away. "No," she said. She gave a shake of her head, meeting his eyes. "It doesn't matter now, Da. I've found out somethin' wonderful, a secret I'll only share wi' you. I'm a witch, Da. There was a sea witch there the day I was brought ashore at Ballaness, an' she knew what I was! She says ye know her – Megan was her name."

Sam sighed. He didn't tell her he had just left the witch. Deception burrowed deeper into his life with every day.

Chapter 12

Rose only had half her attention on the letter she was transcribing for the RAF officer who had lost his right arm.

"And so, dearest Jane," he said, "I came to understand that the moon really is made of cheese, and that one day I will fly again – in a chariot studded with seashells, pulled by a team of giant bats, and I will mine the moon for cheese."

Rose had actually begun the sentence before she realised what he was saying. Her pen faltered, but she didn't look up.

"It's alright," the man said. "I'm only teasing. I knew your mind was elsewhere. No need to send for Dr. Baird."

Rose blushed. "I'm so sorry," she said. "Now, where we were?" she continued briskly. "There was something on my mind, but you have my full attention now. Mining the moon for cheese, indeed!"

They laughed, and she knew she was forgiven. He had given her an idea, though. Dr. Baird was interested in the psychological well-being of his patients. He probed the wounds in their minds as well as their bodies, and sought to heal them. He was the very man to ask for advice. When she had finished the letter and put it in the box with others to be taken to the post office later, she sought out Dr. Baird. He was treating a patient. She tried to look busy in the ward, which was in reality the dining room of the great house, by tidying vases of flowers and straightening bed covers, until she had an opportunity to speak with him. Finally, as he made his exit, she went after him.

"Dr. Baird! Might I have a word?" Her heart was pounding. The likes of her didn't converse with the doctors. If she had any worries about a patient, she would have spoken to one of the nurses, who would have carried her message up the line of command. The man stared at her blankly. He had probably never noticed her before. "It's personal," she said. "Not my health, but my daughter's. And not anythin' tae dae wi' her body, Doctor, but her mind." Since coming to volunteer at the big house, Rose regretted her lack of education. She saw women younger than herself doing meaningful work and getting paid for it. She was interested, and felt she was just as capable as they were. Rose loved her children, but sometimes she wished her life had been different.

Dr. Baird pushed his glasses up his nose. "Well," he said kindly, "you've come to the right person. Please come to my office, and we can chat. I can spare ten minutes."

Rose smiled her gratitude. As she walked behind him, to the dressing room adjoining a bed chamber now given over for use as a treatment room, Matron appeared and requested her services in bathing a patient. "I'm afraid," said Dr. Baird, "that I have asked Mrs. errr…"

"Hailstanes," said Rose.

"Hailstanes! What a delightful name. Forgive me, Matron, but I have asked Mrs. Hailstanes to help me at the moment. It won't take long."

Matron faltered in her reply. "Of course, Doctor," she said, watching their backs retreating into his office. Dr. Baird closed the door firmly behind him.

At the doctor's invitation, Rose sat in the leather chair on the other side of his desk, wringing her hands in her lap. "My eldest daughter – she's fourteen – was lost for four days. She's back, and she's healthy enough…but changed. She went behind mine an' her father's backs, an' took her wee sister tae the May Day Fete at Ballaness. Somethin' happened while she was there – Sadie, my other lassie, didna see it, whatever it was – an' she ran away. She'll not tell us what happened."

Dr. Baird nodded. "I see. You say she's changed – in what way?"

Rose considered. "She's quieter. She was aye a bit cheeky, Helena, an' with a temper. But now she's biddable."

"Many parents would be delighted by that."

Rose smiled wryly. "Many's the time I've wished for it, Doctor! But it's not natural. She won't look me in the eye, her that was sae bold. An' the not knowin' what happened is worryin' me sick."

"I understand your concerns," said the doctor. "Whatever happened has greatly upset her, and she can't bring herself to talk about it. Such things can take time and require strength and patience on the part of those who wait for light to be shed on the matter. It's probably best if you continue to be the mother you've always been. Carry on as normal, making it clear you are there to offer support at any time, whenever it may be that she decides to speak."

Rose looked away, guilty at never having been that kind of mother to Helena. She fought against a desperate urge to spill the whole story to this kind man, or if not all of it, at least to say that she was not Helena's real mother, that the girl had always been closer to Sam, and that she believed she had told Sam things that neither of them would share with her; that, not for the first time, she felt excluded and not needed. That would take a lot more than the few minutes left of her allocated time, though, and said more about her state of mind than Helena's.

"Thank you, Dr. Baird," she said, forcing a smile despite the tears stinging her eyes. "I'll do that."

"If you do find out what happened…I would be interested to know. She may be fully herself again once it's out in the open, or she may be changed for good. I'm interested in the effects our experiences have upon us."

"Of course, Doctor. That's why I spoke tae ye. I thought she might be like some o' the patients, trau… traum…"

"Traumatised. She may well be. But not by the same experiences as these brave men."

"Oh no, never that! Well, I'll not take up any more o' yer time. Thank you again, Doctor."

As she left his office, Matron appeared from the shadows at the side of the stairs. "Mrs. Hailstanes! I'll not ask in what way you were aiding Dr. Baird. But you haven't seemed quite yourself since the incident concerning your daughter."

Rose hesitated. She had respect for Matron, but knew her to be a disciplinarian and a stickler for the proper order of things. She had guessed her reason for being in Dr. Baird's office, despite the good man's connivance in trying to make it look otherwise.

"I apologise, Matron. I love my duties here, an' I'll pull myself together an' get on with them now." She didn't meet the older woman's eye. She tried to slip away.

"There's usually only one reason girls of that age run away," said her superior.

104

Rose stopped, feeling Matron's stare penetrating her back. She turned round.

"Helena ran from the fete because something happened, Matron."

"And she ran away to it in the first place."

"She took her sister there for an adventure, a treat. She had every intention of returning that afternoon, I assure you."

"She might have had some tryst planned. With a boy."

Rose coloured. The thought had crossed her mind, but only briefly.

"We live very quietly here, Matron." Even as she said it, she recalled that her own younger life, while not quite so secluded as Helena's, had been equally devoid of chances for romantic encounters, until...

"Well," said the woman, pursing her lips and drawing herself up to her full height, "whether she planned it or not, you'll likely find that's what's happened. And you'll know soon enough."

Rose clenched her fists and strode away, her head held high. Helena might have many faults, but whatever had happened had been by chance, she was sure of that. *Please God,* she thought, *let it be anything but that.*

When Rose returned home later that day, she found Helena busy preparing vegetables for the evening meal. She had already gutted the fish her father had caught. Sadie was sitting at the kitchen table doing her homework, and she had set the boys tasks to do outdoors. They had some help, she told Rose – she had invited wee Billy MacTaggart, the evacuee from Glasgow, to tea. That was alright, wasn't it?

"Aye," said Rose. "He's a poor wee soul." She watched as Helena carried on with her work, trying to read her expression, but it was closed. The girl usually had to be nagged to do the slightest thing. Could she have done something of which to be ashamed? Despite her distrust of her, Rose didn't believe it; but there was still the possibility that something had been done to her against her will. She bit her tongue against probing again, especially with Sadie there at the table. At least Sadie seemed back to her normal self, apart from being upset whenever Lady Craigendon's death was mentioned; goodness, the lassie had screamed and cried her eyes out when she first heard. Still, the news had broken on the night of Helena's disappearance, when Lady Craigendon's ambulance had been found crashed into a tree on a quiet country road. Sadie seemed strangely affected every time the incident was mentioned.

Rose shook her head to dispel the disquieting thoughts which left her barely able to think straight these days. She would try to do what Dr. Baird had said. "Thank you, Helena. I do appreciate your help around the place. Have ye seen tae Grandpa?"

"Of course," said the girl, smiling. She had taken Grandpa a cup of tea and had stayed to chat to him.

"What did ye chat aboot?" asked Rose. She wondered if Helena told the old man her secrets, since he was unable to share them. She hoped not. He had enough burdens to carry.

"School an' that," answered Helena.

She was pleasant and polite, yet her eyes were far away, and she was... Rose grappled for the word...*docile*. She was docile. Things were far from right.

"Well, ye must tell me aboot yer day. Ye know I'm aye interested tae hear yer stories." She swallowed after the lie came out – but she would be, she told herself, she would be. If Helena had changed, so would she. Yet something nagged at the back of her mind.

When Sam came home later, he wasn't alone. "The Reverend's just parkin' his car," he said. "He stopped me at the gate, said he had come tae see how Helena was."

"How kind," said Rose, but her brow creased. She was flustered. "Tea's nearly ready, though, and the place stinks o' fish!"

"I'm sure they eat fish in the manse, Rose," said Sam. "Anyway, he'll not bide. He never makes long calls."

"You make it clear ye have little time for him, Sam."

"I think he's an old hypocrite."

"He's no older than you are!"

Sam hesitated. "I used tae think he liked ye."

Rose looked at him. "He does. He's always got on wi' Da an' me."

"Not like that. I mean, I think he *liked* ye, Rose."

"Oh!" she said, surprised. "Really? Well, that's not fitting for a man of the cloth." She coloured slightly. In truth, she was flattered that Sam thought such a thing, true or not. Was it possible he might have been jealous all this time?

"I think he's always had an eye for the lassies, Rose," said Sam, his expression serious, his eyes searching.

Rose looked shocked and opened her mouth to speak, but Rev. O'Neill rapped at the kitchen door just then and entered without being invited. He always did that, and would have even if he hadn't already spoken with Sam about his intended visit. Folk thought he was trying to catch them out. Rose, despite being flustered, had had time enough to prepare, though; she had cleared the kitchen dresser of clutter while she conversed with Sam, slipped the family Bible out of the drawer and laid it there as if the good book held pride of place in the room and in the family's hearts. It was well known that to test his flock, Rev. O'Neill never carried his own Bible. At some point in his visit, he would request theirs in order to read a verse or two and deliver a prayer, and a lecture would ensue if it was not readily to hand.

"Good afternoon, Reverend," said Rose. "How kind of ye tae call. I'm just preparin' the tea in here… would ye like tae come through tae the sittin' room?" The parlour at the front of the house was hardly ever used. The minister was usually content with the kitchen which had comfortable chairs drawn up around the fire, but it was only polite to ask. Rose was surprised, therefore, when he said that the privacy of the sitting room would be more suited to the purpose of his visit, and that he hoped the children were occupied elsewhere. He was usually glad to see them. Although folk made fun of him and his empty-headed wife, they pitied their childless state, and were happy to let him fuss their offspring in his condescending way. Helena and Sadie were favourites, despite Helena's behaviour at her christening, when she had screamed the kirk down and trailed his clerical collar off as he held her in his arms. Even more flustered, Rose led the way through, she and Sam hastily pulling the dust covers off the furniture, and Rose returning to the kitchen to fetch the Bible, setting it gently on her mother's sideboard as if it was an altar. Then she offered a cup of tea, but the minister refused it. They all sat down. She and Sam looked at him expectantly.

He cleared his throat. "I, like everyone else, was relieved to hear of Helena's safe return," he said. "Tell me… has she said anything of what happened to her?"

"Not a word," said Sam. "The trail o' what happened leadin' up tae her disappearance stops at you, Reverend."

Rose shot her husband a look and laughed nervously. "Honestly, Sam, ye sound like the policeman we dealt wi'!"

Sam was silent, but his gaze never left the minister's face. A beat fell. Rev. O'Neill swallowed, and when his voice came out, it was higher pitched than usual.

"I wish I could help you more than I can on that score, but I can't. Anyway, it's all in the past. The girl is back safe and sound, and no harm done. We must all look to the future now. As ye know, I was discussin' her future with her at the fete, and I've come tae discuss it with you now."

Sam's hands clenched his knees. "If it involves Helena leavin' hame, Reverend, ye can think again. We dinna want tae know."

Rose was claimed by conflicting emotions. "I think we should hear what Rev. O'Neill has tae say, Sam," she said. Despite the seemingly reformed Helena, in spite of her determination to be a better mother to her, the thought of Helena being out of her house was still appealing.

Neville O'Neill glanced at her gratefully. "We all know Helena's difficult beginnings," he continued, "or rather, we don't. We have no idea where she came from, but tae my mind, there's good blood in the lassie. She's bright beyond her years and stands out in every way among the other local bairns."

For a brief moment, Jeanette swam across Sam's consciousness. He had dammed that part of his life up, but occasionally the defences were breached. The truth was, Helena was as intelligent as her mother had been, and was the double of Jeanette when in her human form. She was a bitter-sweet memory to him now, never dwelt upon, for he had been sentimental neither as man nor beast, and life was too busy for the luxury of pining over a lost love and another life. He had another partner, another family now. He looked across at Rose and saw that her face was stricken.

"All the Hailstanes bairns are fine," he said quickly.

"But of course!" blustered the minister. "I didn't mean to suggest…" He cleared his throat again. "I have the feelin' Helena was born for higher things, is all. I believe it may be God's will, and I will be His instrument in helping her tae achieve her full potential. Helena should be a teacher."

Sam barked a gruff laugh. "Well, Reverend, we need waste no more o' yer time. We canna afford it, and we don't accept charity."

"Sam, we should hear what Rev. O'Neill has tae say," hissed Rose. She faced the minister. "There may be some way we could repay ye, through time, like." She smiled, looking from one to the other, her eyes appealing to both men.

"Helena needs tae stay here, Rose," Sam said, and added, "Now more than ever."

Rose searched her husband's eyes, wondering for the umpteenth time what had passed between him and his daughter that she wasn't permitted to know.

All three occupants of the room jumped as the door swung open and Helena herself stood there. She had been out for some fresh air with her siblings and wee Billy before tea.

"Hello," she said. Her face was shadowed by a wary expression rarely seen. She didn't look in the direction of Rev. O'Neill.

He stood up, holding out his hand and advancing towards her. "Helena, my dear lassie! Mrs. O'Neill and I were so relieved tae hear ye had returned safely."

Helena shrank from his hand, saying nothing, but staring at the marks on his right cheek.

"The Reverend has been in the wars, Helena," said Sam.

Rose looked from her husband to his daughter.

"He's come tae repeat his offer o' helpin' ye tae become a teacher," Sam continued. "I've pointed out that we require no such help. Isn't that right, ma lassie?"

Rose's head was beginning to swim. She looked from face to face – the barely suppressed anger and disgust in her husband's, the nervousness and something more in the minister's, the wariness – and could that be *fear* on Helena's? Helena was never afraid. Why should she fear such a generous offer? The blood drained from Rose's face in realisation, and an instant later, returned to blaze red on her pallid cheeks. She thought she might faint, but with her certainty came a surge of empowering anger. She stood up and crossed the room, taking Helena's hand in her own, studying it, caressing it.

"I've always had trouble gettin' this lassie tae cut her nails, you know, Reverend," she said. "She prefers them long. Like claws, I often say. It's a fortnight since we last fought about it, and she still hasn't done it." She stared pointedly at the minister as she spoke, her eyes straying to the marks on his cheek. She glanced at Helena, who stared at the floor from under her long lashes, and she knew she had the truth of it at last. Sam had been trying to tell her before the minister arrived. Why had he not done it sooner?

Sam was gazing at her with undisguised admiration. He crossed the room to stand with his wife and daughter, putting an arm round their shoulders. "I think you should leave now, O'Neill."

As the man rose shakily to his feet, head bowed, Helena spoke. "Maybe we shouldn't be so hasty."

Rose shot her a startled look. She saw Sam blanch.

"I think Rev. O'Neill's offer of money to aid my studies is very generous, and will do, circumstances bein' what they are. His private tuition won't be necessary, of course."

Rose stared at Helena. The girl was suddenly in total possession of herself. She held her head high, hands calmly clasped, the hint of a smile playing about the corners of her mouth. Rose was afraid, then. She had never feared her before, but this sea change after days of silence and docility... At least she could see that Sam was equally shocked, that he had not expected this.

"Helena!" he said. His chest was heaving, and he had broken out in a sweat.

"I think the Reverend would be only too glad to meet our conditions," she said.

Rose found her voice. "*Our?* We make no conditions, Helena, for we will have no part in this, no matter what has happened!"

"Indeed we will not!" hissed Sam.

O'Neill's face had been twitching as changing emotions chased across it. His countenance settled now into a sneer. "Blackmail! Ye've nurtured a viper in yer bosom! She should have been flung back tae the sea and drowned that day at Ballaness!"

Sam stepped towards him. Rose threw her arm in front of him to deter him, but he shouted at the cleric: "She wouldn't be tryin' it if you hadn't given her reason! And you a man o' the cloth! Never mind that, in fact, there's no man should interfere wi' an innocent lass, no matter his title or station in life!"

Helena was undeterred. "I think..."

"You, young lady, think nothing!" said Sam, rounding on his daughter. "This is for adults tae sort out." His clenched fists twitched, and his body, barred by Rose's arm, leaned towards the cleric, taut with rage.

Neville O'Neill drew himself up to his full impressive height, looking down his beak-like nose, a hawk surveying potential prey and deciding if it was worth the effort. "It would be the word of a girl known tae be wild, frae God knows where and what parentage, against mine," he said. "An undoubted little bastard brat against a man of God."

Rose couldn't hold Sam then, but she flung herself between the two men. "That would solve nothing!"

"Indeed it would not," said O'Neill. "It would merely add assault tae yer slanderous accusations!"

Sam was purple in the face, unable to speak. Rose turned to the minister. "I think you had better go, Sir."

He picked up the hat he had left on the sideboard, next to the family Bible. "It's you I feel for the most," he said to Rose. "There was a time when, low in birth as ye might be, I thought of offerin' for ye in marriage, Mrs. Hailstanes."

Three pairs of astonished eyes stared at him. He smiled in triumph. "Of course, that was before ye disgraced yerself, and had tae take what ye could get. An' why he foisted this bitch on ye when ye lost yer own, I could never understand. Ye had lost one, so he thought he would bring ye another? I always believed there was more to it than that."

Rose's entire body went rigid. She glanced at Helena, who was gazing at her with sheer incredulity on her beautiful young face, and at Sam, whose murderous expression had been wiped from his visage by the minister's words. He was paler than his wife, and shaking.

"Get out!" he cried. He picked up the Bible and flung it at the minister's retreating back.

Sam placed his hand none too gently under Helena's elbow, his other pinching her shoulder, and he bundled her through the kitchen and into the yard. The boys and Sadie, who had just come in, stood saucer-eyed and silent, aware something had happened. Sam had left Rose to recover in the sitting room, sipping a glass of whisky from her father's bottle. As he went through the doorway, the smell of burning followed him. Cursing, he went back indoors and removed the fish pie from the oven.

"Sadie, boys – set the table and serve yourselves. The rest of us will eat later."

Outside, Helena was sulking near the barn.

"I cannot believe what just happened in there!" he said.

"Neither can I!" she said. "Fancy you and Ma havin' a shotgun wedding! Nae wonder Grandpa doesn't like ye. Or me." Her brow creased as she spoke the last two words, and she regarded Sam in puzzlement, waiting for him to say something.

"The past is the past!" he blustered. "Whatever happened between me and your mother is our business!"

"So... ye took me in because ye lost yer own baby?"

"Aye!"

"I was just a replacement?"

"No! Look, Helena, things are never that simple..."

"Did ye know my mother, Da?"

Her words took the wind from Sam, but the lie fell from his lips as part of the lie he had been living for years. "How could I? Ye were found floatin' in a basket!" He studied her, judging correctly that she wanted him to say that yes, he had known her mother, that there had been someone in his life besides Rose, and that yes, he was her real father. If true in the way that she understood it, it would have made him a philanderer with two women pregnant by him at around the same time. That was what O'Neill must have suspected all along. Sam believed Helena would forgive him, though, just to know that she was his. He was well aware, since her escapade in Ballaness, that she was troubled by the question of where she had come from. At least Megan, in her well-meaning interference, hadn't told that much; but she had put other harmful ideas in the girl's head. He still hadn't told her that he had met the sea witch.

"Look, Helena – what did ye think ye were playin' at back there? Ye were tryin' tae blackmail the minister!"

"And why not?" his daughter cried. "I want a chance at life! I dinna want tae be shut up here until I'm an old maid!" Tears of frustration sprang to her eyes.

Sam fished a clean hanky from his pocket. "Blackmail isn't the way tae go about it, lassie."

"I wasn't blackmailin' him! Not tae start with. If ye had only left me tae set the conditions – take his money, but not his 'tuition', oh no, not wi' his hands all over me…" She shuddered in disgust.

Sam took a deep breath. "I asked ye if anything had passed between you and Rev. O'Neill, and ye said no. I guessed it, though, even before ye came back. Surely ye can understand that we had tae refuse his money? It's a matter o' decency and honour. Tae take it – even settin' conditions, as ye call it – would be like colluding, Helena. We would be no better than him."

"Ye've ruined everythin', though!" she spat. "I summoned him tae dae my will, and ye ruined it!"

Sam blinked, taking in her words. "I hope you don't mean what I think you mean."

"If I'm a witch, why shouldn't I use my powers? Megan said as much."

"I think she told ye that ye need tae learn tae control them."

"How would you know that, Da? I didn't tell ye that!"

Sam folded his arms. "Ye're smart, Helena, but not that smart. Ye come back here after four days, an' tae me ye're puffed up wi' pride aboot bein' a witch, while ye act as if butter wouldn't melt tae everybody else… I already knew, Helena. I was one step ahead o' ye. I met Megan before I knew ye were back. She thought ye'd been home for two days, though."

Helena frowned. Then, to his surprise, she shrugged and looked triumphant. "No matter," she said. "What's important is that you know it's a real thing, Da. Magic, I mean. Why else would Megan have told me tae tell you, and not Ma? Unless there's somethin' else ye're not tellin' me?"

Sam cursed Megan and all her meddling in his life. "I lived at Ballaness a while before I came here. I knew her, like she said. Everybody did. That's all." A movement at the corner of his eye alerted Sam to the presence of Sadie.

"How long have you been standin' there, wee lass?" he asked.

The child was staring at her older sister. "Helena put a curse on Lady Craigendon," she said. The words tumbled out then, as if a dam had been burst: "She stopped her ambulance, an' tried tae get her tae give us a lift tae the fete, but Lady Craigendon was angry an' said no, an' she would tell you and Ma, an' she drove off an' nearly knocked me down, an' Helena went quiet an' queer an' mumbled stuff…an' that night we heard that Lady Craigendon was dead!" She stopped, taking gulps of air.

Sam floundered, and looking at his eldest daughter, he saw she was equally thrown by Sadie's words.

"I didn't mean anythin' by it!" cried Helena. "I didn't even know, then, that I…"

Sam raised a hand to quieten her. "Now listen to me, both o' ye!" Sam said. "You will never repeat this to anybody, do ye hear? Whatever ye think happened, Sadie, and whatever ye overheard just now, it's nonsense! Folk will just laugh an' make fun if ye breathe a word o' it! Not even tae Ma, Sadie – ye must promise."

Sadie's face reddened and creased into a whine, and he pulled her to him, burying her head in his chest. "There, there, ye're not in trouble. It's just best for everybody if we keep quiet." Over her head, he looked at Helena. She gazed back at him, eyes huge with genuine shock.

Helena climbed the ladder to the hayloft, her legs shaking. The old mattress which had been Sam's bed when he first came to Loch Duie was up there. She had made a den of the hayloft at the water bailiff's cottage, and had insisted on taking the mattress with her when they moved to the farmhouse. This was her territory, the place where she went to read and daydream. Sadie wouldn't follow her there because she was afraid of the spiders which wove their webs thickly on the low eaves overhead, and the boys knew they could only come up and join her by invitation.

So much had happened in a short space of time, and her mind had been so full of schemes and dreams, that she hadn't given much thought to Lady Craigendon's death, of which she had learned the night of her return. She hadn't felt anything about it and certainly hadn't connected it with their encounter on the day of the fete. She could barely remember what she had said when that strange mood had come upon her, just as she struggled to recall the details of the incident with the older boys at school when she was little. She couldn't believe she had caused a death – was Megan right about her needing to control her powers? There was so much she wanted to ask Megan. Helena retrieved her staff from the place she kept it hidden, between the back of the mattress and the wall.

She took up the knife concealed there also, and began to whittle at the ash branch.

Rose was still sitting in the parlour when Sam returned indoors. "Ye knew what Rev. O'Neill did, Sam," she said. "Why didn't ye tell me?"

"I guessed, Rose," he replied.

"There's more to it than that."

Sam sighed and sat opposite her. "Megan confirmed my suspicions. I didn't meet her at Ballaness that day. I was honest with ye aboot that. But I did meet her afterwards, when I came back tae the estate. Then you came runnin' tae tell me Helena was back, and it seemed best not tae mention it, not tae go into the things she had said. At least, not straight away. I was tryin' tae tell ye aboot O'Neill."

Rose took a steadying sip of whisky. "Is there anything else ye haven't told me, Sam?"

When she learned that Megan's spells all those years ago had somehow made Helena a witch, as well as being a shapeshifting otter stuck in human form, she drained the glass in one gulp. "Well," she said, "that explains a few things." She gazed into the middle distance, numb.

Sam kept quiet about Lady Craigendon.

Helena spent a lot of time in the hayloft over the next few weeks, going there after school when her hateful chores were finished. Her interest in all things domestic had been short-lived, part of her plan to have her way in training to be a teacher. If only her parents had seen the sense of taking what they could get from Rev. O'Neill! She passed the evenings as they lightened towards midsummer working on her staff. As she whittled away at it until it was smooth and seemed fitted to the contours of her hand, an extension of her arm, she mused on what kind of witch she was. Megan had called herself a sea witch. Sometimes Helena dreamt of going to live in the old upturned boat Megan had abandoned; it must be heaven to have your own place. Her homesickness for her family when she was lost had soon evaporated.

Midsummer's Eve wrapped the old barn in a golden glow as Helena put the finishing touches to her tool. The sun seeped through knotholes and spilled through gaps between the planking of the walls, and dust motes danced around her as she attempted to carve a raven on top of the staff. She didn't know if Megan's staff had been embellished like this, but it was something she wanted for herself; it didn't work out, though. Her effort was misshapen and odd, the head and lowered wings blending into one meaningless blob. Helena sighed and thought about cutting it off. She decided to work at it until it resembled some sort of head. She gave it round eyes and a nose and, as an afterthought, whiskers. Helena gazed at her efforts quizzically. It was crude and resembled nothing much she could recognise, but it was hers, she had made it, and she was pleased with it. Finally, she gave the staff a coat of varnish to protect it and bring out the beauty of the stripped, straight-grained wood. Satisfied, she left it to dry.

Later, on that longest day of the year, Helena couldn't sleep. Feeling dreamy and trance-like, she stole from her bed and tiptoed downstairs and out of the house. Her toes curled around the rungs of the hayloft ladder as if she had been accustomed to scaling it barefoot. She retrieved her staff and headed to the edge of Loch Duie. A light breeze caressed her cotton nightgown and made her flesh tingle, and the sharp shingle pierced her soles. She extended her right arm, staff pointing at the loch, and her spirit seemed to hover over the water. "I am a water witch," she said to herself. "I am the Lady of the Loch." Yet in the instant that the knowledge came to her, Helena shuddered and lowered her arm.

"I do not want to stay here all my life!" she cried aloud.

PART THREE

July 1942

Chapter 13

On a hot July morning a few weeks later, Rose turned and waved at Sam from where the road began to rise up towards Craigendon House. She had felt his eyes following her and Helena, and understood his anxieties. She had won at last, though. *"The lassie has tae have some kind o' life, an' somethin' tae keep her busy, tae stop her gettin' intae trouble,"* she had reasoned with him. *"She's leavin' school. Ye canna expect her tae hang around here all day, every day."*

She called on the girl, who had walked ahead, to stop and wave to her father, then she made a shooing motion with her hands towards Sam and watched for a moment as he strode away towards the woods. Helena was already walking again, eager to be at the big house, where Rose had secured her a job as a maid. Her enthusiasm surprised Rose, who had expected resistance since Rev. O'Neill had put grander ideas in her head. She had assured the housekeeper that Lady Craigendon had promised employment for Helena just prior to her death. That wasn't exactly true, but nobody could gainsay it, and Rose was well known and respected by the staff. She crossed her fingers when she thought of the white lie, and of the day to come.

The two of them were damp and tousled from the heat by the time they walked through the servants' entrance at Craigendon House. Mrs. Bailey, the housekeeper, eyed them with displeasure and told Helena she had best take five minutes – no more – to wash her face and hands and put her hair in order. She wasn't in a position to boss Rose around, but well aware that Matron would say likewise, she joined her daughter in the servants' privy. After tearing a brush through her own unruly curls, she pulled the pins from Helena's long hair and let her thick plait fall, tucking in stray hairs and winding the plait back into a coil at the nape of her neck as quickly as she could. They had been practising the style for a week now, and but for the heat, it would have been perfect that morning. As usual, Rose didn't waste time trying to go gently with the styling, and as was also customary, Helena complained bitterly.

"Ye'll have tae learn tae dae it yerself," Rose mumbled through a mouthful of pins.

"I hate it! I don't see why I have to keep it up. I like my hair free."

"Those days are gone, lassie. Ye should have it cut, really."

Helena gave Rose a look of such sullenness that she decided not to needle her any more. It would do neither of them any favours to send her to work in a bad mood.

Helena presented herself to Mrs. Bailey in the kitchen, and Rose took the back stairs to the first floor to commence her hospital duties. As she came out into the grand entrance hallway with its panelled walls and great baronial fireplace, she was passed by the aged butler and an even more aged estate worker who was sometimes pressed into service as a footman in these staff-impoverished times. They threw open the double doors which formed the principal entrance of the house. Lord Craigendon appeared at the top of the staircase then and strode down with an eager air seldom seen since the death of his wife. He adjusted his cuffs as he did so, and at the bottom he paused to peer in the mirror above the mantel, smoothing his iron grey hair. Intrigued, Rose concealed herself behind a pillar. She heard the crunching of tyres on the gravel of the driveway. His Lordship stepped outside to greet the visitors, whoever they might be; when he ushered them into his home a few minutes later, Rose felt the blood rush to her cheeks and drain to her feet just as quickly. She leaned against the pillar for support.

Helena had been given an old-fashioned black dress to wear, and a white apron to put over it. It had belonged to previous maids and was well-worn, but it fitted perfectly although a little long, skimming her ankles, and Helena loved it. She had never worn black before, apart from Megan's old cloak, and she was desperate to see her reflection. She would like to see herself in that dress with her hair tumbling down. As she worked her way through the mountain of potatoes Mrs. Bailey had given her to peel, she mused on what the dress would look like out by the loch on a windy day, the skirt billowing, her hair flying, and her staff in her hand...

Helena knew she could survive the menial tasks a maid had to do because of two things – the thrill of seeing inside Craigendon House, and the secrets she nursed to herself like a family of newborn infants. She nurtured them whenever life was mundane, feeding them with fancies of what she intended to do. She wouldn't be stuck at Craigendon forever, not once she had practised some more and discovered her path. Her staff, now empowered with spells of her own devising, lay waiting for her, concealed in her den. She smiled to herself, her hands working automatically as she allowed her mind to roam.

"You're a quick worker, lass, I'll give you that."

Startled from her reverie, Helena jumped and cut her thumb with the knife. Mrs. Bailey reacted quickly, grabbing her hand and forcing it under the cold tap.

"Careless!" she cried. "Don't spoil your good work by bleeding all over it! This is no place for daydreaming, even if your hands are still doing the work they were given. Your mind must be on the job at all times, ready to heed what's going on around you and to jump to it when given orders. Is that clear?"

"Yes, Mrs. Bailey," said Helena, thinking of her staff and how ironic it was that she had done all that work to whittle and carve it without injury, while nearly slicing her thumb off peeling potatoes.

Mrs. Bailey bound her injury; her head bent close to Helena's chest. Despite her sharp manner, her touch was gentle. She took care not to cause more pain. It struck Helena how rough Rose had always been with her. She understood matters better now, though; she had obviously not made up for the loss of Rose's own child. It had been Sam's idea to take her in, a clumsy attempt at substitution, and it had gone wrong. She should be thankful that he himself had taken to her as if she was his own.

Mrs. Bailey finished binding her thumb and told her there was work to do upstairs. "Lord Craigendon, for some reason, has decided not to entertain his guests in the Duie Drawing Room. It's the finest room in the house, so I assumed... Anyway, the dust covers must go back on again. I'll get Mary McDowall to help you."

She led Helena out of the kitchen and up the servants' stairs. Helena glimpsed the entrance hall as they ascended the back stairs to the upper floors, and the opulence of it made her gape in wonder. She craned her neck through the doorway revealing the next floor, seeing a long corridor richly carpeted, with vases overflowing with flowers set on pedestals along the length of it. They carried on to the floor above, where Mrs. Bailey led her out into a corridor not quite as grand as the one below, but still finer than anything in Helena's experience. Her feet sank into the patterned carpet as they walked along to a room at the far end where a doorway stood open.

Helena followed Mrs. Bailey through it, finding herself in a bedroom with heavy oak furniture, including a four-poster bed straight from a fairy tale. A young woman dressed like Helena was taking clothes from a suitcase and placing them in drawers. Absorbed in her work, she didn't notice them enter. Helena knew Mary McDowall from school. She was two years older, and her brother was one of the boys who had bullied Helena that fateful day not long after she started school. As a result, there was enmity between the families. Mary McDowall fancied herself, and Helena had little time for her. She was amused to see Mary sniff some garments she held, inhaling deeply before placing them in a drawer with dreamy reverence.

"I take it you're nearly finished here?" Mrs. Bailey asked, making the girl jump.

"Aye! I mean, yes, Mrs. Bailey." Mary took in Helena's presence, and scowled.

"You'll know Miss Hailstanes – Helena," said the housekeeper. "I need the two of you to go the Duie Drawing Room and close it up again. Put the ornaments in storage, cover the furnishings and paintings and close the shutters."

Mary looked curious. "Is that not where the guests are?"

Mrs. Bailey sniffed. "Lord Craigendon decided otherwise. Just as it was decided that Captain Carmichael would not be accommodated in a ward with the other patients." She glanced around. "You've done a good job of the room in a short space of time. Come now, and show Helena what needs doing downstairs."

The two girls glanced at each other tight-lipped. They descended a floor and walked along the flower-filled corridor where Helena breathed the scent deeply and felt she was floating. She glimpsed her reflection in huge gold-framed mirrors as they went, and she longed to stop and look properly. At the far end, Mrs. Bailey threw open a set of double doors.

Light exploded into the corridor and flowed over them where they stood. Helena gasped.

The room within was a corner one, with long Georgian windows on two sides giving magnificent views over the estate. Loch Duie sprawled among the hills in all its splendour, shimmering in the morning heat haze. Helena watched as a huge bird, larger than any she had ever seen, swooped down on the loch and rose with a fish clasped in its talons. Mighty wings beat the air as the bird spiralled upwards and turned in the direction of the manor house. For a moment, Helena thought it was going to fly through the open window; she felt as if it was coming straight at her. It soared up and away, however, and she forgot about it as she turned her attention to the room, which was dominated by furnishings covered in royal blue. The wallpaper was patterned with birds of sky blue flitting between blue trees, and vases and other ornaments complemented the decorative scheme. It had not one, but two, enormous fireplaces. Helena could barely take it all in.

"I've had the crates and boxes of covers brought back up. Don't stand there gawping, Helena! Set to it, girl!"

Mrs. Bailey departed and Mary curled her lip at Helena. "So, the cleverest lassie at Craigendon School has to settle for goin' into service after all?"

Helena didn't bat an eyelid. "Ye've been left school two years, what would you know?"

"Only that ye thought ye were better, bein' a pupil-teacher, but look at you now."

Helena bit her tongue. She worked harder at controlling her temper these days. She couldn't believe she had really been responsible for Lady Craigendon's death. She didn't want to be. It was a coincidence, she had convinced herself, but a sobering one after what Megan had said about the need to control her powers. "Just show me what I have to do, Mary," she said.

"Oh, I will. I'm in charge, see? I don't trust you wi' these priceless treasures. I'll pack the ornaments away; you cover everything up."

The maids set to work, not speaking. Helena wanted to ask after wee Billy, who lived with the McDowalls. She would miss him now she had left school. He could barely read when he arrived after the Clydebank bombings in March, and she had been assigned to help him. He was a poor wee soul, and she was fond of him, but she decided it was best if

123

Mary didn't know that. Standing on stepladders to cover a mirror, she was taking advantage of the chance to admire her reflection covertly, when she caught sight of something which nearly caused her to fall off. Above the fireplace behind her, reflected in the looking glass, she noticed Lady Craigendon's portrait for the first time. It looked as if it was a few years old, and the image wasn't the same as that of the middle-aged woman who had argued with her on the country road on May Day, not long before her death, but it was unmistakable. She had been a handsome woman when this was painted, proud and fierce looking. Helena had often heard it said that she was hard; but there was something else in those eyes, too. Helena thought she could detect hurt. She dismissed the notion. How could you tell that from a painting?

Giving herself a shake, she climbed down the stepladder, ashamed to find that her legs were shaking slightly. As she worked her way around the room, covering paintings and furniture, she glanced uneasily at the portrait. Every time, the eyes were looking straight at her. Abruptly, she hauled the stepladders over to the fireplace and climbed, dust sheet in hand. She heard a snigger behind her.

"Freaked by the eyes, are ye?" asked Mary McDowall, her hands busy wrapping an antique vase. "She knew everythin' that went on, that one. Missed nothin'. And she'll know what's goin' on here now."

"What dae ye mean?" asked Helena.

"As if I would tell you!" Mary pouted. "But the eyes are only an artist's trick. Does smart Helena Hailstanes not know that?"

Hands trembling, Helena pulled the sheet over the painting, noticing the artist's signature as she did so: F. Carmichael.

"Look at the state o' you!" laughed Mary. "Don't fall off the ladder, will ye? I wouldn't want ye to hurt yourself or anything."

Helena never could stand humiliation. She stood stock still on the ladder, staring at Mary with loathing, all trembling gone in the emotion surging through her. Her fists were clenched, and so were her teeth, fighting the words she longed to set free. They sprang from her mind, though, and the vase slipped from Mary's hands and fractured into three large pieces on the floor.

🐾

Chapter 14

On the ground floor, in the rooms converted to wards, Rose Hailstanes went about her duties with head bowed and eyes glancing nervously around everywhere she walked. She sat down to act as scribe for the kind officer with the injured arm again. He always requested her. If she wasn't available, he said his letter could wait. Rose was flattered by this. The officer was younger than she was, and he often asked her to transcribe words of love to his girl, but she knew when a man liked her. She felt his gaze on her head as she bent over her writing pad, and she had seen his eyes travel down her legs, which were shapely. The bearing of children had improved her figure rather than the reverse, fleshing out her bones and adding curves where awkward angles had been. While she had no thoughts whatsoever of encouraging him, she basked in this knowledge and felt rejuvenated by it.

She greeted him and sat at the table, laying out her pad and pen.

"We are distracted again, sweet Rose," he said. "Is all well with your family?"

Rose forced a smile. "Very much so, thank you. My eldest daughter is below stairs at this minute, having entered service here this morning."

"Excellent!" said the officer. "Well then, shall we begin?"

He had just started to dictate when Matron bustled in, looking flustered.

"Might I have a word, Mrs. Hailstanes?"

Rose glanced apologetically at the officer. "Excuse me. I'll be back soon." She hoped she would be. Surely Helena hadn't got herself into trouble already?

"We have a highly irregular situation," said Matron. "A patient arrived this morning who is also a personal friend of Lord Craigendon. He has asked to be given a guest room rather than a hospital bed, and now he is requesting a scribe."

Rose felt weak. Thank goodness she had an excuse. She controlled herself, hoping to suppress any signs of agitation. "As you can see, Matron, I am already employed."

"I know, and I wouldn't ask. But no-one else is available, and His Lordship is most insistent that this gentleman be given every attention. He is here with his mother, an old family friend." Matron was clearly uncomfortable with the situation.

Rose thought quickly. "I think, Matron, that if this gentleman is to be treated more like a guest than a patient, then surely someone among the household staff can be found to attend to his needs? It doesn't seem right for me to abandon one patient in favour of another just because he claims privilege." The words tumbled out of Rose and surprised herself. She had been raised an estate employee's daughter, and usually thought nothing of subservience. For a moment, she wondered if she had gone too far, but to her relief, Matron smiled.

"You are quite right, Mrs. Hailstanes. I'll inform Harris the butler that he needs to look to his own staff for non-medical matters outside allocated hospital areas. Thank you."

Rose blushed at the rare complicity and approval of Matron. She went back to work feeling a burden had been lifted. From what she had just heard, and what she had had the presence of mind to suggest, it seemed she might easily avoid Francis Carmichael after all. He would claim no more privilege over her.

Mrs. Bailey tutted as she stalked away from the butler. It was beneath both their dignities to do what was being asked, he had said, but Matron was adamant. Such a pity Captain Carmichael's batman was still being treated in another establishment; the man was needed here, if the captain chose to be a guest and not a patient. The arrival of the Carmichaels had caused so much extra work already.

The housekeeper made for the Duie Drawing Room at her usual brisk, though dignified pace, but on hearing a crash she broke into a run. Entering the open doorway, she heard Mary McDowall cry, "I'll say it was you!" The new girl, Helena Hailstanes, was up a stepladder over one of the fireplaces. She noticed Mrs. Bailey, and Mary followed her gaze and turned round.

"If you're referring to that broken vase at your feet, Mary McDowall, you'll not be able to lay the blame anywhere else. I've caught you red-handed!"

Mary's lips moved as she sought to explain herself. Finally, she blurted out, "It was still her that did it, though!"

"What utter nonsense! Helena is at the other side of the room, up a stepladder!"

Mary was scarlet. "She...she threw it at me!"

Mrs. Bailey folded her arms and pursed her lips. "I know where that vase stands. I placed it there myself yesterday. I am appalled that you would lie like this, girl!"

Hot tears sprang to Mary's eyes. "She still did it, though! She's fey, she's a selkie! You dinna come frae these parts, Mrs. Bailey, you don't know! Floatin' in a basket, she was..."

"What drivel are you talking now, girl? Have you lost your mind?"

"She... she *does* things! She attacked my brother like a wildcat when she was five years old, and she's totally bewitched the evacuee laddie stayin' wi' ma folks. She taught him tae read, an' he won't stop talkin' aboot her...She *made* the vase slip from my hands, I felt it, like it had a life o' its own..."

"That is enough, Mary McDowall!" cried the housekeeper. She turned to Helena, who stood silently on the stepladder, fists still clenched and tension in every muscle. "I see no blame attaches to you, Helena. Please come down. I have a special duty for you." She turned back to Mary. "Gather up the pieces and place them in a bag. We will have the vase mended, although its value will be greatly diminished. Then finish the room. Helena is required to assist Captain Carmichael in transcribing a letter for him." On seeing Mary's stricken face, she added, "Thank you for confirming her skill with letters." She didn't say that, having seen the adoration with which Mary handled the captain's belongings, she would not have sent her anyway; besides which, she doubted if the girl was up to the task.

After washing her hands and straightening her uniform, Helena followed Mrs. Bailey along yet another corridor. She knew she was on the same floor as Captain Carmichael's bedroom, but they had taken a different back stair, and she didn't know where she was in relation to it. They stopped outside a door and entered when a deep male voice said, "Come!"

Peering from behind the housekeeper's back, Helena found herself in a small parlour. It was plain in comparison to the Duie Drawing Room, but more cosy and welcoming. She noted the padded window seat, with its view over the walled garden, and she thought how grand it would be to sink into it with a book.

"Ah. I take it you've brought my scribe?"

Helena jumped and noticed the man in the winged armchair by the fire for the first time. He was contemplating her while sipping from a glass of whisky, his brown eyes fiery above the rim while the amber liquid trickled into his mouth. She saw his Adam's Apple rise and fall as he swallowed. He put the glass down and pinched the sides of his trim moustache with the index finger and thumb of his left hand.

"Yes, Sir," Mrs. Bailey replied. "This is Helena. I'm afraid we're short-staffed and she's the best we can spare...She's educated, and helped latterly as a pupil-teacher."

"No need for apologies. Helena will do very well. Thank you, Mrs. Bailey."

The housekeeper nodded and left. Helena, for once, was lost for words. She hadn't been prepared for any more than serving duties towards the gentry, and had been told she would not be doing that type of work immediately. If she came upon His Lordship or any guests in the course of her work, her instructions were that she should avoid them, if possible, or if not, curtsey and continue on her way, eyes lowered. She therefore slid her gaze away from Captain Carmichael's bold stare, although it was hard, because she wanted to look at him. Her heart beat faster and her hands trembled slightly. She grasped them in front of her.

"I wish I could paint you, my dear," said the Captain. "You are charming, quite charming, standing there with the light coming from the side like that." He stood up and walked towards her. "Alas," he continued, "I can paint no longer." He thrust out his right hand. It was bandaged. "Four fingers missing," he said.

128

Helena cleared her throat, and met his eyes. "I'm sorry, Sir."

"Thank you," he said. He lifted his left arm and ran a finger down her cheek and under her chin. "Exquisite," he murmured. Abruptly, he removed his hand and swiped it down his face, blinking hard afterwards. He walked away from her and resumed his seat.

In a different voice, one which did not sound laced with the warmth of the liquor he had been drinking as it had a moment ago, he said, "The writing table is over there. My things are on it. Let us begin, Helena."

Rose's day was over long before Helena's. When the girl arrived home, she was tired, but with a dreamy, contented air which took her mother pleasantly by surprise. She went for a swim before tea and sat at the table with her damp tresses smelling of fresh air and sunlight, smiling to herself. Rose felt triumphant, as she watched Sam stare at his daughter, incredulity written in every crease of his familiar face. She had been right. This would be the making of Helena – broaden her horizon, give her new things to think about and plenty to keep her hands busy.

"So, what dae ye make o' the big hoose, Helena?" she asked.

"It's like stories come tae life," Helena replied. "So beautiful!"

"And what did Mrs. Bailey have you do?"

"I started in the kitchen, wi' hundreds o' potatoes tae peel," said Helena. "They were for the hospital as well as the household. Then I went upstairs tae help shut up the Duie Drawing Room, for Lord Craigendon decided tae entertain Captain Carmichael and his mother elsewhere."

Rose's smile faltered. Helena fell quiet, as if thinking about what to say next.

"Then what?" prompted Sam, eager for all her news.

Helena hesitated, then seemed to make up her mind. "Well, I had tae dae that wi' Mary McDowall. An' she smashed a vase, an' tried tae blame it on me. But it's alright," she hurried on, "Mrs. Bailey arrived, an' saw it all, so I'm not in bother. Honest." Helena had decided her part in the affair was perfectly justified, and that Mary had deserved it. She looked from one parent to the other. "In fact, I got given a special job." She paused for effect. "I was sent tae write a letter for Captain Carmichael."

Rose lowered the teacup she had been holding into its saucer, where it tinkled into place because of the sudden tremor in her hand. Sam leaned back in his chair and clapped a fatherly hand on Helena's shoulder, beaming.

"Well, well. My lassie makes her mark on her first day!"

"Serves that snooty Mary McDowall right," Angus mumbled, through a mouthful of pancake.

"And what did ye write for him?" asked Sadie, eyes wide.

"Oh, I couldn't give that information," smiled Helena. "It's *confidential*. Isn't that right, Ma?"

Rose was staring through her. She forced herself to focus. "That's right. We can't discuss what we do for the patients. Not that you should be working with the patients, Helena. I ought to have a word with Mrs. Bailey about this…"

Helena groaned. "Oh, don't, Ma! Captain Carmichael isn't really a patient. He's a guest of Lord Craigendon, a family friend. And it feels good tae be able tae use ma learnin'. Please don't speak tae her!"

"Of course yer mother won't do that," said Sam, staring pointedly at Rose. "It's excellent for ye tae get a chance like this."

Rose raised herself unsteadily from the table. "I'll make a fresh pot of tea." As she turned her back on the family, the better to hide her distress, Jamie changed the subject.

"There's otters arrived in the River Duie," he said. "I've never seen an otter. Can we go and look after tea?"

She glanced round to see Sam's proud expression evaporate.

Chapter 15

Rose and Sam set out together once the children were in bed and safely asleep. Sam had told them otters were unlikely to be seen before dark to stop them going looking. That was just what he and Rose were doing now, late as it was, the long summer day beginning to slip into night.

"Ye surely don't think it could do any harm for them tae see an otter?" Rose asked.

"Who knows what it would mean?" he replied. "It could spark memories for all of them, or instincts, like Helena rememberin' how tae catch fish when she was hungry enough tae feel the need." He had told Helena sarcastically that her actions must have been one of the "gifts" of her sea witch heritage, and refused to comment further, other than forbidding her from mentioning it to anybody else.

"And what about you?" asked Rose.

"I've learned tae be a man. I'm more man than otter now."

"So... you wouldn't go back? Tae yer Jeannette? Even if ye could?"

Sam stopped and faced her. "She's long gone, Rose. I have a man's lifetime now. And anyhow, I swore my vows and meant them. I would never leave you or our children. All of you... you are my life. I've maybe never said it, but ye are."

Rose felt a rush of warmth towards him, and stood on tip-toe to kiss his cheek. "Thank you. I dreaded ye goin' away tae fight, ye know. I would have missed you, an' worried myself sick." There were uncharacteristic tears stinging the back of her eyes. He was a good man. She pushed away thoughts of someone less worthy.

"I'm grateful for the chance Tully gave me," he said, "and for you stickin' by me even when ye knew the truth." Sam was secretly thankful that farming was a reserved occupation, and while he wouldn't have wished ill on his father-in-law, whose condition meant he was needed on the farm, he had dreaded being called to fight. His unusual family needed his guiding hand and protection. He didn't like to think what would have happened without him to stand between Rose and Helena, for a start.

They walked on in silence towards the point where Loch Duie tumbled into the surrounding countryside and became the River Duie, and they followed its course downstream, eyes peeled. By now, they were using a torch in case they stumbled. Suddenly, Sam put a hand on Rose's arm to halt her. She shone the torch on the water, but he covered the beam and directed it away. Rose could see nothing in any case. Sam pointed to his ear, and she understood that he had heard and interpreted sounds she could not. Sure enough, a few seconds later, she discerned a shape emerging from the river and heard the ripple of water as the creature pulled itself on to the bank. She was surprised by its small size, although not sure what she had been expecting. The truth was, she had always tried not to think about the relationship between these animals and her husband, or indeed her children. They saw the silhouette slither into the undergrowth, and that was it. Nothing more. Rose could read wistfulness on her husband's face.

She was close behind them, and they had no idea. Helena ducked behind a bush as her parents began to make their way home. She had heard them leave the house and decided to follow, because it was so unlike them to go out together like this. Sam often went to check on things at night, but not Rose. Helena had taken to wandering out at dusk, concealed in her cloak and armed with her staff. She went barefoot, feeling empowered by the earth beneath her feet. When she spread her arm and swung her staff low over the loch, she felt a surge of energy and practised sending out her intentions, experimenting with her craft and her calling.

She had meant to venture out this night in any case, for she had seen the way ahead. Bonny lasses bewitched without magic, Megan had said, and she knew the truth of that now; but magic would enhance matters, ensure that lust became love. Now that her staff was complete and she knew herself, he would be in her power. Rev. O'Neill might have been, too, despite her lack of preparedness at that time, if her parents hadn't intervened. She would have to be more careful than she had been at the tea table earlier, guard her countenance and her words, for her mother was a woman, too, and no fool.

There were never many signs of romance between her parents, but as she trailed them, she heard them whisper and saw Rose peck Sam on the cheek. She only caught a few words. They were talking about the otters. She wasn't much interested in the otters, but Mary's outburst earlier had reminded her of the selkie legend. Helena knew she was a witch. She was a water witch, the Lady of the Loch. Yet she had been rescued out near Ailsa Craig. It was urgent that she speak to Megan – for couldn't she be both water witch and selkie? Helena pondered this as she waited while her parents paused at the river's edge, silent, their torch dimmed. They must have seen an otter, she supposed. Then she tailed them back in the direction of the house, breaking away at her favourite spot on the loch. It was late and dark by now. Thrusting out her arm with the staff extending from her hand, she concentrated her thoughts on Megan. She had discovered that she was billeted at Fernglass, with Mary McDowell's family and wee Billy MacTaggart. She sighed. Something was wrong tonight. The connection with her element was weak.

Helena turned and jumped as she almost bumped into the figure who had come up behind her. She let out a stifled cry, only to have a hand clamped over her mouth.

"Sshh, your father is still out! What do ye think you're doing?"

Helena flooded with relief as she recognised Megan's voice. "I've been wanting tae see you, trying tae summon you!"

"I know. Rab has been reporting. Did ye not think o' that?"

"I've never seen him!"

"He knows how tae use stealth, too, missy!"

"Then why didn't ye come and find me?"

"Cheek! Think I'm at your bidding or convenience, dae ye? I wanted tae see how far ye would take this charade."

"What charade?"

Megan waved her hand in a gesture which took in Rose's appearance. "All this! A staff, if you please!"

Helena stiffened and drew herself up to her full height, which wasn't impressive. The Hailstanes children took after their otter lineage – small,

133

but lithe. She thrust her chin up at Megan. "I'm only claiming my identity! I have powers, I'm a witch like ye said!"

"And ye're fallin' intae the trap I did, lass! Can ye not see – I told ye so I could help ye, so ye could learn frae my mistakes! The first lesson is this – ye have gifts, not powers."

Helena let a beat fall. "But ye told me nothin' much."

Megan sighed. "I meant tae get back tae ye sooner, but I have tae be careful. I heard talk aboot ye today, so I sent Rab tae find ye."

"What talk?"

"I bide at the McDowall's farm, remember," Megan replied. "That hoity-toity bit, Mary, was sayin' ye're after an officer already, on yer first day."

Helena's cheeks flamed in the darkness. "I was sent tae scribe for him. I wasn't after him. But I can tell he likes me, an' he might give me a chance tae get away frae here, see life!' she exclaimed.

"And what if he wants what O'Neill wanted? And like O'Neill, no chance of marriage? Ye're playin' with fire, wi' him and magic both. There – I've warned ye, Helena! But I think ye might be more like me than I realised, an' ye might have tae learn for yourself."

"Who says I want marriage? That's what the likes o' Mary McDowall would be after! I'm cleverer than that, I'll make use of what I can and go only as far as I want!" When there was no immediate reply, she added: "Am I a selkie, Megan? Are you? For selkies can bewitch, too, can they not?" When there was no reply, she thought Megan had gone. Then a match struck, and Megan's face was illuminated as she lit a cigarette.

"No, ye're not a selkie," she said. "I've told ye as much as I can."

Helena took a deep breath. "Megan…ye said I've done things all my life, not realisin' it was because o' my powers…I was angry at Lady Craigendon. I cursed her under my breath. And she crashed, and died. Did Rab see? Did I cause it? I can't really believe it, because I would never wish harm like that."

In the darkness, the tip of Megan's roll-up quivered. "What exactly did ye say when ye cursed her, Helena?"

"I can't remember. I was so angry, it just came over me…it was somethin' about stoppin' her tellin' my parents that I had tried tae hitch a lift tae Ballaness."

"So that was May Day, just before the accident?" Megan was taking quick, nervous puffs.

"Aye."

Megan hesitated. "I'll be honest. I don't know. Rab was wi' me in Ballaness then. We knew ye intended tae come, but not how ye would manage it. So she refused ye a lift? Ye wanted tae silence her, an' she was silenced forever, so ye might have been the cause. But it could just be a coincidence. Ye say ye never intended that she should die, though?"

"No!" cried Helena.

"Then I'm thinkin' it wasn't your fault. But ye never know. It's all the more reason tae heed ma warnin', Helena – be careful what ye ask for, because ye don't know how your wish might come about. Stop meddlin' wi' things too big for ye, lass. Remember ye have *gifts*, not *powers*, an' use them well. I have to go."

Helena saw the tip of Megan's cigarette receding into the darkness, but she heard nothing, for she walked the night as stealthily as Helena herself. She turned to head home when she became aware of something slithering on to the loch's edge near where she stood. She pulled her cloak closely around her. The creature seemed fairly small, like a little dog, with short legs on which it darted away once clear of the water. It must be an otter! So, at least one must have migrated up-river to Loch Duie. Despite her lack of interest earlier, Helena wished she could see more. Then, to her astonishment, the animal was followed by a much larger shape lumbering on to the shore, which even in the darkness she knew to be her father. He must have stayed out for a swim after his walk. Helena stood still and silent, her hooded cloak blending into the night. Sam was so close, she felt the drips of water when he shook his head as he made his way up the shore. That wasn't all, though. Something flew from his mouth, hitting the shingle with a damp slap. Helena's keen sense of smell noted the distinctive tang, and she was amazed to realise it was a fish.

Rose was brusque at breakfast next morning. Sam assured her he hadn't eaten the raw fish she had detected on his breath when he eventually came to bed last night, but as far as she was concerned, it was a step on the slippery slope. Her mood wasn't helped by Billy MacTaggart turning up looking, not for her sons, but for Helena; and no doubt for food, which was finished. She had no time to cook more. Helena slapped some jam on two slices of bread for him, folded them over, and ushered Billy outside. Through the open kitchen window, Rose heard her promise that she would continue his reading lessons, despite the fact she had left school, and she saw the grin on Billy's face as he walked away, scuffing at stones on the ground. Well, so be it; Helena could come to no harm spending her spare time with Billy, and she would do no harm, either. The laddie never seemed to have had much attention in his life, so who was she to grudge it now, if Helena chose to humour him? Anyway, she seemed genuinely fond of him, and that was to be encouraged in a selfish nature like hers.

Thus Rose mused as she and Sadie cleared away after breakfast, before she called for Helena to hurry up and they set out for Craigendon House. They spoke little on the road, each preoccupied with her own thoughts. Once through the door of the servants' entrance, they went their separate ways, Helena to report to the kitchen and Rose to head for the hospital. After picking up the list of volunteer duties for that morning, she went in search of Matron. Approaching with courage because of their new-found complicity the day before, she asked to speak with her.

"It's about the request from His Lordship's guest, Captain Carmichael," she said. "My daughter, on her first day at work as a maid, was sent to scribe for him."

Matron gazed, uncomprehending. "It was your suggestion that one of the household servants should do it, Mrs. Hailstanes."

"Well, yes, but I didn't expect it would be my daughter, a fourteen-year-old girl, on her first day at work. I didna think they would send a maid, let alone a new one, tae dae such a task."

"Granted, I would have thought others might have been asked first, but the household staff is so greatly diminished by the war that it doesn't really surprise me. In a way, it's a feather in her cap for your daughter."

Rose swallowed. "Undoubtedly, Matron, but as a mother I have tae consider whether she is… mature enough tae handle this. Ye'll not have forgotten that we…had some bother… not that long ago?" She hated herself for raising this with the woman who had implied Helena had been up to no good, but she had thought it over in the night.

"Yes?" the older woman's face was eager now, eyes narrowed in her desire for information.

"It wasn't what ye thought," Rose continued hurriedly. "She had no tryst tae make with a boy. But… a man tried tae take advantage. A much older, married man. And that was why she fled the fete, and got lost."

"I see." Matron glanced away, considering.

Rose thought she had managed that rather well. She let the silence lie between them.

"I hope you aren't suggesting that Lord Craigendon's guest, an officer injured while serving his country, might not be honourable?" asked Matron.

Rose blanched, caught off-balance. "I…oh…no! Only that Helena might be nervous in the situation of being alone with a man…" Rose felt the heat rising up her neck to her cheeks.

"Ah," said Matron, her face clearing. "Forgive me, Mrs. Hailstanes. I failed to see where your concern lay. But I'm not sure what can be done about it."

Rose had thought about this, too. Taking a steadying breath, she said, "Mindful of the staffing difficulties here and in the house, I wondered if I might…if I might offer my own services to the Captain at a set time which wouldn't interfere with my hospital duties."

Matron nodded her approval. "That's most generous of you, Mrs. Hailstanes. I can see no difficulty with that. I'll speak to Mr. Harris, and convey that you will be available after your duties end here, in order to save you going and having to return. Would that be suitable?"

Rose forced a weak smile. "Thank you, Matron, yes." She had put herself in the lion's den to save Helena, for she had been in no doubt of the direction in which that little minx's thoughts lay, and she could see no other way. She had discerned her daughter's plans, and was equally sure of the turn of Francis Carmichael's mind, no matter what the intervening years may have wrought. Francis Carmichael was no stranger to Rose.

When she had finished her shift, Rose reported back to Matron to see if Captain Carmichael required her scribing services. Matron greeted her with a hint of hesitation.

"Ah, yes, Mrs. Hailstanes… I regret to say your kind offer was met with refusal. The Captain was most insistent, when Mr. Harris put the plan to him, that only Helena would do. She appears to have acquitted

137

herself well yesterday. I must say, it's commendable in a girl her age, and perhaps you are worrying unnecessarily." She smiled kindly.

Rose faltered. "Well, you understand a mother's concerns," she said, biting her lip.

"Of course. And I must say, having had a chat with Mrs. Bailey earlier, I admire that you have taken in one not your own and raised her with such care. I think we know what that jaunt to Ballaness was all about, don't we?"

Rose stared, taken by surprise. It had been one thing for the scattered neighbourhood of Craigendon estate to know and gossip, but it was old talk; it was another thing altogether for staff new to the house to be finding wonder in the story of Helena's rescue from the sea. To have talk like that going on within the four walls where she and Helena worked was alarming.

"Yes, well... Sam and I, we did what... we could... Would you excuse me, Matron? If I'm not required, I'll be gettin' on my way."

When she left Matron, Rose went straight to the kitchen. She didn't quite know what she was going to do or say, but on finding that Mrs. Bailey would be busy above stairs for some time, she was glad. It was the little McDowall chit who told her, sitting at the table mending household items, and when she enquired casually after Helena, the girl informed her sulkily that she was away attending on the Captain.

"It would be so much better if the Captain was in the hospital," Rose said. "I mean, he can't be a well man."

"Four fingers blown off," Mary replied. "But no other injuries, he's able to get about and all. Dinna see why he shouldn't be more guest than patient, especially with his mother here."

"Ah yes, Lady Carmichael. She was gracious and rather beautiful, so they said, last time they were here." Rose was thankful that the cook was too busy in the scullery to pay heed to her efforts to engage the maid in gossip.

"She still is," said Mary. "Now, of course, she has no husband." The maid winked, warming to the conversation.

Rose sat down at the table and leaned forward conspiratorially, dropping her voice to a whisper. "And are the guests... conveniently situated... upstairs?"

Mary giggled. "Mother and son have been given rooms at a considerable distance from one another," the girl answered with a smirk. "It threw His Lordship when the Captain said he didna want tae be in the hospital."

"What happened?" asked Rose.

"Well, Mrs. Bailey said she would have the room next to his mother's made up, but Lord Craigendon said no, the Captain was a wounded officer and would benefit from somewhere more peaceful. So, he's at the other end of the corridor."

"While His Lordship and Lady Carmichael are closely quartered, I'll bet," grinned Rose.

"Och aye, second floor overlooking the loch. He's only given *her* the suite of rooms belongin' tae Lady Craigendon, next door tae his – and his wife not three months in the grave!"

Rose shook her head. "Scandalous!" she said. In truth, she couldn't have cared less. "Does the Captain keep to his room, then?"

"No," answered Mary. "There's a wee sittin' room round the corner." Her face suddenly turned sullen again. "That's where your Helena is now."

Rose hid the triumph she felt. "I'd best be gettin' along, Mary," she said. "Nice tae have had a wee chat with ye."

Mary eyed her in some surprise. It seemed just to have dawned on her that she had been familiar with the mother from the family which her own held in enmity, whose daughter she had fought with only yesterday, and that she had been perfectly friendly. She shrugged and recommenced her mending.

Rose scuttled from the kitchen and made up the back stairs before she could change her mind. She could orient herself roughly by what she knew of the outside of the house – she had grown up roaming around the grounds, after all – that was how she had met him. Propelled by this thought, she reached the correct floor, and emerging, walked the length of it praying that she met no-one. At the end, she followed the corridor round to the right, walking slowly now, listening for voices. It was a laugh which alerted her to the correct room, a man's laugh, and she stopped and clutched her stomach, overwhelmed. Then she squared her shoulders and rapped at the door.

"Come!"

Rose entered.

Chapter 16

Sam was about his duties in the woods that morning. He was overseeing the felling of more trees required for the war effort. The estate had large areas of woodland. Part of it was officially designated a forest. Yet the extent of the pillaging made him sad. He accepted it was necessary, but it ripped the heart out of Craigendon, leaving denuded patches which wouldn't recover for generations. It affected the habitat of creatures, too, of course. At that thought, he felt suddenly weary and sat down on a log.

He hadn't set eyes on an otter for years until last night. That had been part of the suitability of Loch Duie, known to both him and Tully – that he would be well away from his own kind, and even those creatures who were not otter-folk, who couldn't take human form. The boys had learned of a family – a mother and her cubs – on the River Duie, and sure enough he and Rose had seen the mother last night. He had been glad they were on the river and not the loch itself. On returning to the cottage with Rose, he had decided on a midnight swim, as he sometimes did. In the course of that, he had discovered there was an otter living by the loch. It was a male, and its prowess in the water caused him to yearn for times long gone. He had been unable to resist the temptation to fish. He longed for the taste of raw fish, freshly killed. When it came to it, though, he hadn't been able to bring himself to eat it. Sitting on a log in the midst of the woods now, sky clearly visible where once the tree canopy had shut it out, he cradled his head in his hands in an agony of anxiety.

"Hangover, is it?"

Sam jumped. "No, Sir!" he said, removing his cap while scrambling to his feet, and inclining his head to Lord Craigendon. "Late night, Sir, that's all."

His Lordship smiled, then frowned. "Looking bare around here, isn't it?"

"Needs must. It's a sorry business all round, war."

"Yes. Only sad I'm too old now to do my bit. You must feel that way, too, essential though your work is."

"Of course, Sir." Sam recalled his conversation with Rose the night before, and didn't meet his employer's eye.

"Anyway, at least it means I still have a water bailiff, which is just as well, for we have poachers...of a sort."

Sam looked at his employer, puzzled. "What sort might that be, Sir?"

"Otters, Hailstanes. I hear they've moved into these parts. Might even be in the loch already. We can't risk the population growing and spreading."

Sam felt every muscle in his body tense. "It would take a lot to make any impact on the loch, Sir."

"Even so. Keep an eye. It might be best to act quickly, before they breed and things get out of hand."

Sam kept his voice steady. "Aye, Sir."

Up at Craigendon House, Rose clasped her handbag in both hands to stop them from shaking. "Forgive the intrusion," she said, "but I've been sent to scribe for you, Sir. I'm a volunteer in the hospital. My daughter is needed elsewhere."

Francis Carmichael, who had been slumped in his chair, sat upright and stared. He seemed unable to speak. Rose turned to Helena, who sat at the table, pen in hand. "A wee word outside, please. I'll be right back, Sir."

Helena rose slowly from the table and dipped a faltering curtsey to the Captain. Rose caught her arm and ushered her out. She closed the door behind them both and whispered urgently in her ear. "Report to Mrs. Bailey that Matron sent me tae replace ye."

Helena shook her arm away. "Did she, though? Why do ye not want me to help the Captain?"

Rose decided honesty was best, as much of it as she could tell. "Because, lassie, we don't want another carry on like that wi' the Reverend! You're young and headstrong and ye don't recognise danger!"

"Oh, so ye're just protecting me?"

Rose returned her sour look. "Maybe I'm protecting him, too. Now, go!"

When she went back into the room, Francis Carmichael was standing by the window, gazing into the middle distance with his good hand over his well-sculpted mouth and chin. She took in the ebony hair with its peppering of grey, cropped in army fashion and not tousled as it used to be.

"We meet again," he said, without looking at her.

"It would not have been my wish," she said.

"I would rather you didn't scribe for me, thank you."

Rose wasn't surprised. "You always did want to avoid awkward situations."

"I'll inform the housekeeper that I will wait until Helena is available, as was my stated desire."

Rose swallowed. "Your desire is what worries me."

He looked at her then. "Good God, woman! It's been... what? Fifteen years? What do you think I am?"

"I know what you are! I wasn't the only one hereabouts, was I?"

"I was young!"

"That's no excuse!"

"I give you my word – your daughter is perfectly safe with me. I simply like the girl, she's bright. Great air of self-possession for her age. How old is she, by the way?"

"Fourteen," said Rose. She watched as she saw the wheels in his head turn. His talents lay in paintbrush and palette. He hadn't been all that intelligent, she remembered.

"Good Lord," he murmured.

"You will not request her services again," said Rose. "If needs must, I will scribe for you." She turned heel and stalked from the room. *Let him think she's his,* she mused. It would solve the problem nicely.

Helena didn't report to Mrs. Bailey immediately. Why should she? The housekeeper would be none the wiser meanwhile. Instead, she took

143

a feather duster from a cupboard to justify her actions if discovered, and she headed for the room in the house she most wanted to see – the library. She had asked questions about it and knew roughly where she was going, finding it without too much bother and hoping nobody was there. Lord Craigendon, she had learned, was not much of a one for books, and anyway, he had Lady Carmichael to entertain. If the other servants' gossip was correct, he would be most attentive to her. Helena smiled to herself. Fancy the old goat, carrying on beneath Lady Craigendon's nose, all those years ago! Her Ladyship sitting for a portrait while her husband became well acquainted with the artist's mother. You never could tell. Who would ever have thought Ma would have been in the family way and Da forced to marry her, after all.

The library door stood open when she found it. She craned her neck in and glanced around. Nobody was there. Helena had hoped to see this room from the minute she knew she was to work at the big house. It didn't disappoint. She crept inside reverently. Closing the door behind her, she walked to the centre of the large, square room and turned in a circle, gazing upwards to take in the glass cases of books which rose almost to the ceiling. She stopped, giddy with pleasure. Then she set her mouth firmly. Not only did she want to see the library for the love of books, she now had a more pressing purpose. She must act before she was missed.

Scanning the shelves, she located the section which contained volumes of natural history. It was a joy to realise she would have to use one of the ladders to reach them, and she took delight in wheeling the highly polished piece of hand-crafted wooden furniture into place. She noticed the braking mechanism on the metal wheels and locked it. Then she ascended with care, selected three likely-looking volumes, and carried them to one of the padded window seats which overlooked the loch. On second thoughts, much as she longed to sit and indulge herself, it was too risky. She took them over to the ornate and, by the look of it, little-used desk in front of the central window of the room, and placed them tenderly there, with her feather duster to hand lest she should be disturbed. Fighting the temptation to linger over the pages, she went to the index in the first volume; she had to repeat the exercise with all three before she found what she was looking for. Flicking quickly to the place, she found herself staring at an illustration of Lutra Lutra – the European Otter. Gasping in recognition at the whiskered face, which was

144

uncannily like the carving on top of her staff, she scanned the text and had to sit down, shakily, in the chair behind the desk.

Relations were strained in the Hailstanes' farmhouse later that day. The family sat down to tea, three of them nursing grievances and concerns which left them uncommunicative. It was a relief to the younger children when Billy MacTaggart knocked at the door. Sadie let him in, and Rose filled a plate and set it in front of him without needing to ask if he wanted anything to eat.

As the lad picked up his pudding spoon to start on his main course, Sam took it from him gently and reminded him about using his knife and fork. Through a mouthful of food, he spoke to Helena. "Will ye help me wi' writin' a letter tae ma aunty, please?"

"Of course, Billy," she smiled. "I think I'm allowed tae help *you*."

She didn't look at Rose, but Sam glanced from his daughter to his wife and asked what was going on.

"She interfered wi' me and Captain Carmichael!" cried Helena.

"Not in front of our visitor!" hissed Rose.

An awkward silence fell on the table again, everybody occupying themselves with eating, avoiding the eyes of their fellow diners.

When the meal was over, Rose sought to avoid any more being said by excusing Helena from helping to clear up. She and Billy disappeared to the barn, writing materials in hand. They climbed up the hayloft ladder and thumped down on the old mattress. Helena sighed, recalling the grandeur of the library.

"Now then, Billy. I'm not goin' tae write this letter. You are – with my help. Alright?"

The boy looked at her adoringly. "Aye, Helena."

She tousled his hair. "Dae ye miss yer aunty? Dae ye miss Glesga?" Helena dreamed of visiting Glasgow, the nearest city and yet out of her reach. Other people from Craigendon went there and back in a day, by train. She couldn't even go to Ballaness without it causing untold trouble.

Billy was chewing his lip, staring at the pencil in his hand as he twiddled it round. She had sensed his unhappiness for a long time. "I miss my Maw," he said.

Helena reached out and gathered him to her. The pencil clattered to the floor, unheeded. There were tears in both their eyes. "Where's yer Da, Billy?" She knew his mother had been killed in the Clydebank blitz.

"I dinna have one," the boy sniffed. "I never have. My aunty and uncle have no time for me because of it. Nobody has. Folk in Glesga call me names."

"An' they call ye names here, too," Helena sighed, kissing the top of his head. She had sought to protect him from the bullies at school, all those healthy country children, well-fed and glowing with fresh air and sunshine, picking on puny wee Billy with his stick-like limbs and milk-bottle skin.

Billy shrugged and nestled closer to her. "It's no' sae bad, bein' called a Weegie. I dinna even care aboot bein' called Weegie Weasel. It's better than what they ca' me in Glesga."

"Why dae ye want to write tae yer aunty, Billy?"

He looked up, tear-stained eyes imploring. "I wondered if she would ask for me tae be moved away frae the McDowalls. I want tae bide wi' you."

Helena smiled. "Ye canna just decide for yersel', Billy. Ye would have tae sort it oot wi' the McDowalls and the folk in charge o' evacuees. We weren't asked tae take any, because we've no room."

He bit his lip. "I could sleep here in the barn. I thought maybe you could ask yer Ma an' Da, an' fix it, Helena."

"Oh Billy," she replied, "there's many a thing I would like tae be able tae fix!"

146

Chapter 17

The following day, Helena walked alone to Craigendon House. It wasn't one of Rose's days for volunteering. The one thought in her mind, even greater than the hope that Captain Carmichael might send for her despite Rose's interference, was that she had to get back to the library. How was she to achieve this? For yesterday, a bitter-sweet truth had been confirmed there, and she needed to learn more. She bent all her concentration to the memory of the library in her mind, willing herself back there.

Up in the tree canopy close to the roadway, Rab the raven peered between branches, hidden by copious foliage. Not too far away, Megan leaned against a trunk, rolling a cigarette. She had been working since dawn already. Since yesterday morning, she had had an uneasy feeling, and recognised it as being connected to Helena. Her thoughts wandered to the mirror she kept under lock and key in her suitcase, along with her wand, in the room she shared with three other Land Army women in the McDowall's farmhouse. One of them had discovered her with the mirror once, exclaimed over it, told the others. It was a family heirloom Megan had said by way of explanation. Well, that was true as far as it went. She dreaded to think what they would make of the wand, and took greater care after that. Her wand magic was becoming less effective in any case. *"As she increases, I decrease,"* she thought. Helena was becoming master of her craft, of those gifts inherited by accident from Megan; and so, Megan's own abilities waned faster these days than they had before. She lit her roll-up and took a calming draw.

As Helena tied her apron strings, Mrs. Bailey appeared and said she had a special job for her, one she was sure she would relish; and yet, she must remember she was there to work and not yield to the temptations on offer. She said it sternly, but with a twinkle. She led the way without saying where they were going or what Helena was to do, but Helena knew exactly where they were going. She couldn't believe it had come about so easily. She composed herself for a little play-acting, and didn't disappoint the housekeeper in her awe-struck exclamations when she threw open the door of the library.

"Now then, lass," said Mrs. Bailey, "it's a long time since this place has had a really good going-over. I want you to open the cases and dust the volumes – all along the rows, on top, and their spines, and the shelves, of course. Then dust and polish all the furniture. I know you love books, so I know you'll see that this room is given the shine it deserves. But no dawdling, mind!"

Helena blinked in surprise as the housekeeper winked. She actually winked. Helena marvelled, wondering at her powers. Had she brought this about by sheer will-power, as she walked to work that morning? Or was it going to happen anyway? The one thing she knew for sure, though, was that she had won Mrs. Bailey over, and she didn't think magic had been involved in that. It came as a revelation that despite her sequestered life and those who feared her strangeness, there were those, like Billy and Mrs. Bailey, who genuinely took to her.

Now, however, her superior recollected herself and added primly, "Get as much done as you can in two hours. Then report back to the kitchen. And really, don't open the books, Helena. If there's one which takes your fancy, I will ask permission for you to borrow it." She nodded and left.

Helena gazed around in no less awe than yesterday, but was already scanning the shelves for volumes on folklore. Then she gave herself a reprimand, deciding to begin work and hope to come across them in the course of that – she didn't want to lose Mrs. Bailey's favour. It would be better if she could take books away for a proper, leisurely perusal in any case. Her task, therefore, was far from a burden that morning, and she didn't have to let her imagination roam to be able to endure it. It was a pleasure to see gold-embossed titles gleaming freshly from newly-dusted spines.

After about an hour of hard work, when she still hadn't discovered what she sought, the door handle turned and someone entered. She was up a ladder, coughing from the dust and looking grimy, when she turned to see Captain Carmichael. Quickly, she brushed herself down and descended, bobbing a curtsey when she reached the floor.

"Begging your pardon, Sir. I was sent to clean here, but I can leave…" she kept her eyes lowered, long dark lashes much in evidence against the creaminess of her skin.

"That won't be necessary, Helena. It's a pleasure to find you here."

"Do you want me to write for you, Sir? I'm sure Mrs. Bailey would understand if I interrupted my cleaning…"

Carmichael waved a dismissive hand. "Thank you, but your mother is my designated scribe now."

Helena suppressed her annoyance. "Very good, Sir. Ye'll not mind if I continue…"

"Not at all. As you were, by all means."

She climbed the ladder again. He came to the foot of it and gripped a rung half-way up. "Are you quite safe up there?"

"Yes, Sir. The wheels have brakes." She carried on dusting, not looking at him.

"You look very different to your mother."

Helena hesitated. She could have told him the story of the baby in the basket, but now she knew that there was so much more to it.

"I'm dark like my father," she said. She spoke matter-of-factly, her voice betraying nothing of the emotions she felt, caught between joy and fear at the thought of rich brown fur…The duster trembled in her hand.

"Does he work on the estate here? For Lord Craigendon?"

Helena made an effort to steady herself. "Yes, Sir, he's the water bailiff."

"Oh – I thought that was a chap called Tully."

"That's my grandfather, Sir. Father took over when he had a stroke. A series of them."

"I see. I'm sorry to hear that. Have your parents been married long?"

"Well…all my life, of course. They don't go in for celebratin' anniversaries as a rule." She smiled at the thought of them having to marry because a baby was on the way. Prim and proper Rose and her quiet, mannerly Da – it was still astounding. Her face fell as she remembered she hadn't been the expected baby.

"And are there others? Children, I mean."

"Oh aye, Sir – I have two brothers and a sister."

"That must be fun for you. I was an only child."

"It is, Captain Carmichael." Helena thought a moment, then climbed down the ladder, hitching her skirt up rather higher than was necessary. She faced the captain at the bottom. "I'm sorry if you were lonely as a child, Sir," she said. She gazed at him frankly.

He laughed. "What a funny little thing you are, Helena." He stretched out his injured right hand and chucked her under the chin with his thumb.

Before he could withdraw it, she grasped his wrist gently and pulled his hand back towards her. "I would like to do as I do for my brothers, Sir, and kiss it better for ye," she said, brushing the bandage with her lips.

Carmichael pulled his hand back as if he had suffered an electric shock. "What do you... how did that...?"

Helena thought he must be angry. She bit her lip. She had misjudged. Instead, a smile of wonder came over his face.

"I've had no feeling there," he said. "But I felt that. I felt it, Helena!" He put his arms round her waist and began to dance her clumsily round the room. That was how Mrs. Bailey discovered them when she returned, hoping not to find Helena injured at the bottom of a ladder, because she hadn't told her about the braking mechanism. Outside on the windowsill, an aged raven, white feathers striking amongst the black, cawed and rose into the air.

That evening, Megan stole away from the McDowall's farmhouse with her mirror concealed in a bag she had made out of sacking, and which she used to gather herbs and wildflowers for use in her medicines. Mrs. McDowall was a country woman from a long line of such, and knew of these skills; her grandmother used to try her hand at her own medications for common ailments, she said. Therefore, she was content to allow Megan to use the scullery from time to time for this purpose, although Megan suspected it was more out of meanness and to gain free remedies than anything else.

Megan loved to escape from the house in the evenings, and this gave her a great excuse. The women with whom she shared a twin-bunked room, much younger than she was and full of swooning over film stars and trying new hairstyles, were tiresome company. She was patient with them, though, laughing inwardly at finding herself a mother figure on occasion, and taking her current circumstances as due penance for her wrongs. Megan had broken faith with her kind, and this was part of her punishment.

The scents of evening wafted around her, and she inhaled deeply. She could just catch a tang of salt sea air borne upon the westerly breeze. As always, it filled her with longing and sadness. She knelt down and gathered a few heads of Self-Heal, savouring the feel of the delicate purple flowers between her fingers. Then she headed for a favourite ash a little way from the river bank, sat with her back against the trunk and drew out her mirror. Putting her fingers to her lips, she gave a low whistle, then whispered softly, lest anyone should be around, "Rab!" He would hear her, wherever he was. He could no longer enjoy the comforts of a cottage fire, living as he did in the wild now to protect Megan's new persona – the strange woman who lived in the up-turned boat had been known for her pet raven, among other things. She had sought to leave that person behind.

Sure enough, within five minutes he came flapping to her lap to receive his reward, and to settle under her arm. He had never minded doing this since he came to understand that Megan's interest in Sam and his family was now for their good. Of course, she had always used him to view other people and matters, too, and she did this first to steady her nerves – if seeing the evidence of war he had witnessed that day, in one form or another, even here on the Scottish home front, could be classed as steadying nerves. She shuddered at the coastal defences he had flown over, and hoped they would never need to be used.

Then she directed her thoughts to what she was most interested in, and they both gazed into the mirror as their reflections began to transform into various scenes involving Helena. She saw her walking to Craigendon House that morning, and felt rather than read the thoughts in her head, the overwhelming wish to get back to the library. It gave Megan a jolt, a warning of something significant. When she finally witnessed the girl in the library, she understood it all, sighing at first, then sitting up abruptly, eyes wide.

The atmosphere in the farmhouse that evening was even worse than it had been the previous night. Helena had come home with a written warning about her behaviour with Captain Carmichael, and her wages had been docked from the time of the incident, although she had been made to work at menial tasks for the rest of the day. She hadn't eaten. She had taken herself off to the barn, where she shed hot tears of humiliation, anger and disappointment – for all was ruined now. If only Captain Carmichael hadn't told Mrs. Bailey about her kissing his injured hand, she might have got away with it. She could have laid the jigging round the library entirely at his door – in fact, it had happened at his instigation, after all. It took two, so why should she carry all the blame? No doubt she would have been told to steer clear of him at all costs, to leave any room he entered without conversation; all of which would have been hard enough to manoeuvre around, but this...this! The disgrace of it, and the pity, the waste of opportunity...not to mention the fact that she liked the captain, she really did.

The realisation caused Helena to stop crying. Did she really want to use someone she genuinely liked in the way she had planned? Rev. O'Neill was one thing, Captain Carmichael entirely another. He had mostly behaved with propriety towards her. She remembered Megan's warning, and for the first time considered what harm she might unleash while trying to fulfil her selfish desires. Now that she was calmer, the impact of what had actually happened began to dawn on her. The touch of her lips had caused feeling to return to dead nerves. Was it waiting to happen, or had she brought it about? For she had meant her words about helping him, even if there had been an ulterior motive. Whichever it had been, serendipity or her doing, Helena was glad for Captain Carmichael, and somewhat humbled. This was a new emotion for Helena. She lay on her back watching a particularly beautiful spider, at peace in the centre of its web, which vibrated gently in the breeze creeping through a crack in the barn.

Sam found Rose distraught in their bedroom. She had disappeared from the kitchen without eating and without attempting to clear up after the family. Events had left him struggling to cope. Helena was a problem, he had to admit that now – her headstrong wish to escape her life at Craigendon leading her to behave as she did towards two important men. As if trying to blackmail Rev. O'Neill hadn't been bad enough, she had behaved atrociously towards a guest of Lord Craigendon. She was a child no longer. She was a young woman determined to use her wiles, and that upset him in a way he couldn't comprehend.

He sat on the edge of the bed they had shared for more than fourteen years, and stroked his wife's head as she lay, her face buried in the pillow. "I wish I had listened tae ye, Rose. I'm sorry, I really am. There's no excuse for her – except that I do think I'm tae blame for tryin' tae keep her here. I never thought she would have such a longing tae get away." He fished a clean handkerchief from his pocket and offered it to Rose. She accepted it and turned to look at him.

"I wanted out into the world once, too, Sam," she sniffed. "I had dreams. Goin' to work at the big hoose was a step in the right direction for Helena. If only *he* hadn't turned up like a bad penny..."

"Captain Carmichael? If not him, it might have been somebody else, through time. Strikes me that she's determined. I've not dealt wi' her yet. I don't rightly know how tae, Rose."

Rose was looking through him, lost in her own thoughts. Suddenly, she wailed. "But what did he think he was doin', lettin' them get into a situation like that, when he thought..." she trailed off.

Sam frowned. "What are ye talkin' aboot, Rose?"

She blew her nose and stared at her stockinged feet. "I hoped I would never have tae tell ye, Sam."

Up in the hayloft of the barn, Helena had pulled out her staff and was caressing the carving on top with her index finger. She ran it over the head, traced around the prominent eyes and tapped the nose. She took her pinkie and brushed each whisker. She had managed to carve an otter's head when she had wanted to carve a raven, entirely by chance. Or had it been chance? She was beginning to feel fearful of the force which seemed to surround her and cause things to happen, as if there was more to it than her will alone. Something fed off her will, bent it sometimes, warped it. "I think Megan knows more than she's ever told me," she whispered. "And I think I understand why Da is as he is, and

Ma is as she is. And Da *is* my Da. He really is." She wished she had behaved herself in the library and found those volumes on folklore.

Back in the bedroom, Sam paced the floor while Rose looked on, letting it sink in. "Are ye cross wi' me, Sam?" she asked, after a while.

"Why should I be?" he asked. "Ye told me it was somebody doin' work at the big hoose, an' ye didna even have tae tell me that much. I just assumed it was a workin' man, that was all."

"I didn't lie, exactly. He was there tae paint Lady Craigendon's portrait, that was his work." She sighed, and swallowed. "I did lie about us only...once, ye know. It was more. I didn't want ye tae think me a hussy. I loved him, or thought I did."

"It doesn't matter tae me, Rose," he said, rushing to her side and placing a hand on each shoulder. "Not now, and not then. I wouldn't have thought badly o' ye. Otters have different ways, and... any man, even one not a proper man, so tae speak, would have known ye for someone deceived, Rose."

"Thank you, Sam."

"Thank you for tryin' tae protect Helena from him."

"I didn't trust her, either, Sam. I haven't, not since what happened wi' O'Neill."

Sam looked away. "Right enough. So, ye let this Captain Carmichael think she was his?"

"Aye. So what he was doin' touchin' her face like she said, I don't know..."

"Rose," he said, "did it not occur tae ye that he might be pleased to have such a fine daughter?"

Chapter 18

Helena woke at four o'clock in the morning. She had fallen asleep, exhausted by emotion, in the barn, and no-one had bothered to come looking for her. She was still clutching her staff. She stroked again the crude carving of the otter. They were fine creatures, according to what she had read in the library on her first visit there. Now she understood a lot about herself – her need to swim, the love of toads' legs and the knowledge of their poisonous skin, the catching of fish when she was young and later, when she was starving… and her ability to run faster than anybody else she knew. There were many other things she had to learn, of course, but for now, tired and with aching limbs, the waters of Loch Duie called.

Sam was up and out by five that morning. He had meant to do last night what he now set out to do; but for one thing, Rose had needed him, and for another, he had been a tad afraid of what he might find, not to mention how he might react. Best to begin in daylight, he thought, see if there really was anything about which to be concerned.

He began by swimming, of course, for his own good as well as to serve his purpose that morning, but he saw nothing of note in the water. Once dried and dressed again, he set off around the loch shore, looking for signs of otters. He had a keener sense of smell than most humans, having retained that otter part of him, and it wasn't long before he detected the scent, like that of freshly cut hay, which gave them away. He walked a long distance, noticing large mounds of dirt and gravel dotted along the shore, smiling to think of the busy paws rejoicing in such activity. Noting signs of den building along muddy stretches of the bank, Sam veered off into the woods in places where the trees crept close to the loch, and found one or two holts. On a part of the loch where a low rocky ledge rose from the water, he discovered a nest made of branches and twigs, but not built by any bird.

Tired, he sighed and sat down to think there, removing his boots and socks and letting his feet dangle in the refreshing water. It was impossible to say how many otters there might be living on Loch Duie. An otter's actual territory was small, but a single otter could range large distances. However, he had been able to distinguish between the droppings of many animals already; they left them to mark their territory and warn others off. Having only covered a fraction of the loch's edge, he guessed there were many more. They were probably fleeing the increased activity the war brought to waterways lower down, where camps of various kinds had been established in the countryside and there was much more traffic than there used to be. Otters hated the fumes and poisons which came with so much human activity. Sam shivered. He himself had been part of that activity for so long. The big question, of course, was – were these otters of his kind, of that ancient line which could take human form? Even if not, there was still the dilemma that Lord Craigendon would not tolerate disruption of his fish stocks, and the thought of causing harm to these creatures, be they of his lineage or not, made Sam's stomach contract with fear.

Now that she knew the truth, Helena had no idea what to do with the knowledge. It was too huge to comprehend. So, after her swim, she headed for home, seeing Sam leave but hiding until he was in the water. She had a sickening feeling as she saw him swim with such ease and speed that his head was soon just a dot out in the loch, and she ran her hands down her wet tresses and the damp nakedness of her glowing skin as if to reassure herself that she was still as she had always known herself. She had not sought any toads to treat herself that morning, despite her gnawing hunger from having hardly eaten the previous day, and she went to the kitchen in search of breakfast. Puzzled that Rose wasn't seeing to it, she cut blocks of porridge from the drawer reserved for that purpose and added water, setting it to heat while she went upstairs to get ready to face the day ahead. The thought that grieved her most this morning was that she had lost Mrs. Bailey's good opinion of her for ever.

Francis Carmichael had barely slept. He cursed himself for a fool. He should not have given the girl away. She had no idea he was her father. Of course, she shouldn't have behaved like that towards him. No woman should have so little self-respect as to act in that manner. Yet even as he thought it, a pang of shame seized him as he remembered how grateful he had been for several maids who had done far worse. More than that, there had been young women like Rose, innocent and respectable, whom he had pursued with false promises in order to have his way.

Rose was the only one who had ever claimed to be carrying his child, though. It was Rose's responsibility, he had told her fifteen years ago, just as he would have told any others. He was a different class – what did she expect? Lady Craigendon's portrait had been nearing completion by then, and he left the estate soon after. He hadn't expected to return, ever. Her Ladyship had found out about his mother and her husband. He had known for a while. Lord Craigendon wasn't his mother's first conquest, although it was rumoured she was his first affair. Maybe she had been his only one – he saw adoration in the man's eyes whenever he looked at her. He had obviously been carrying a torch for her for years. She was a widow now, showing her age, and she could do worse. It added impetus to his wish to sort out his own matter in this backwater. When Harris brought a tray to his room, he asked for a word with Mrs. Bailey.

Megan was waiting, looking out for Helena. She was pleased to see she was alone. Coming out from the cover of the trees, she called her name. The girl stopped and stared at her as she walked towards her. There was no eagerness in her look, no welcome. Maybe not surprising, Megan thought, considering their last encounter, in the dark by the loch. At least there was no apparent hostility. When she was closer, though, she saw that Helena's expression was one of wariness. It gave her a second's pause, but she ploughed on regardless. No time for pleasantries, for passing the time of day.

157

"I've seen it, lass. You and Captain Carmichael's hand...the kiss."

"So what? I've been punished for it. There's nothin' you can say can make it any worse."

Megan hesitated. She hadn't expected the girl to be so...flat, lacking in spirit. They held each other's gaze. Megan could sense curiosity in Helena's searching eyes, as if they would burn into her soul.

"I won't beat about the bush, lassie. You're a healer. I think I might have been, too, if I hadna been sae stupid when I was young, and selfish. All I can do now is pedal my ointments and cough mixtures, and it doesn't take a witch of my lineage tae dae that... But you... you brought life tae a hand that was... dead."

"And what's the point in that, when I canna make his fingers grow back?" asked Helena, suddenly showing some of her old spark. "I know I canna dae that, I just know it, for I would wish with all my heart tae be able tae dae it!"

Megan seized her by the shoulders. "And that's what makes ye a healer, Helena! That you have that desire. For him, tae feel anythin' there was better than feelin' nothin'. Please, lass, let me help ye. Let me guide ye. I don't want ye tae make the mistakes I've made!"

"Megan," said Helena, "are you my real mother?"

Up at Craigendon House, Francis Carmichael regarded Mrs. Bailey kindly as she stood uncertainly in his bedroom. "So I assure you," he was saying, "the girl merely did for me what she would have done for her brothers if injured. She said that was what she wanted to do, as she took my hand. In my excitement at sensation returning, I failed to tell you the whole story, and undoubtedly gave the wrong impression." He knew he hadn't misjudged what Helena was about, but Mrs. Bailey only had his word for it, and it was the word of a gentleman, her employer's guest. She could not gainsay him. To his relief, her face seemed to clear and he saw that she wanted to believe his version of events.

"I thank you for clarifying that, Sir," she said. "It was still foolish, wrong behaviour towards her elder and better, though, and her punishment must stand."

"I hope," he said, "that does not mean termination of her employment? For that would make me feel very bad. I would beg you to reconsider."

Mrs. Bailey sighed. "In other times, it would have done, Sir," she said, "but not with a war on. We have few enough staff. She has been punished in other ways."

Carmichael thought he had best leave it at that. "Very good, Mrs. Bailey. I would very much like to see Helena. The sensation has remained in my fingers – what's left of them. As you can see, Dr. Baird has even seen fit to dispense with the bandages. In as much as I can be healed, I have been. I believe I will be able to use my hand again."

He saw the housekeeper's eyes stray to his fingers and knew what she was thinking – how on earth could those stubs be of any use? He smiled. She would see. They all would. But first, Helena.

Helena was far away as she tied on her apron and tidied her hair. Megan had been taken aback by her blunt question. After hesitating, she had said she wished more than anything that she was her mother. Helena had searched her face, had tried to probe her mind, but the former sea witch had been inscrutable, a mask pulled down. *"I know Da is my real father, and I know what he was,"* she had said. Megan had asked how she knew, and if she had spoken with him. Her only advice had been that she must, straight after work. It was his place to explain matters. She would help, if he asked it. So Helena had drifted into Craigendon House in a fog of confusion. She didn't hear Mrs. Bailey when she first spoke, and looked at her in some alarm when she repeated her name loudly.

"Sorry, Mrs. Bailey," she stammered.

The housekeeper appraised her cautious countenance with approval. "You've had a lot to think on, Helena, and no doubt you have. It can't be easy to come here today. However, I've been speaking with Captain Carmichael, and he has shed more light on the situation. It was wrong and foolish to treat a gentleman, a guest of His Lordship, as you would one of your brothers, but I understand now that this was what you meant, and nothing... untoward. Captain Carmichael would like to see you."

Helena stood wide-eyed, struggling to reply. "I'm very grateful to the Captain, and to you," she managed at last. She meant it. The situation was salvageable after all, but she wouldn't play it as she had intended to, not even if Carmichael had rescued her for that purpose. She could see that her demeanour was pleasing to the housekeeper.

159

"Well then," said Mrs. Bailey, "Eleven o'clock, in his private sitting room. Don't be late, and make sure your tasks are completed by then." She proceeded to issue orders for the morning's work.

So it was that three hours later, Helena presented herself in the sitting room which overlooked the walled garden. She looked tired and subdued, and Francis Carmichael hesitated, having only witnessed previously the vivacious sprite who the day before had plainly tried to seduce him.

"Helena! My dear girl!" he blustered after a moment or two.

"Captain Carmichael, Sir," she said, not meeting his gaze.

He drew a breath. His lips formed words he didn't speak. Finally, he managed, "Perhaps yesterday would be best forgotten. Only, a miraculous coincidence happened. But the way it happened stands between us as an awkwardness."

The girl looked up then, misery in her eyes.

"Please, let me continue. You are a beautiful young woman. More than that, you are engaging and intelligent. But there can be nothing of… that nature… between us."

To his surprise, he saw her shoulders sag with relief, as she gave a tearful smile. The sight gladdened him. She had seen the error of her ways. She was a good girl, he had no doubt of that. He was an attractive older man who had paid her attention, and it had just been a lapse… He shuddered to think how his younger self would have taken every advantage of that, how many men in his position yesterday might have reacted, and ruined her.

"Come, my dear. Let there be no more awkwardness between us. Let me show you something."

He ushered her to a draped object over by the window. With a flourish, he pulled the covering sheet away to reveal an easel. On it was a rudimentary sketch. Carmichael watched as colour returned to Helena's pallid cheeks. He saw emotions flit across her lovely face as the implications dawned… pleasure and surprise first at beholding her own face, then the question as to how he had drawn it.

"A work in progress, of course," he said. "As is the artist. But he has feeling back in the stumps of his fingers, and he can just about manage to control a pencil… he thinks he will be able to do much more, in time.

160

And all the circumstances of this miraculous happening have given him hope. So much hope, Helena!"

They fell into each other's arms, then, just two human beings overjoyed at the wonderful turns life could take. Francis Carmichael kissed the top of Helena's fragrant head with more affection than he had shown anybody for a long time.

Chapter 19

Megan had to ask for permission to leave work. It was, she said, family business. Tam McDowall hadn't bothered to enquire further, too busy grumbling about her absence and the extra work it would give him. She knew fine well it wouldn't mean extra work for *him*. She told her Land Army colleagues that she was going to see the doctor about women's troubles. Their sly glances didn't escape her. No doubt they were deciding whether she might be pregnant. She knew they whispered about her evening ramblings. As she left the farmyard that afternoon, she saw wee Billy MacTaggart staggering under a bucket of pigswill that she should probably have been carrying. She hesitated, but much as she liked Billy and bemoaned the way he was treated as underfed, unpaid labour, she had to go.

She headed westerly, in the direction of the Hailstanes' farm, rehearsing what she should say, how much. It was raining lightly, and she was glad of her mac; she turned up the collar, but her scarf was no protection for her hair. She felt her curls become damp and heavy under her sodden head covering. It was twenty minutes of fast-paced walking, and she was dishevelled when she arrived. Before approaching the door, she sheltered under a nearby tree and lit a cigarette to calm her nerves. She hoped that Sam might be about the croft rather than engaged in his other duties, but she had no way of knowing. She was sure Rose would be at home with her father, and if she had to tackle them alone, then she would. Rose and her father, both. It was time.

Stubbing out her roll-up and squaring her shoulders, Megan walked round to the green-painted back door, looking out for Sam in the yard but not seeing him. She rapped with a confidence she didn't feel. She heard a scrabbling of feet, and the door opened to reveal Sadie.

"Hello. I've come for a word with your mother and father, if you could tell them, please."

Sadie was staring at her in some puzzlement. Megan thought she might just get away with it, that the child wouldn't quite be able to place her. Then, without speaking a word, the girl ran through the empty kitchen shouting that the fortune teller was here to see Ma and Da. Megan heard a clatter of feet on the wooden treads of the stairs, and Sam appeared, coming down the hallway.

"It must be serious if ye've come here," he said as he reached her, speaking low. "Is it the otters?" He flicked a warning glance at Sadie, who stood regarding Megan with mingled curiosity and awe.

"In a manner of speaking," Megan replied. "I need to talk to you, and your wife. And also your father-in-law. In private."

Sam frowned. "My father-in-law isn't a well man. He's bedridden, and he lost his power of speech with the last stroke..."

"I know," said Megan. "But it's important you all hear what I have to say."

"Sam? What's going on?" Rose had come up behind him.

The two women stared at each other. Rose's expression was one Megan had seen just a couple of months ago, on May Day, so like Sadie's when she had first seen her outside her tent at the fete... and it was the child who broke the silence now.

"You look..."

"Please!" cried Megan, interrupting. "I have to speak to the adults. No children, not for this."

"Sadie," said Sam, "be a good girl and play in your room for a while." He turned back to Megan. "The boys are out. A bit o' rain never stops them."

Sadie thrust out her lip, but shrugged and ran away upstairs.

"I'm sorry, Megan, forgive me. Please come in oot o' the rain. Rose, this is Megan that ye've heard me mention. Megan, my wife, Rose." The polite introduction was surreal under the circumstances.

The two women nodded warily at each other. "You're the sea witch," said Rose.

"I was," the other woman replied. "After the way I treated Sam and his family, I left that life in shame. I've not lived the life of a sea witch

163

since. I live in the world as most men and women know it, and try tae dae ma bit for it. Especially in these times."

"What dae ye want with us?" asked Rose, an edge to her voice.

Megan smiled wryly as she watched her slip her arm through her husband's and pull him close, in a territorial display. "I need tae speak tae you first, then your father, Mrs. Hailstanes."

"My father is sick, and has nothin' tae dae wi' this. Well, apart frae rescuin' Sam after what ye did…"

Megan held up her hand. "All in good time. This is important, please hear me. Helena knows what she is, or was. She knows ye really are her Da, Sam."

Sam's jaw went slack and he clutched the back of the nearest chair for support.

"I think we should all sit down," said Megan.

"How do you know this?" There was ice in Rose's voice. "How do we know you're not just tricking your way in among us…"

"I'm not interested in your man!" cried Megan. "Can we just get that straight?"

Rose stared at her. "What is your interest in my father, then? He doesn't even know you!"

"Your father is no stranger to the hidden world, Mrs. Hailstanes," said Megan. "Maybe he hasn't told you everything, Sam neither. Sam knows fine William Tully had dealings wi' the Sea Witch o' Ballaness."

Rose fell silent. She still felt a sense of betrayal, after all these years, that Tully had manipulated Sam into marrying her, knowing full well what he was and where he came from. Now it seemed there was even more to the tale.

"I need to speak to him," said Megan.

"He can't answer you," said Rose.

"He can hear me," said Megan.

"I don't see what…" said Rose.

"This way, is it?" said Megan. She was on her feet and heading for the stairs before they could stop her. She took them briskly and paused at the top, seeing the old man in the bed, facing the window with the view of his beloved loch. Closely followed by Sam and Rose, she walked quietly into the room and looked down at him.

His eyes were closed, but he opened them slowly and jumped when he saw her, his walking stick sliding from the coverlet and crashing to the floor.

Rose rushed to his side. "Da, I'm sorry, this woman…" she blustered.

"Do I look familiar, Mr. Tully?" Megan asked. Their eyes were fixed on each other. "I'm not the same one. That's a myth among your kind – the ancient witch whose beauty never fades. Well, it's half true. The waters of St. Bride's Spring do help tae renew the youth of such as we, but I stopped bathing in them in shame at what I did tae Sam and Helena, and the others… The Sea Witch o' Ballaness always bore a daughter. We're mortal, too, and in time, her daughter took her place. She selected a man for the purpose of conceiving the child, but she wanted nothing of him, only the girl. That was my first mistake. I wanted to possess Sam, to keep him. But never mind that. My mother didn't make that mistake. She was never going to stay with a man. But you didn't give her the chance, did you, William Tully? You threw her out before she could explain. So as not to spoil your reputation."

There was silence in the room. Rose's mouth fell open. Sam looked from one woman to the other. Megan pulled off her scarf, and her blonde curls bounced free, spiral tendrils even more pronounced because damp. Sam thought back to an early spring morning fourteen years ago, a young woman in a river, hair floating, and he had thought it was Megan…

"Hello, Father," said Megan.

Later, downstairs, after the old man had wept and held her now work-callused hands in his feeble, shaking ones, Megan sat sipping tea. Her half-sister couldn't take her eyes off her. Sam studied them both, wondering that he had never realised it before. They weren't all that alike, however; it was more obvious when you saw them together. They both had Tully's hair, apparently, the curly hair he had had as a youth, before falling prey to early baldness. Apart from that, there was a mild facial resemblance, a similarity of colouring, but nothing striking. Megan was the younger by seven years, but she looked older, sun-wizened and sinewy from her outdoor life. She was subdued now, spent with the emotion of revealing what she had never told a soul.

She was the child of Tully and the housekeeper he had employed after his wife died. Her mother had selected him as the father of the daughter she knew she would bear, for that fair curly hair which wasn't unlike her own. She didn't love him. The Sea Witch o' Ballaness was supposed to make her choice of mate for practical reasons. Megan blushed as she said it. She often wondered if it made her better or worse, that she had sought Sam for love of him. Her mother hadn't rushed Tully, who was heart-broken after losing his wife, had worked for him fully two years before he succumbed, going back and forwards between her boat-house and his cottage. In that time she had been kind to little Rose and taught her the rudiments of keeping house. It only needed to happen once between Tully and the sea witch, and she conceived. He was ashamed and said it would never happen again, and she concurred, nursing her secret close as Megan grew within.

She planned to leave his employment before the pregnancy began to show, but Tully guessed her state and dismissed her, blaming her for his shame at betraying the memory of his wife, and fearing for his reputation. It hadn't happened here; the events had taken place on an estate closer to Ballaness, where Tully was an assistant water bailiff, four years before the outbreak of the Great War. He only realised the woman was a witch when she cursed him as she fled into the wind and rain. This much Megan's mother had told her. She had cursed him with an old age filled with infirmity, long and drawn out and dependent on others. Megan knew he had tracked her down afterwards, that he had kept a wary eye on the house-boat. The child, he believed from the legend, would be offered as tribute to the faerie realm. He would have had no interest in her in any case. She had not been wanted by him, Megan assured Rose, but he had shown remorse today, and she was touched.

Half an hour later, Rose waved Sam and Megan away from the farmhouse. She had one hand on Sadie's shoulder. The child had appeared while Megan was crying, and Rose had ushered her to her room again, with milk and oatcakes, saying the grown-ups still needed to talk. *"The fortune teller looks quite like you, Ma,"* Sadie had said. *"I thought it when I saw her at the fete."*

Rose laughed at the coincidence and went back downstairs, determined to take control of the situation. *"What are we to tell the boys and*

166

Sadie?", she wanted to know, and *"Since your mother cursed my – our – father, Megan, can you do anything about it?"* They had decided that the children should be told nothing meanwhile, but Megan updated them on the story of Captain Carmichael's hand and Helena's part in its healing. She could do little to help, she feared, because her gifts were draining as Helena's grew – but Helena might be able to help her grandfather.

Rose smiled as she waved, subduing her resentment at Sam and Megan's shared history. They had agreed that Sam should go to meet his eldest daughter alone, but would walk Megan to the point where their paths diverged. *I have a half-sister,* Rose kept saying to herself. She remembered the pretty woman who had come to look after them when her mother died. Rose had liked her. Then, one day, she hadn't come. Tully had told her she wouldn't be back, and Rose supposed she had died, like Ma, and had grieved all over again. The smile on her face was becoming rigid. *So now I suppose I have to share my father with Megan as well as my husband.*

Sam and Megan hugged when they came to the fork in the road. "I always valued your friendship," he said. "In the old days, before…"

"I was wrong, Sam, in everything," she replied. "I was a stupid lassie. Left on my own too young, with too many powers. Or rather, gifts. There's a difference. It took me a long time tae realise that. Helena has tae learn the difference now. I've told her."

"Well, you're family, and I hope you'll feel free…"

She put a hand on his arm, to silence him. "I'm not sure Rose is ready tae see things that way. Not yet. Maybe not ever. But one thing I said tae ye before – clumsily – was that Helena is like my daughter. So much of what was mine has passed to her. She's my heir, Sam, the nearest I'll ever have. Please don't let me be cut out of Helena's life. Things aren't ever likely tae get easier between her and Rose, ye know. It was always a bit much tae expect o' yer wife."

"Aye," said Sam. The word came out like a sigh. "I'll be seein' ye, then, Megan."

Sam saw Helena walking towards him. Her head was down, which wasn't like her, and she walked more slowly than usual. He didn't blame her if she was in no hurry to reach home, after the way things had been. He called to her from some distance, rather than startle her by coming upon her suddenly. The girl raised her head and he saw her pleasure at seeing him. They both quickened their pace. When they drew near, no words were necessary. The truth was there, hanging in all its pain and glory in the air between them. Sam held his arms open, and his lassie ran into them, sobbing on his shoulder.

PART FOUR

July – August 1942

Chapter 20

July 1942 was drawing to its close, the summer nights already darkening significantly earlier than just a month ago at midsummer. Helena slipped from her bed, seeing by the light of the full moon shining into her and Sadie's bedroom. She looked down at her half-sister, who looked even younger asleep, her fair curls spread out on the pillow. How she envied her innocence! Ma and Da saw no reason for her siblings to be told, ever. Helena had known the truth for three weeks now. She had asked questions about her biological mother and Sam's past. She knew she was a witch – and a human – only because of Megan's incompetence. It had taken the shine off everything. She felt like an unnatural freak, much the way others had always viewed her. Da said their ancestry was noble, sprung from the hidden folk of the Faerie Isle. She needed to see for herself. If she was ready, he said that tonight was the time.

Silently, she crept out of the room and along the hallway to her parents' bedroom, where she had left warm clothing earlier that day. A lamp was burning. Sam was waiting for her, already dressed, but Rose was in her nightgown.

"Ye're not coming, Ma?" Helena asked.

"No," Rose replied, "best leave this tae you an' yer Da." Helena bent over the bed and kissed her, and Rose flushed in that way she did when emotional, a red rash spreading from throat to forehead.

Helena pulled on the trousers she wore for dirty work about the farm, and a sweater knitted by Rose the previous Christmas. She and Sam tiptoed downstairs and donned boots in the kitchen before heading out into the night. Loch Duie shimmered, a trail of silver moonlight cleaving its unruffled surface.

"Bomber's Moon," Sam remarked.

"If it wasn't for the hospital up at the big hoose, I might forget there was a war on," said Helena.

"Aye, we're far removed and not sufferin' like most," Sam replied.

Helena took a deep breath. Now was as good a time as any. "I don't want tae stay safe here forever, Da. When I'm old enough, I want tae dae my bit. I'm good wi' the officers."

"Let's hope this war doesn't go on much longer," Sam said. "Have ye seen any more o' Captain Carmichael?"

"Not since he showed me he could draw again, with his injured hand. He's treated more like a guest than a patient."

Sam chose his words carefully. "Ye've only helped in the hospital three times, Helena," he said. "Dinna get carried away, lass."

Helena decided against saying any more. Megan had returned to the cottage to persuade Rose to allow Helena to volunteer in the wards on her day off. Rose didn't think for one minute that the flighty girl would want to, but she did. *"She has to follow her path,"* Megan had said. *"She's a healer. She knows it now."* As they walked on the grass verge at the loch's side, not betraying their presence by stepping on to the shingle, Helena thought about her staff, lying in its hiding place in the hayloft, and wished that she had it with her. Sam had forbidden it; he and Rose didn't like the fact she had one, and were afraid of what might happen if Helena became overwrought. He had already experienced what she was about to, having discovered what he needed to find out, and although he knew so much more about it, it had been traumatic, he said – moving, stirring and disturbing all at the same time. Helena decided not to remind him that her emotions produced effects without use of her staff.

They arrived at a clump of low bushes with a convenient gap in the middle. Helena did as she was bid and lay at one side of the gap, concealed from view of the loch, while Sam lay at the other. They had a clear vista of a large section of water. It stretched before them still silvered by the moon, but the surface here was not calm, for something disturbed it, creating a long wake. Soon, there were other such signs of activity, and as her eyes adjusted and focused, Helena could make out the tiny heads breaking the surface of the water. Sometimes, they came together and there was much splashing. Intent on the loch, she jumped and stifled a cry as something rushed past her. She saw its diminutive but lithe and strong form, observed its grace and speed and watched it

171

enter the water silently, its wake ploughing a furrow in the moon trail on the loch.

Helena felt detached. It was interesting, enchanting even, but it didn't go any deeper. Glancing across to where her father lay, she could just make out the rapt expression on his face, and knew that he was feeling involved in a way she could not. This may have been how she came into being, but she couldn't remember any of it, and would rather not.

A sudden flash drew her eye to a bright shooting star. The Perseid Meteor Shower had begun a few days ago and would grow in strength over the following weeks. She scanned the sky for more before returning her attention to the loch; and this time, she did cry out. Sam uttered an urgent, "Shush!" Helena clamped her hand across her mouth to stop any sound from issuing, as she watched the procession of naked bodies walk dripping from the water, their skin milk-white in the moonlight. Some of them sat down on the grass verge not far from where she lay, while others chased each other, continuing their water games on land. Some of them danced and cavorted, seemingly in a world of their own, glorying in their strong-limbed beauty. They were fully human, which startled her even though it shouldn't have done, for she and her father were the same. Surely, these were not the creatures she had seen swimming in the water a few minutes ago? Helena could identify with these no more than she could with their furred and clawed alter egos. She felt sick, horrified. Bile began to rise in her throat.

Out on the loch, there was a disturbance. The waters became ruffled and began to churn, and waves chased to the shore. The otter-folk noticed and ceased their chatter and activities. There seemed to be some confusion among them as to this strange phenomenon. Helena Hailstanes, Lady of the Loch, rose and fled for home with the speed of her ancestral race, before her engulfing emotions caused more havoc.

Rose handed a cup of tea to Helena as she sat hunched in a chair by the fire. Sam was talking to her, appealing to her, saying how beautiful these otters were, how noble, in whichever form they took, human or animal. Helena regarded him as she might have looked at a stranger, noting his large brown eyes, which were also hers, and which she had until now regarded as an attractive feature. Rose wrapped an arm around her shoulders and drew her close in a rare maternal gesture. Helena looked her into face and knew that, for once, this her step-mother understood more than her father did, for Rose must have felt as Helena did when she first found out.

"Sam," said Rose, "that's enough for one night, dear. We need to drink up and get to bed. Helena has work in the morning, and she's not used to being out late then working like you are."

Helena drank deep and said nothing of her midnight wanderings, barefoot with staff in hand. At this moment, she would have given anything to be normal – nothing of creature, nothing of witch, nothing of the hidden world about her. Daylight, and mundane tasks, were all she wished for, life as others lived it. She wished she was ordinary, just the water bailiff's daughter.

Into the silence around the dark, unlit fire, a soft knocking came at the door. "Not tonight," sighed Sam. "Not news of poachers tonight!" He crossed the room and opened it a crack. Megan pushed past him and entered.

"I was wakened by Rab tapping at my window," she said. "I knew it was urgent when he did that." She walked over to Helena and dropped to her knees beside her chair. "I'm so sorry, sweetheart. Sorry for all my meddling that led tae this! This is why I want tae help ye, why ye must follow your path."

"My daughter has had enough to deal with tonight," said Rose. "And you have meddled quite enough in her life, don't you think?"

Megan sighed. "She needs me, Rose."

"I think you're the last thing my family needs."

"Like it or not, Rose, without me, you wouldn't have a family. And don't forget that, also like it or not, I'm part of it."

In the morning, up at Craigendon House, all talk was of the bombing sustained by the Midlands. That Bomber's Moon which had revealed a hidden world to Helena had brought hell on earth to human beings hundreds of miles away. She thought of wee Billy MacTaggart and other evacuees, and the horrors they had known. When would it be Glasgow's turn again? As she went about her duties, which that day were as mundane as she had wished the previous night, the thought crossed her mind that maybe it was better to be an otter, or at least some creature which didn't have to deal with the problems of being human. She glimpsed her reflection in a mirror, those eloquent eyes which reflected back her confusion, and she thought it might not be so bad to slip out of this human frame and into the loch as a care-free creature after all.

Rose was on the ward, happily immersing herself in a new duty. Some St. John Ambulance cadets had arrived to sort through hundreds of books which had been donated from all over the region. Some were to be kept here for the patients, and others sent to other hospitals. Many were tattered and needed some mending. The young people, all around Helena's age, had travelled down from Glasgow for work experience. They would help to organise the books, going through them and turning corners back up where they had been used to mark the place, unsticking pages, mending bindings. They were to stay for three days to gain further experience of a convalescent hospital, and had the added thrill of being billeted in Craigendon House itself. Although they were in the servants' rooms on the top floor, rooms rarely used as there were so few who lived in now, it was a grand adventure for them.

Mary McDowall was sent to find Rose, and inform her that Captain Carmichael required a scribe, once her duties were over. It was the first time he had sent for her – she had no idea what he had been doing for help with his letters meanwhile. She assumed he had made another arrangement, from wishing to have no further dealings with her. She knew he had shared with Helena the return of his ability to draw, but nothing more had been heard from him, and she was glad. Rose spent the allocated time with her charges, then dismissed them. She washed her face and combed her hair, despising herself for doing so.

He was waiting for her in his sitting room. She barely acknowledged him as she went straight to the table and laid down her writing materials.

"Please, Mrs. Hailstanes," he said, "Leave those and come and sit here."

Rose still didn't look at him. "I'm your scribe," she said. "We have no other business with each other."

Carmichael sighed. "I haven't much need of the services of a scribe, actually," he said, getting up and walking to the window. "My mother is here, and I have no-one else beyond a few colleagues who are all serving, if they're not dead already. My wife and my children died in the London Blitz. They were visiting friends."

Rose turned to look at him, startled to realise she had never thought of his circumstances, never considered he might be married. He had his back to her, tension in the set of his shoulders.

"I...I'm right sorry, Sir," she stammered.

"There's no need for formality after what we've been to each other. Call me Francis, like you used to."

"How... how old were your bairns... Francis?" she asked, softly.

"Sebastian was seven and Angus five."

Rose thought of her own healthy boys, one of them also Angus. "I'm right sorry," she repeated.

He waved his injured hand and sat down again. "Please... join me and let us forget the past and look to the future."

Hesitantly, Rose walked over and sat facing him in the other winged armchair.

"Helena is a fine girl. She has spirit, and intelligence. I should like to know her better," he said.

Rose sighed and gripped one hand in the other to stop them shaking. "There's no reason for ye tae know her, Francis."

"But there is. You told me so yourself."

Rose gulped. "I may have let ye think it. But it's not true. She's too old tae be your lassie, Francis, by a few months. I lost ours, and a few days later, we took Helena in. She was... found. She'd been abandoned. She had nobody. I'm sorry. I thought ye liked her over-much..."

"You thought history would repeat itself."

"Aye."

Francis Carmichael fell silent. Glancing at him, Rose saw tears in his eyes. He took out a handkerchief and blew his nose. "Well, maybe I deserved as much. But I'm sorry she's not mine. And I've changed, Rose. There would have been no repeat of what happened between us. Does your husband know about us?"

"Yes, Francis, he does now."

"Did you marry him because you were pregnant? Did he know that?"

"Yes to both questions. We liked and respected each other. And love grows. Love of a kind. I'm sorry that I deceived ye, Francis."

"It's me who should say that to you, for all those years ago. And I do. I am sorry, Rose. Please be on your way. You have your family to see to, no doubt."

Rose trod softly to the door and pulled it shut behind her, leaving a man who looked as if he had just been bereaved all over again.

Megan was working in fields near where the roads converged, and she saw Rose heading home from Craigendon House. She rested her pitchfork and stretched to ease her back, wiping the sweat from her brow. Tomorrow, she would have more fulfilling work, for St. John Ambulance as an organisation was interested in the healing properties of plants, and she had been asked to lead the visiting cadets on fieldwork. It would make a welcome change. She planned to introduce them to chicory, which formed the basis of Camp Coffee, a substitute for real coffee in these days of wartime shortages. She also thought she might get them to gather some tips of broom, and demonstrate the mild diuretic she made with them. Old farmer McDowall was always taking chills and needing his kidneys flushed out.

As Megan mused happily on her plans, a sudden shadow fell over her, and the warmth went from the day. Megan looked up to see a huge eagle just a few feet above her, hovering, something in its beak. She cowered and raised her arms to protect her head as the bird swooped down on her, then flew high again with a great cry in which she sensed triumph. It had dropped something. Megan stared, unable to take in the sight before her eyes. Her heart breaking, she saw Rab her raven, bloodied and broken on the dirt in front of her.

Chapter 21

As Helena prepared to walk home in the light summer drizzle which had begun to fall, a boy she had never seen before appeared and offered to shelter her under his umbrella. "I'm fine, thank you," said Helena. "A bit o' water never hurt me!" She burst out laughing as she said it, as if it was an enormous joke.

The boy looked puzzled. "Well, may I walk with you anyway? I have some free time just now. I've seen you about the house today."

Helena took in his appearance, the black Balmoral cap, the black and white tie over his grey flannel shirt, and the arm band on his sleeve. "Oh, you're one o' the St. John Ambulance cadets frae Glesga!"

The boy straightened proudly and offered his hand. "Tam Watson."

Helena brushed his fingers with hers. Nobody her own age had behaved this way towards her before. She only knew those with whom she had grown up on the estate, and rarely met new young people. "I'm Helena Hailstanes," she said.

Tam grinned. "What a great name!"

"I've never thought aboot it," said Helena, lying. Sam had told her how he made the name up when pressed by the policeman for a surname, thinking of the hailstones hammering off the hull of Megan's home. The name was unique to their family, and she wished they were not so unique after all.

"Course, I've heard it already," Tam said. "Was that your mother supervising us with the books?"

"It must have been. There's not many o' us wi' that name," she replied. "Anyway, I'd best be gettin' along."

"So, can I come, too?"

Helena blushed. "Ye can keep me company a bit o' the way," she replied.

He held the umbrella, which he admitted to having borrowed from a stand in the hallway, over her head. For ease while walking, her hand shyly joined his on the handle.

By the time she reached the farmhouse, Helena's spirits had recovered, thanks to Tam. He had been pleasant company, and she had been interested to hear of his work with St. John Ambulance. He wanted to train to be a doctor, he said, but he would serve his country first if the war was still on when he turned eighteen. His father was a captain in the Royal Air Force. He might be from Glasgow, Helena reflected, but he came from a different world to the one Billy had described.

She walked into the kitchen to find Megan there. She looked as if she had been crying, and Rose was placing something wrapped in an old bed sheet into a crate, with great care.

"Hello. Has something else happened?" asked Helena. She couldn't imagine what kind of drama might have visited itself on the Hailstanes household now.

"It's Rab," said Megan. "He was attacked by an eagle. Killed."

Helena walked over to the table and wrapped her arms around Megan. "I'm so sorry. I know what he meant tae ye. An eagle? I've never seen one."

"I've lived here most o' my life, an' I've never seen one in these parts, either," said Rose. "That's him ready, Megan."

"Thanks. I didna know where tae come. I could hardly take him back tae the McDowall's. Nobody knew aboot him there." She turned to Helena. "I had tae hide him under a bush an' finish wi' my work before I could come here. Yer Ma has been very kind." Her face was drawn and haggard.

"Are ye goin' tae bury him?" asked Helena. "Dae ye want us tae be there?"

"Thanks, lass, but no. It's aye been just me and him, after Ma died. He came tae us when I was a bairn. He replaced the one she had had for many years."

"He wasn't… magical, then? Immortal, or long-lived? Obviously not."

Megan sighed. "He was wise. He was drawn tae Ma, sensing his purpose, she said. He wouldn't have had all that many years left. But he deserved tae die peacefully, not like this. Another consequence o' me turnin' my back on Ballaness and the life I was born to!"

Helena looked thoughtful. "Ye were right tae make the break," she said after a pause. "Not tae punish yerself. If ye had never done anythin' wrong, ye still should have done it. Better tae be workin' good in the world than castin' spells in a backwater."

The two older water bailiff's daughters regarded her silently, lost in their own thoughts.

As Helena bid Megan farewell with her precious, sad cargo in her arms, she saw Billy coming towards the cottage. He and Megan paused to speak a moment. Megan smiled rather too broadly at the boy, no doubt pretending the crate, if he asked, contained nothing of note. Helena welcomed Billy and took the book from under his arm. It was an old one belonging to the boys which she had loaned him to practise his reading. She sighed. She was tired, yet agitated. She couldn't be bothered with a reading lesson today. She knew what she had to do. You couldn't deny nature, after all.

"Can ye swim, Billy?" she asked.

Billy couldn't swim. Nobody had taught him. The only water he had ever been near was the River Clyde. When he saw the sea from the train on his way from Glasgow, stretching for miles and miles, it had made him feel dizzy, he said. Helena thought of her first view, from Rev. O' Neill's car, and understood. Was that only three months ago? So much had happened since the first of May. Well, she knew the truth about her origins now. She wasn't the stupid, naive girl who had gone searching that day, escaping the confines of Craigendon estate.

She hunted out a pair of trunks belonging to Jamie, knitted like her own hated costume, of course. Billy was so thin, she had to tie string round the waist so they would stay up.

"This is what ye need tae build ye up, Billy," she said. "What's the point of livin' near Loch Duie if ye don't take the good o' it for exercise?

I wish the boys were here tae join in, but they're away wi' Da in the woods."

They walked to the water's edge. It was still drizzling, and Billy shivered. "Ye'll be fine once we're in and ye get goin'," she smiled.

Billy recoiled noisily from his first ginger steps into the loch, screeching and running back out. Helena laughed and ran after him, catching him round the waist, swinging him up easily like a bag of potatoes. She could never have done that now with her strapping brothers. She waded out deep with him, half-floating, half-dragging him, ignoring his shrieks, until suddenly, she let him go just as she had with her siblings when they were young. It occurred to her that maybe her method with a fully human child should be different, but to her surprise and delight, Billy began to swim after being cast from her just a few times. Even her brothers had taken more effort than that before their limbs submitted to the rhythm of the water. He didn't have their natural style and grace, but that would come, thought Helena. He didn't have their lineage, after all. She swam after him, careful to restrain her speed and stay close in case he should flounder.

The wee Glasgow boy's face was almost split in two by his grin. He rested, treading water as if he had been doing it all his life. "This is wonderful, Helena! I could stay here forever!"

"Can I swap with ye, then, Billy?" she laughed. "I'll go and make my life in Glesga, an' you bide here."

His face clouded. "I wouldn't wish my life there on anybody," he said. Then he splashed her. "Hey, Helena! They call me Weegie Weasel at school, now look at me – I'm a Weegie Water Weasel!"

Helena's heart melted towards the wee boy, so unhappy in his city life. A water weasel was a Scots name for an otter. How strange that he should say that. She wished he could stay here. She wished her family would adopt him, and he would never need to go back and face the aunt and uncle who treated him badly. She wished she could keep him here with her, and not see the droop of his shoulders as he headed back for the mean McDowalls' farmhouse. Her eyes misted over, and there was a warmth running through her veins, from her yearning heart to the soles of her feet where they paddled her water element, and her lifeblood seemed to become one with the water, and the water was warm like her heart.

"What's happening, Helena?" asked Billy, the first faint alarm she had heard in his voice.

The water around her was beginning to pulse with her heartbeat. She knew it was her doing, and that she had to control her emotions. "Don't worry, Billy," she said. "It's just something that happens in water. A wee disturbance. Get swimming again, and ye won't notice."

She tried to calm herself as he smiled trustingly and flipped over to begin his crawl again. She breathed deeply and followed him, engulfed in affection for this little lad, wishing she could help him, make him happy... It happened suddenly. One minute, Billy was there; the next, he wasn't.

"Billy!" cried Helena. He must have sunk like a stone to disappear so quickly. Helena knew the loch, its vagaries and its moods. There were no hidden currents, nothing to drag a swimmer under like that. She stared around, her heart pounding, completely released from the dreaminess which had claimed her a few moments ago. "Billy!"

The creature broke the surface in front of her with a cascade of ripples. Water dripped from its sleek head and whiskers. Its eloquent brown eyes gleamed.

Helena knew then what had happened. "Billy!" she breathed. He was gone again before she could blink, submerged in the waters he had never entered until half an hour ago. Helena dived and looked frantically around her, but she couldn't see him. Surfacing, she called his name over and over again. The sound of her voice sped across the surface of Loch Duie and rebounded from the hills, but he did not reappear. Panicking, Helena swam faster than she ever had for home.

Megan had just buried Rab deep in the woods when she heard Rose frantically calling her name. She fought her way back through the tangled undergrowth, hitting branches out of the way with her spade. As she came out into a clearing, Rose hurtled towards her.

"Quick, Megan, come tae the loch! It's wee Billy – Helena says she's turned him intae an otter!"

Megan flung the spade down and together the two women ran in the direction of the water. As they arrived, they saw a terrible sight. Not far from the edge of the loch, where she had returned to continue searching for Billy, Helena was under attack from a massive eagle. They watched in horror as the bird dived repeatedly each time her head broke the water's surface. Then they saw that she was struggling with something – Helena had an otter flung over one shoulder, grappling to hold on to it as she tried to stay afloat, ducking to avoid the eagle's talons.

Megan unlaced her boots and kicked them off, running into the water. Rose shed her shoes and did likewise, but her cotton dress and petticoat clung to her legs and she couldn't keep up. She began to flounder, while the former sea witch swam with strength and agility towards the struggling girl.

Then, suddenly, other forms appeared in the water. Megan gaped in disbelief as people she hadn't known were there reached Helena before her. She heard a cry of fear from Rose, and glancing back, she saw that two people had appeared from nowhere to be with Rose also, and they were helping her; a woman, long hair spread like seaweed on the loch's surface, had her arms wrapped around her chest and was taking her back to the shore. Sam was there, struggling to get his boots off, when they brought her ashore. Megan saw that they were stark naked, and understood. Turning back to where Helena was, there was now a ring of ten swimmers surrounding her, waving arms and shouting noisily at the eagle, but one was in the middle with her, and taking the otter from her shoulder. As suddenly as they had appeared, the swimmers were gone, submerged with not a trace remaining. They had taken the otter with them.

Back at the farm, Sam lit the fire and set up the clothes horse to dry Megan's things. She and Helena sat wrapped in blankets, while Rose, in her dressing gown, cleaned the wounds on Helena's head and shoulders. The eagle had managed to peck her, and the otter's claws had left deep scratches.

"I'm sure it was him," she was saying. "It was wee Billy."

"He wanted to stay with them, lass," said Sam. "They told me that."

"Ye gave him the life he wanted and needed," Megan added. "Ye didna mean to, but it's part o' yer nature. And better than causin' harm when ye're roused."

"But I have caused harm!" cried Helena. "What dae we tell everybody? Billy will be missed by bedtime!"

There was silence while they all thought, eventually broken by Sam. "We could say we know nothing. We never saw Billy after his reading lesson, after he left here earlier."

"It's lucky the boys and Sadie didn't see it," said Rose. The children had witnessed them come dripping back to the farmhouse, and had been sent to do tasks with the promise of an explanation later. "Sam's right. Nobody knows but us."

Megan was frowning, deep in thought. "I think it's best tae stick close tae the truth," she said. "Helena's been injured, an' your other children know it. An' people will notice her head at work. That'll draw comment. It would mean making up another story."

"Not really," said Helena. "I went swimming and was attacked after Billy left."

Megan sighed. "The police need tae be informed. They'll search for him, ask questions. There are people who would normally have seen him pass by on the way back tae the McDowalls'."

"What dae ye suggest then?" asked Sam. "Because we either leave it until he's missed, or we have tae report somethin'."

"Helena took him swimmin'," said Megan, "after his readin' lesson. There was an otter in the water close by, the eagle was after it and Billy panicked."

"Let folk think he drowned?" ask Helena.

"Yes. We need tae stick as close tae the truth as possible. The eagle made Billy panic, he went under and it turned and attacked you before ye could save him."

Sam stood up. "I'll away up tae Craigendon House. I'll inform His Lordship and ask tae use the telephone tae inform the police."

Helena doubled over, sobbing. "He's lost tae us!" she cried.

"He's found a life he wanted," said Megan.

"And they want him," said Sam. "He's not a misfit any more. Think on that, Helena."

Chapter 22

"Hello. Good to see you back at work," said a quiet voice behind her.

Helena jumped, startled from her sly investigation of the interesting piece of furniture beside the sofa in the informal family parlour in Craigendon House. The small table had a drawer which was actually a silk bag on runners. She had asked about it before, and been told it was for ladies' work – embroidery and the like. It had been empty then, but there was a work in progress on a hoop in it now, fine stitches making up a floral bouquet. Lady Carmichael was certainly making herself at home.

"Don't worry. I won't tell."

"You certainly won't. You shouldn't be here!" said Helena, laughing and swiping at the intruder with her duster.

Tam Watson grinned. "Do I get to walk you home later, Miss Hailstanes?"

"I think I might permit that, Mr. Watson."

Someone in the doorway cleared his throat. The two young people swung round to see Captain Carmichael standing there. It was the first time Helena had seen him since he had shown her his drawing.

"I'm sorry, Captain, Sir, I...we..."

"At ease," Carmichael smiled, "but off you go, boy, before anybody else catches you putting the maids off their work!"

Tam blushed. He stood to attention and saluted. "Sir, yes, Sir!" he said, and marched out of the room, causing Helena to erupt in a fit of giggles.

Carmichael sat down in an armchair, crossing his long legs. "I take it you're walking out with this young chap, then?"

"Hardly that, Sir," Helena replied. "We met the day of… the tragedy, you know. He came tae see me twice while I was recoverin' though."

"It must have been most distressing for you," said Carmichael. "Have your injuries healed?"

Helena avoided his gaze. To add credence to their tale, they had exaggerated the eagle attack, blaming the bird for the scratches on her shoulder also, and she had been granted five days off work to recover. She touched her head where the eagle had indeed pecked her and drawn blood. "Yes, thank you, Sir. The wounds smart when they get wet, but that's all. The loss of Billy is worse." She spoke the truth – he wasn't dead, she knew, but she missed him.

Carmichael nodded sympathetically. "Well then, Helena, I'd best not detain you, or I'll stand accused of putting the maids off their work like your young man. I hear you're volunteering in the hospital now, too?"

Helena was surprised he knew. "Yes, Sir. I find it suits me. I would like tae be a nurse, when I'm of age."

Carmichael smiled. "You have a healing way with you, Helena. Oh, I know it was a coincidence, the feeling coming back into my hand when it did, but you have a manner suited to the occupation. If you ever require my help, you need only ask."

"Thank you, Sir. Tam wants tae be a doctor. He impressed Dr. Baird. He's been allowed tae stay on when the other cadets went home, tae gain more experience," she said, a trace of pride in her voice.

Captain Carmichael stood up and walked to the window, gazing out. "I'm sure that's one reason, Helena. Make sure he treats you with respect, won't you?"

"Why, of course, Sir." She bobbed a curtsey to his back and scuttled from the room, picking up her cleaning things as she went.

Megan leaned on her pitchfork and stared back at the sleek black creature on the gatepost. It was a week since Rab had been killed now, and her loss was still raw, although it had been submerged in the aftermath of events surrounding Billy's disappearance. The police had taken a boat out on the loch and sent a diver down, but they had shaken their heads and said people had disappeared in these waters before, never to be seen again. Parts of the loch were bottomless, they said. Megan had laughed inwardly at the locally held belief, but agreed with them that a body might never be found. She had suppressed the hysteria which threatened to bubble out at that. Poor lad, to prefer life as an otter to life with the McDowalls or his relatives, she had said to Sam later; and Sam had replied that life as an otter was a fine thing, as he well knew.

She would have liked to keep an eye on Billy, know how he was faring. Under other circumstances, she would have spied with her enchanted mirror, but its magical properties were lost to her now, for it was useless without a bird's eye view. Megan stuck her fork in the soil and trailed out another plant heavy with potatoes, then she emitted an experimental low whistle, not looking at the bird on the gatepost. There was a whirring of wings and the creature landed at her feet, cocking its intelligent head and eyeing her. With a rush of joy, Megan reached into her pocket and offered a nut. The raven hesitated, then accepted with an enthusiastic peck which drew blood.

"We'll have tae teach you some manners, sir," said Megan, sucking her finger. The bird fixed her with a haughty stare. Megan inclined her head in a small bow. "I apologise…madam," she corrected herself. "How does 'Rowan' sound?" Rowan the raven jumped on her shoulder; the deal had been struck. Megan's new bird had chosen her as Rab had chosen her mother before her.

After tea in the farmhouse kitchen, Helena and Tam climbed the stairs to Tully's room. "Grandfather," said Helena, "this is Tam. He's a St. John Ambulance Cadet, and he wants tae be a doctor."

Tam stepped forward, and took the old man's left hand in his, perceiving that this was his good side, unaffected by the stroke. "How do you do, Sir?"

Tully stared at him bleary-eyed for a few seconds, before dropping his hand and hitting it away with a scowl. Then he looked at Helena, red-faced, and animal noises, guttural and primitive, came from his mouth.

"I'm sorry," said Helena, rushing to wipe Tully's chin with her handkerchief. "It's his condition." She stared into his eyes. Tully gazed back, tears welling. She took his useless right hand, caressing and massaging it as she had many times lately, now that she understood the old man had taken on more than he bargained for in Sam – because through him, she herself had been foisted on his household.

"Take his other hand," said Tam. "It's a waste of time holding that one, he has no sensation in it."

"I'm well aware of that," Helena replied. "And he might not be able tae speak, but he hears ye," she said, with meaning. She didn't take her eyes off Tully. She longed for him to understand what she was trying to do. Suddenly, there was a spark in his limpid eyes – just a flicker, just for a second. Only she knew the gentlest pressure that his hand applied on hers, like being brushed by a feather.

Helena and Tam dawdled on the shore of the loch as he set off back to Craigendon House. They were holding hands, not saying much, the late summer evening wrapping itself around them in the pinks and purples of sunset, intensified by the heather coming into bloom on the hills. When the time came to part, they stood awkwardly, before Tam took her other hand also, bent and brushed his lips against hers.

"Will ye be mine one day, Helena?" he asked.

"I'll be a nurse before I'm anybody's," she laughed, disentangling her fingers and running away. She glanced back to see him smile and shake his head as he turned and plodded onward. Helena breathed the scented air and sat down on a rock at the water's edge. She felt almost peaceful for the first time in days. Checking to see there was no-one around, she slipped her skirt and blouse off, then her underwear, and waded into the loch. She hadn't had a chance to swim today. Soon she was immersed in her element, and despite no hunger pangs, she permitted herself some toad's legs when an unfortunate creature happened along to tempt her. As she sat licking the juices from her chin, she saw the dark shape out in the water, with the wake trailing behind it. It came straight for her, and she saw that it carried its own toad in its mouth. It pulled itself up on to the rock beside her, and dropped the toad in her lap.

Helena's heart nearly burst with joy. "No thank you, Billy," she said. "I've eaten. Ye'll not go hungry now, ay, wee man?" He looked back at her, eyes sparkling with mischief. "Not going tae change an' keep me company as Billy?" she pleaded. "Like old times?" Nothing happened. The otter-boy sat with her to enjoy his supper, then he held out one paw which she cradled in her palm, stroking it with the index finger of the other. Then he was gone. Helena sighed.

She had just struggled back into her petticoat, still damp and hair clinging, when she heard a voice she had thought never to hear again.

"Hello, my dear. My, those are nasty scratches on your shoulder. You blamed the eagle, but I don't think the eagle caused those, do you? It was the nasty little otter."

She snatched up her skirt, blouse and shoes and ran.

Rev. O'Neill's shadow loomed over the shore in the sunset as he watched her disappear.

Sam was shutting the chickens in for the night when he heard it. It was a sound he had thought he would never hear again. His breath caught in his chest and his heart pounded. He tried to carry on with his work, but he couldn't concentrate; he had to know. Finding Rose in the kitchen, he said he had to go out to check something, a matter he had forgotten about.

"At least say good night tae wee Sadie, ye know what she's like," said Rose.

He was trembling slightly as he kissed his youngest child, perspiration beginning to bead on his brow.

"Are ye alright, Daddy?" asked Sadie.

"It's a warm night," said Sam. "You get tae sleep."

He went back downstairs. "Where are Helena and the boys?"

"Out and about. Not far, I don't think. It's a nice night, and they'll be drawing in fast soon."

"I'd rather they were all in."

Rose looked at him. "What is it, Sam? Are ye expectin' poachers?"

"In a manner o' speakin'," he said. "Poachers, hunters, it's all the same, isn't it?"

Puzzled, Rose went to call her brood, disturbed by her husband's words and the look of him, while he disappeared into the gloaming falling on Loch Duie.

Sam knew the sound could only have come from one place. He headed to Craigendon House, putting one weary foot in front of the other, for recent events had left him sleepless with worry. It was late, almost dark, when he approached the house by the estate workers' favoured path through the woods. He veered off to the stable block, senses alert. All was quiet now, apart from the gentle snorting and snuffling of the horses, but mingled with their scent and the smell of hay, Sam could detect something else. As he walked through the archway, the noise started up again – a loud, deep baying which reverberated through the night and set his heart racing.

He didn't realise anybody was there until his colleague MacAllistair, the elderly but still fit gamekeeper, loomed large out of the murk of the surrounding buildings.

"Hailstanes! Good God, man, what are ye doin' creepin' around here at this time o' night?"

Sam licked his lips, his mouth dry. "I heard… that….". He inclined his head towards the noise.

MacAllistair scratched his beard. "Aye. Thanks tae you, they're off again! I had just got them quietened." He sighed. "His Lordship was goin' tae send for ye in the mornin'. He managed tae get them on loan from another toff, miles away. He sent me for them wi' the horse box."

Sam leaned against the wall as the baying continued. "Are they what I think they are?"

"They're Otter Hounds," MacAllistair replied. "Magnificent beasts!"

Chapter 23

As it happened, there were two reasons for Sam to return to Craigendon House early the next day. His Lordship sent a stable hand down to summon him, and Tam Watson appeared with an unexpected request from Captain Carmichael – he wanted to meet with Rose and Sam. Sam was surprised, suspicious and anxious, and glad he already knew why he had been summoned on one matter, awful though it was.

Helena and Tam strode ahead of the adults, shoulder to shoulder, their foreheads almost touching when they whispered to each other.

"Young love," said Rose, to break the silence between her and Sam.

"Speaking of which," said Sam, "now that they're out of earshot, what dae ye think yer old beau wants wi' us?"

Rose glanced at him. "I can only imagine it's tae dae wi' Helena. It's certainly nothin' tae dae wi' me, Sam, I assure ye."

"But he knows she's not his!"

"He still likes her, though. He told her yesterday if she ever needed any help..."

"An' what did he mean by that?"

"We'll find out soon enough, Sam. But he's a changed man. I misjudged him. Dinna fash."

His Lordship's summons had to be obeyed first. With heavy heart and gritted teeth, Sam returned to the stable block to be formally introduced to the newest guests at Craigendon. He took off his cap as he approached Lord Craigendon where he stood gazing into a stall, and squeezed it to stop his hands from trembling.

"Hailstanes! I gather you've heard them already – hard not to, couldn't believe the noise – but aren't they incredible?"

Sam stared at the four shaggy dogs clawing the top of the lower half of the stable door with huge paws, slavering for the titbits His Lordship was feeding them. They were light in colour, a mixture of white and tawny patches, rough-coated with hair over their eyes. They had a look about them of a teddy bear Rose had knitted for Sadie, with loops of wool in place of fur, and Sam reflected that they looked like cuddly pets. He knew differently, however, for he had seen what they could do. He had had one on his tail, literally, when he was a boy. His playmate had not been as lucky.

He swallowed hard. "Ye're intent on huntin', then, Sir?"

"That I am. I know we could track them down and shoot, but we may as well have some sport. I would like to present Lady Carmichael with a paw, won in the hunt as it would have been in the old days."

"I didn't know ye wanted tae move against the otters at all, Sir. They're hardly disruptin' the fish stocks, an'…"

Lord Craigendon clapped him on the back. "As I said before, best to take early action. And it was an otter which led to that little lad drowning, your children's friend. Shocking thing. Revenge for him, ay what? It shouldn't be so hard to track them down and flush them out, with these boys."

"The eagle was more to blame for Billy's plight, beggin' your pardon, Sir," said Sam.

"That's another quarry I'll be after, before it starts on my livestock," His Lordship replied. "Why in heaven's name are these creatures coming among us now?"

Sam held his breath a moment. "Despite the fact it attacked my daughter and her friend, it's a magnificent bird, Sir. A Golden Eagle. It must be because of the tree clearances makin' the estate a better place for them tae thrive."

"Whatever, Hailstanes, it isn't welcome," said the gent. "It has to go before it attracts a mate. I have my sheep to consider. They've even been known to attack grown deer. The Glorious Twelfth is drawing near, and I intend to bag more than pheasants this year. Then, if not before."

Sam choked back his nausea. He hated any kind of hunting for sport, something nobody else on the estate understood. "As you say, Sir. If that's all for now, I have someone to see."

191

The Lord was absorbed in tousling the animals' heads. "Of course, of course. I'll let you know when the event is to happen. Some morning, soon."

Sam shot his employer's back a look of disgust, and made for the manor house.

Francis Carmichael adjusted his tie and cuffs and stood rehearsing what he wanted to say. When the knock came at the door of his sitting room, he cleared his throat. "Come!"

Rose and her husband entered. The man was younger than he had expected, but Carmichael took in the weariness in his eyes.

"Good morning, Mrs. Hailstanes," he said. "Mr. Hailstanes, I'm pleased to make your acquaintance." He held out his hand. Sam took it wordlessly, although his eyes were eloquent.

Rose broke the silence, careful to follow his formal lead. "Ye asked tae see us, Captain Carmichael, Sir?"

"Please, be seated," he said, indicating the sofa. He turned his usual armchair so that it faced them squarely, and sat down, wanting to grip the chair's arms but acutely aware of his missing fingers. Then he began to speak. He told them of his regard for Helena, that he thought her intelligent and capable, and that he would like to see her advance in life, that he would like to help her, if they would accept.

"The war may be over by the time she is of age to train as a nurse – pray God that it is, and that we're victorious – so it might be harder for her to be accepted. She would stand a better chance if she could continue her education. I would like to help with that. As Mrs. Hailstanes knows, I've lost my own children, and… well, I would like to make recompense for past wrongs. You are a good man, Mr. Hailstanes, Sir, better than was I."

As Sam continued silent and awkward, Rose spoke. "That is a most generous offer, Captain," she said slowly. "Sam – well, neither of us – would like to see Helena going far from home, though, and she cannot continue at the school here…"

"Of course not. There is a senior secondary school in Ayr, though. There are a number of schools in Ayrshire, and you could have your choice. I would pay the fees at any. None are required for the senior secondary, though. It's simply a continuation of the type of schooling she has had here, and I thought she might find it easier to fit in there. But I would pay for lodgings and other expenses. She could come home at weekends. She would gain her Leaving Certificate, which would stand her in good stead for a number of careers, should she change her mind about nursing."

Sam spoke at last. "Are you able to give me your assurance, Sir, that your interest in Helena is as selfless as you say?"

Rose gasped. "Sam!"

Carmichael held up a hand to reassure her. "It's a reasonable question. I give you my word, as an officer and a gentleman, Mr. Hailstanes. I wouldn't seek to see your daughter under any circumstances. If she wished to see me, and you gave permission, I would be delighted to know at first hand of her progress. But I would instigate nothing. My motives are as I have stated."

Rose looked from one man to the other. "Sam…we've known these past three months that she needs tae spread her wings…"

Sam held out his hand to Carmichael, and clasped the injured limb offered in response more firmly than before. "Then I'm happy to accept. Thank you, Captain Carmichael, Sir."

At Sam's request, Rose went to find Megan after work. She was still labouring in the fields, but she quietly pointed out to Rose the sleek bird watching her from the wall. Megan was glad for her. "Be sure tae bring her later tae show the children," she said, issuing Sam's request for Megan to come to the farmhouse. Then she remembered. "Och, he's asked ye tae come sae late, though. He wants the bairns in bed. I'm not sure why."

As she walked on towards home, Rose was surprised to find that her resentment of Megan was waning. She smiled to herself. Life was looking up. Helena would be leaving home, and despite the change in the girl over the last few weeks, that could only make things easier.

When Megan arrived that night, Sam told the womenfolk in his life about the proposed otter hunt. "He plans it for one morning soon," he said, "We need tae go and warn the otters not to linger at daybreak, tae get back tae the holts an' stay in until after dark. Dig deep and hunker down all day. Especially Billy, who came tae see Helena last night."

"Did he really?" asked Megan.

"He did," Helena replied. She seemed about to say something else.

"Was he well?" prompted Megan.

"Oh aye. He stayed as an otter, but I could tell he was happy. It's just...somebody else was there, by the loch. I don't know how much he saw. I'm sorry I haven't told ye, Da. I didna like tae mention his name. It was Rev. O'Neill."

Sam drew his breath in on a whistle. The name was indeed forbidden in the house, and the family no longer went to church. "What's he up tae, prowlin' round these parts at dusk? Did he try tae touch ye?"

"No, Da. I ran whenever I saw him."

"So there was no conversation between ye?"

"No, Da." Helena bit her lip on the half-truth. Sam noted it, but said nothing more. He would question her later.

Megan watched Helena pull on her sweater before they set off. She had learned of Captain Carmichael's generosity, and was pleased and grateful, yet Megan sensed something was amiss. They set out into the early August darkness surrounding Loch Duie, Sam leading the way. Having heard about O'Neill being in the vicinity, they had unanimously agreed that Rose should stay home with the children. Megan saw Helena jump as the key turned in the lock behind them, for this was unheard of in these parts, where His Lordship's game and fish were the only things usually considered under threat.

"Are ye not takin' yer staff, lass?" she asked her.

"I didn't think I would need it," Helena replied.

"We could stay out. I could give ye some instruction. It's high time, I've neglected my duty towards ye."

"Maybe not tonight," was all Helena said.

Rowan the raven was on Megan's shoulder, but she hopped over to Helena's. Megan felt a heaviness in her heart. Helena flinched and shrugged the bird off. They made their way to the spot where Helena and Sam had viewed the otters' transformation before. Megan began to tense the closer they came, and she trembled slightly as they lay in the grass behind the bushes. It took her back to another life, far away on the

194

shore at Ballaness. She looked at Helena, the waning moon casting a silver sheen down the length of her lustrous hair, and she thought of Jeanette, her true mother, sitting on a rock by the River Dunn.

Before long, they heard a disturbance in the water, and the procession of dripping figures came out on to the bank. Sam rose slowly and went forward. He had instructed the others to wait, since he was the only one who had spoken with the otter-folk so far, on the day they came for Billy. Megan held her breath, and she knew that Helena did, too.

Sam hoped he would see those he had spoken to on the day they rescued Rose as she attempted to help Helena. He was afraid they would all run for the safety of the water at his approach, but although they drew together in twos and threes, some holding hands, they stood their ground. He took his bonnet off and wrung it in his hands. He meant respect by it, but even as he swiped it off his head, he had to smile to himself, for it would mean nothing to them.

He cleared his throat. "I spoke with some of you on the day Billy came to you. Ye helped my wife, and my daughter. I thank ye for that. In the way that Billy is now one of you, because a witch wished it on him as he wished it for himself, I have been a human for many years, and my daughter, too. In our case, it was against our will. We were cursed by a sea witch down at Ballaness. Both my daughter and the witch are here with me. We have resolved our differences, and none of us mean you any harm. As you know, Billy was not cursed, but given the life he craved by an act of well-wishing. It was my daughter's doing."

A woman stepped forward. She was lithe yet muscular, and Sam felt a pang for Jeanette. "Welcome," she said. "We knew you for what you were. If you have come for Billy…"

Sam raised his hand to dismiss her words. "No, no…we understand how things stand. We've covered for Billy's disappearance. We've come tae warn ye."

"Warn us?"

"Have ye heard o' Otter Hounds?"

The otter-folk looked at him and at each other and shrugged their shoulders.

"Ye're lucky, then," he continued. "Twice, when I was a boy…" He thought better of it and cleared his throat. "They're dogs bred for huntin' otters. Men have brought them here because they want rid of all of you. I suggest ye don't venture out until much later in the day, and definitely not first thing, no matter how hungry." His words reminded him of Billy. Sam cast his eyes around the group, seeking him, wondering if he looked the same as he always had. He heard a noise at his side. Helena had joined him.

"Where is Billy?" she asked.

The otter woman looked at her, from her head to her feet and back. "You retain a look of one of us, my dear."

"She looks like her mother," said Sam, a crack in his voice. "About these Otter Hounds…"

"Where's Billy?" Helena asked again.

"He can't change his form," the woman replied. "Your magic didn't go that far. He's no doubt fishing. He can't eat enough," she laughed. "He's happy, be assured o' that, lass."

Helena thanked her in a faint voice and retreated to the bushes. What she had suspected about Billy had been confirmed.

"The hunt…the Otter Hounds…" said Sam.

"We'll take care. Thank you," said the woman.

With that, they turned from him, back to their own business. Sam knew he had been dismissed and it pierced his heart. He walked past his companions in silence, and they followed after him.

Chapter 24

Ten days later, Megan tossed and turned in her sleep, hearing the deep baying of the Otter Hounds up at Craigendon House. She was certain the noise carried all over the estate. Lord Craigendon had led three unsuccessful hunts so far. Megan had witnessed them passing once, the dogs shambling along, noses to the ground, hardly lifting their great pads off the path. They looked amiable enough apart from their imposing size, but although they had caught no otters, they had caused other devastation. Highly trained, they were obedient when under supervision, but one had escaped the run Lord Craigendon had ordered to be made for them, and the McDowalls' chicken coup had been destroyed in the massacre which ensued. They had been more upset about their hens than about wee Billy MacTaggart.

One of the Land Army girls with whom Megan shared a room was snoring softly. Megan buried her face in the pillow, something tugging at her semi-consciousness. Suddenly, she was wide awake. The sound of the Otter Hounds was nearer than usual. Their baying wasn't coming from Craigendon House. She became aware of another noise, a light tapping at the window. She stole from her bed in the close, enveloping darkness of the room and lifted the curtain. The blackness outside was a continuation of that inside. She could see nothing, but she understood. Rowan was tapping at her window. The dogs were getting closer, and now she could detect human voices, calling to them. It could only mean one thing.

Her snoring companion woke with a snort and stirred. "What's going on?"

Megan hesitated. "I think His Lordship's got those dogs out."

197

"I'm sick o' them!" groaned the young woman. "Lumberin' aboot, covered in mud – clarty beasts!"

"Ssh!" hissed Megan. "Go back tae sleep. I'm goin' downstairs for a smoke."

Under the circumstances, all she could grab was her dressing gown from the foot of the bed, stumbling around in the dark. She felt her way along the corridor and down the stairs, avoiding parts she knew to creak because she had done this before. Usually, she had been prepared with clothing stashed somewhere, but this circumstance was unforeseen. Surely Sam didn't know about it, either? She retrieved her boots from the back porch where the outdoor things were kept, and slipped them on over her bare feet, and her jacket over her night things. Rowan flew to her shoulder, a whoosh of wings in the night, and she stroked her sleek head and fed her a nut from her jacket pocket.

"You really are one bright bird," she whispered. "Come on."

Megan could hear that the hunt was still behind her as she headed for the Hailstanes' farm, but she knew their path would diverge towards the loch soon. If it wasn't for the exertion she keenly felt, she might have been running on the spot, so total and disorienting was the dark. His Lordship must be frustrated and desperate to venture out on a moonless night like this. She had no idea how long she had been walking, half-running, when Rowan swooped down and halted her. Somebody was ahead of her; she could hear their footsteps on the well-trodden path, two sets by the sound of it, heading away from her towards the loch.

"If that's Helena and Sam, go and let them know I'm here, too!" she hissed to the raven. "Go tae Helena! She'll understand." She was becoming breathless. Rowan sped to do as she bid.

Megan caught up with them at the water's edge, where they were better prepared than she, torches in hand. Out from under the tree canopy, stars blazed in the inky summer sky and reflected dizzyingly on the calm surface of Loch Duie. "Did ye hear the dogs?" she asked.

"Who wouldn't?" said Sam. "I feared this!" He shone his torch tentatively along the loch shore, but it didn't penetrate far into the night. A shooting star sliced the darkness to the north east.

"Perseid meteors," said Megan.

"We would need a fireball to see anything on a night like this," sighed Sam.

Rowan squawked, but remained on Helena's shoulder where she had landed a few minutes before. "What about the mirror, Megan? Could it help?" the girl asked.

"I couldn't get it from the case under my bunk," said Megan. "Anyway, it only gives a bird's eye view. Rowan would have tae have seen the otter-folk, tae give us any clue where they might be – and in what form. And we're just gettin' used tae workin' together."

"They'll be in human form, if shootin' stars are aboot," said Sam. "We always used tae enjoy such nights for changin' shape."

"Will they not be okay, then, Da?" asked Helena.

"Far from it." Sam shook his head. "They won't stay that way when they know people are aboot. They'll take on otter form again."

Just then, there was a burst of several bright meteors. They exploded like fireworks across the sky, and briefly lit up a patch of loch shore.

"Did ye see that?" said Helena.

"What?" asked Sam.

"I'm sure I caught a glimpse o' the otter-folk!"

"That's impossible," said Sam, "Nobody could see by shooting stars…"

Megan gave a short laugh. "Ha! She's a witch, remember."

Sam turned to face her. "So did you see them, too?"

She shook her head sadly. "My abilities aren't what they were. Truth is, my gifts wane as Helena's grow." She heard a sharp intake of breath.

"I didn't know that, Megan. I didn't know my magic diminished yours. I wouldn't have wanted tae take anythin' from ye."

"I think ye would have liked the thought o' it once, lass, so I'm pleased tae hear ye speak like this," smiled Megan. "It's just the way it is. My own fault, for ma muddled use o' magic. For what I did, meddlin' in matters I should have left alone. I've known the consequences for a long time."

Helena struggled to take in what she had just learned, but dismissed it. There were more important things right now. "Well, I'm sure of what I saw. They're not that far away. If we're goin' tae warn them, we might be on time."

Megan noticed that Helena was leaning on something. "Ye've brought your staff! Good thinking."

They set off in the direction indicated by Helena, who strode ahead. Megan noted how sure footed she was, her staff tapping the shingle, and she realised that she had traced this path in darkness many times. As she had been the Sea Witch o' Ballaness, Helena was the Lady of Loch Duie indeed. They could hear the Otter Hounds in the distance – they seemed to have gone in the opposite direction.

"They won't have such a strong otter scent if they're in human form," said Sam. "The hounds have likely scented a holt further away. That might just give us the time we need."

"But they must be able tae hear the dogs, too," said Megan. "Would they not think it would be better tae stay as they are?"

"Unlike me, they've never been hunted by dogs," Sam replied. "They dinna really know the danger. They listened to my advice aboot not comin' oot in daylight, but I could see they weren't really worried. It's not the dogs they'll fear. It's bein' seen. They'll change back."

"Anyway," said Helena with a wry laugh, "what would His Lordship think if he saw them, naked and cavorting in the dark? That he had a witches' coven meeting on his estate, that's what!"

They hurried on, Rowan flying to and fro, spying and returning to them to urge speed.

Lord Craigendon lashed out at one of the Otter Hounds with a whip. "Confounded animal! Get on the scent!" His words were slightly slurred.

"Turn them around, old chap, try this way!" said a voice in his ear.

Despite his own inebriation, Lord Craigendon recoiled from the whisky and cigars on his friend's breath. It was during a small dinner party which ran into the early hours that the subject of his lack of success in the otter hunts had come up. One of the guests gave his opinion that they had been setting out too late, that the hunt should begin at the crack of dawn when they might catch the animals out hunting their breakfast. That would let the dogs get a good scent of them. Then, even if they managed to get back to their holts, the hunting party would jump on the ground above them to dislodge earth and frighten them out into the jaws of the hounds... *"Well,"* His Lordship had said, *"It's nearly the wee sma' oors o' the mornin' already. What better time than the present?"* So it was that they had wakened the stable lad at around three o'clock to help them, and set out on a noisy rampage in the darkness, drink-fuelled hopes high.

On his friend's advice, His Lordship turned the dogs around and off they went. The hounds stopped suddenly and sniffed the air. "They have something now," he said with certainty, as they took off again in their lolloping gait, noses to the ground.

The otter-folk themselves were unaware of the two parties converging on them. They were admiring the shooting stars of the Perseids, as they lay flat on a grassy bank, gazing upwards. Nestled on the shoulder of their highest-ranking female, the one who had spoken with Sam, was Billy, who did not have the ability to become human, as she had informed Helena. His adoptive mother nuzzled his pelt with her nose, reveling in his comforting scent.

As they shambled their way among the trees near the loch shore, one of the dogs stopped and raised its great shaggy head towards the canopy. Lord Craigendon followed its gaze, directed his torch, and laid his hand on his friend's arm to halt him. He pointed. On a low branch not far ahead of them, the silhouette of a great bird loomed in the torch's beam, its back to them.

"It must be that damned eagle," he whispered. "Sleeping. Well, I'll make sure it never wakes!"

"It would be in a better roost than that if it was asleep," replied the other. "They don't usually hunt in the dark, but it must be on to something... Maybe the same quarry as ours, old man..."

"Be damned if I'll allow competition!" barked His Lordship.

He raised his gun, and before his friend could stop him to warn of the noise, he fired at the silhouette of the mighty bird.

Sam, Helena and Megan froze. "Why would they shoot?" said Sam. "They let the dogs tear the otters apart." He shuddered as he said it, and Megan laid her hand on his arm.

Seconds later, they heard a number of splashes.

"Well, that's done it," he hissed. "If the noise of the dogs didna worry them, that has. That's a sound only a human can make, and one intent on killing! They're headin' back tae the water. They'll try tae swim for their holts, and the hounds will follow!"

The drunken hunt party was seized by bloodlust now. Careless of what they did or how much noise they made, they ran to find the fallen Golden Eagle. Lord Craigendon was boasting of having it stuffed for the entrance hallway. Torches to the ground, they sought its body. When the outline of a man lying on the pathway came into focus, they stopped dead in their tracks. The Otter Hounds, on the scent of otters and baying with bloodlust of their own, ploughed onwards toward the loch.

Megan was becoming breathless, and her bare feet were blistering inside her boots. "There's only one way tae save them now!" she cried. "Helena, we need magic!"

"What are ye goin' to do?" the girl asked.

"I can do nothin'," she replied. "It's beyond me. It's down tae you, lassie. Sam, for heaven's sake, stop! We canna warn them now."

They all pulled up, breathless, bending to gulp air into their labouring lungs.

"I don't know what to do," gasped Helena.

"Calm yourself. Think of the water flowin'. Hear it, feel it," said Megan.

The cool night air and the sight before them had a sudden sobering effect on the hunt party. "Well, I'll be damned!" said Lord Craigendon.

The body lay face-down on the beaten dirt of the woodland path.

"Let me through!" said one of his five companions, who had been quietest of the party until now; a somewhat unwilling member, Lord Craigendon had thought. Captain Francis Carmichael pushed his way to the body and knelt down, feeling for a pulse. "Nothing," he said. "He's dead." He turned the deceased over.

Lord Craigendon's knees almost gave way, and he leaned against a tree trunk. "It's the parish minister," he gasped. "It's Rev. O'Neill."

They switched off their torches, and Helena closed her eyes. She thought back to other nights when she had stood on the banks of the loch, peaceful nights when her intuition had lapped with the water and she had known her connection, had known that she could bend her witch's will to her desire. Those desires had been selfish, the foolish wishes of a girl drunk on a new awareness of herself. Yet she had learned that her earnest desires for the good of others could work in ways totally unforeseen by herself. She thought of Billy, of the danger he was in. She delivered herself up to the mystery of it all.

Trance-like, she bent and pulled off her boots and socks. Barefoot, she walked out into the water until it lapped around her waist, staff held high above it in both hands. Her feet were firmly planted apart on the silty bed of the loch's shallows, her stance powerful. There was a sudden burst of meteors overhead; she was illuminated for a few seconds, and her companions saw her there, staff raised above the water, swaying as wavelets, increasing in strength, raced towards the shore.

She said nothing; her lips didn't even need to move. Her will was beyond words, her ability to send her will an impulse of mind to water. All that she desired, she sent out from her very heart, mind and soul, a trinity of purpose unsurpassed in magic, or prayer, or by whichever name it went. It made the incantations of wise women and the mutterings of kirk congregations seem like ineffectual mumbo-jumbo. She was in the power of the great spirit which dominated the universe, its gift to her that her mortal feet should be allowed to tread its pathways.

A mist began to rise from the water around her. It had a different quality to the darkness, for it ate it and replaced it with something even more impenetrable. It was a wall around the loch, and Helena had never felt so alone, for she knew she was the only human being within it. She sighed as she sensed her father and Megan being cut off from her. She was the solitary water witch, as Megan had been down at Ballaness. A tear ran down her cheek.

"I definitely shot upwards, at the bird on the branch!" Lord Craigendon mopped his forehead with a handkerchief.

"The bullet must have ricocheted and hit him," said Francis Carmichael.

"But what the devil was he doing out here at this time of night? He hasn't even got a torch on him!"

The hunt party clustered around the dead cleric's body, stunned into sobriety. They had forgotten their purpose and the Otter Hounds until they heard strange yelps. His Lordship shook himself as if from a bad dream and called the dogs back. Several times, he whistled and yelled, but there was no response. Leaving Captain Carmichael with the lifeless minister, the other men headed off to find the Otter Hounds. As they shone their torches ahead of them, the beams hit a green mist rising from Loch Duie. It swirled like poison being shaken in a flask, but it didn't move beyond the shore of the loch. They found the dogs staring at it in silence. The nose of one was bloodied.

"Do you think he had a run-in with an otter?" asked Lord Craigendon.

His companion shivered. "No. He's not been scratched. Looks like he's been punched." He stretched out his hand towards the mist and withdrew it with a startled gasp.

"It's like a solid wall! I think he must have run into it!"

The others tested the mist, either tentatively or boldly, as if their companion was mad. Their fingers met with something cold, hard and impenetrable. Gripped with primal fear, they took off away from the loch, the dogs at their heels.

Megan and Sam stood watching. "Good girl," said Megan.

"Will she be alright in there?" asked Sam.

"Fine," Megan answered lightly. "She's exercisin' her gift, and it's in the good of others. This will protect the otters. It should put the fear intae the hunters, too!" She sighed longingly.

A pinpoint of light appeared in the mist. It began to grow, like a torch beam increasing in strength. It came towards them.

"What's happenin' now?" asked Sam. "Is this her comin' back tae us?"

Megan frowned. "I don't know." Her heart began to race as the beam enveloped her, and only her. "I have tae go tae her, Sam!"

"What's wrong?"

Megan didn't answer. She kicked off her boots and waded into the light, into the loch.

Like Helena before her, she didn't feel the cold water as it rose up to her waist. What she did feel was a peace she hadn't known in a long time.

Helena was waiting for her. "Hello, Megan. You'll have tae get us out of here and put things back tae rights," she said.

"I told ye, Helena, I can't…" but as she said it, she felt the power of water surge upwards through the soles of her feet. Her limbs tingled, her fingers flexed with purpose. "What have ye done, lass?" she said in wonder.

"My will," said Helena. "It isn't my will tae be a witch. I have other gifts, enough tae get by and maybe do well in a normal life. I want a normal life, Megan. I've willed it all back tae you. It's your birthright, not mine." She handed Megan her staff.

The two women hugged.

As Sam, Megan and Helena made their way back to the farm, Rowan riding on Megan's shoulder, they heard voices behind them. They stopped and listened; who could it be? The hunt party would have gone in the opposite direction. They were startled, therefore, to hear Lord Craigendon's voice calling to them.

"Hallo? Who goes there? Stop! We know you're there!"

They stood still and glanced at each other. Sam whispered to Megan and Helena that they should creep away. He could explain himself being out, but not them.

"It's Sam Hailstanes, Sir," he said loudly into the darkness, which was beginning to lighten, shining his torch in the direction of Lord Craigendon's voice. He picked out five men and the four great Otter Hounds coming towards him. He tried not to tremble at sight of the dogs.

"Ah, Hailstanes. We were just heading to your place for help! There's been an accident!"

"Oh no, Sir? What kind of accident? Is someone hurt?" asked Sam.

"Worse than that," said Lord Craigendon, coming up to him. "I've… that is, Rev. O'Neill…has been shot dead. Come with me."

Stunned into silence, Sam followed the hunt party back through the trees.

"Heard us out, did you?" asked His Lordship.

"I heard the dogs, Sir."

They stopped where they had left the body of Rev. O'Neill. It was no longer there, though. Where it had lain, there was the sad corpse of a magnificent Golden Eagle. While the others stared in disbelief, Sam smiled to himself.

Dawn wasn't far away as Sam returned home. There were still one or two meteors visible, the tail end of the peak night of the Perseid shower. He met Megan, hurrying back to the McDowalls' farm before she was missed, Rowan swooping and soaring around her.

"So, all yer powers are back?" he asked.

"Helena has returned my *gifts*," she corrected him.

"She's never goin' tae be ordinary, though, is she?"

"No. I think she'll probably be extraordinary. But on her own merits."

"What will you do, Megan?"

"I'll see out my war duty as is only right," she replied. "Then I'll think aboot it. The world is changin'. The days of solitary women livin' alone in upturned boats are passin'. Maybe I need more of a normal life – or the semblance of one – tae dae some good in the world. Helena's made me think that."

"I'll be seein' ye, then, Megan."

"Aye, Sam, ye will. I'll be seein' what I can do for Tully. He is my father, after all."

Back at the farmhouse, Rose was waiting for him. Helena had gone to bed to try to get a few hours' sleep before work. Sam filled her in on what had happened after he had parted company with his daughter and Megan.

Rose could barely speak at first. "How many kinds of hidden people are there?" she asked. "And why did O'Neill choose tae live most of his life as a human, when he could still become an eagle? A Golden Eagle here would have been noticed before now!"

"We'll never know," said Sam. "There are creatures who do, because they stumble upon circumstances which suit them. It's many years since I would have wished tae be any different, Rose."

She smiled. "What happens now?"

"His Lordship is like a man shell-shocked. They all are. We've agreed the events of this night will never be mentioned."

"But what aboot Rev. O'Neill, when he's missed?"

Sam shrugged. "He was one for wanderin' the estate at night. There are all sorts of dangers. Loch Duie is deep."

He took Rose in his arms and kissed the top of her head.

The next morning, when she heard of Rev. O'Neill's demise, and of his long deception, Helena wasn't totally surprised. She recalled seeing the huge eagle from the Duie Drawing Room on her first day at Craigendon House, although she hadn't known what she was looking at; now she understood that O'Neill had revealed himself to her in his true form. "We knew other creatures could change their form, Da," she said. "Like the selkies ye told me about when I was a wee lassie. And there was something about him... Anyway, there's more tae Loch Duie and Craigendon than meets the eye."

"Is there?" Sam asked.

"I've often sensed it," she said, "without bein' able tae put ma finger on it. Ballaness can't be the only place in this big world where the air is thin, where other worlds break through."

"The world of the hidden peoples, ye mean? The fae folk?"

"I think there's more than this world and one other, Da, and I don't think the fae folk are behind it all."

"I was just an otter," said Sam. "One who could become a man. Then I was stuck as a man. I've never really thought aboot it all. It's too much."

"Dinna fash, Da. And neither will I, any more. I've chosen the only world I want, and ye can let me set forth in it now, and dae ma bit."

The water bailiff and his daughter smiled.

EPILOGUE

Five years later, Rose, Sam and Megan helped Helena with her cases as she moved into women's accommodation at the University of Glasgow. She had spent a year training as a nurse after gaining her Leaving Certificate from the school in Ayr, but her ambition was to be a doctor. Thanks to Francis Carmichael's continuing generosity, and her own hard work and intelligence, she was able to do this. Rose was training to be a nurse, now that her father had gone to his rest and the children were growing up. Sam was proud of both of them. Megan, finding it harder to fit into society than she thought, returned to her travelling friends after the war. Earlier that year she had become Megan Fa, the wife of one of them.

Tam Watson, his experience as a St. John's Cadet invaluable, had already embarked on his medical studies, and was waiting to welcome Helena. She greeted him cordially enough, but she had her career on her mind. The water bailiff's daughter was going places – at last.

THE END

Other novels, novellas and short story collections available from
Stairwell Books

Carol's Christmas	N.E. David
Feria	N.E. David
A Day at the Races	N.E. David
Running with Butterflies	John Walford
Foul Play	PJ Quinn
Poison Pen	P J Quinn
Wine Dark, Sea Blue	A.L. Michael
Skydive	Andrew Brown
Close Disharmony	P J Quinn
When the Crow Cries	Maxine Ridge
The Geology of Desire	Clint Wastling
Homelands	Shaunna Harper
Homeless	Ed. Ross Raisin
Border 7	Pauline Kirk
Tales from a Prairie Journal	Rita Jerram
Here in the Cull Valley	John Wheatcroft
How to be a Man	Alan Smith
Know Thyself	Lance Clarke
Thinking of You Always	Lewis Hill
Rapeseed	Alwyn Marriage
A Shadow in My Life	Rita Jerram
Tyrants Rex	Clint Wastling
Abernathy	Claire Patel-Campbell
The Go-To Guy	Neal Hardin
The Martyrdoms at Clifford's Tower 1190 and 1537	John Rayne-Davis
Return of the Mantra	Susie Williamson
Poetic Justice	P J Quinn
Something I Need to Tell You	William Thirsk-Gaskill
On Suicide Bridge	Tom Dixon
Looking for Githa	Patricia Riley
Connecting North	Thelma Laycock
Virginia	Alan Smith
Rocket Boy	John Wheatcroft
Serpent Child	Pat Riley
Margaret Clitherow	John and Wendy Rayne-Davis
Sammy Blue Eyes	Frank Beill
Eboracvm: the Village	Graham Clews
O Man of Clay	Eliza Mood

For further information please contact rose@stairwellbooks.com

www.stairwellbooks.co.uk
@stairwellbooks